# Other Books by AJ Adaire

*Friend Series*

Sunset Island - Book 1

# Awaiting My Assignment

by

AJ Adaire

Desert Palm Press

# Awaiting My Assignment
Friends Series Book 2

Copyright © 2013 by AJ Adaire

ISBN-13 9781494790677
ISBN-10 149479067X

This is a work of fiction - names, characters, places, and incidents are the product of the author's imagination or are used fictitiously. Any resemblance to actual person living or dead, business, events or locales is entirely coincidental. All rights reserved.

No part of this publication may be reproduced, distributed, or transmitted in any form or by any means, including photocopying, recording, or other electronic or mechanical methods, without the prior written permission of the publisher, except in the case of brief quotations embodied in critical reviews and certain other noncommercial uses permitted by copyright law.

For permission requests, write to the publisher, addressed "Attention: Permissions Coordinator," at the address below.

Desert Palm Press
1961 Main Street, Suite 220
Watsonville, California 95076
www.desertpalmpress.com

Editor:  Sue Hilliker
Editor:  R. Lee Fitzsimmons
Cover Design: ©AJ Adaire

Printed in the United States of America
First Edition - December 2013

## *Dedication*

This book is dedicated to my readers. Publishing *Sunset Island*, my first book, and the first in the Friends Series, has been an exciting, roller coaster-like experience. I think the most amazing part of the whole endeavor has been receiving letters from readers. They wrote to tell me how I kept them up at night, reading my story, or caused them to set the alarm to get up early so they could finish the book before they went to work. Others wrote telling me how my book encouraged them to keep searching for the right partner, or how it helped them analyze their feelings over their own loss of someone special. I've read every note I received and responded to those who reached out. Those letters have been wonderful, and I'm very appreciative to those who wrote to me. I also want to thank those readers who took the time to put up thoughtful reviews of *Sunset Island*. Writers and readers alike, benefit from those who take the time to put their thoughts in writing on Amazon and other places.

*Awaiting My Assignment* allowed me to not have to say good-bye to my characters, Ren, Lindy, and Mallory, from *Sunset Island*. Many who wrote said they had fallen in love with those characters, just as I did when I wrote their story. I hope you will enjoy this new group of friends just as much and will enjoy revisiting Ren and Lindy. The third and, for now, final book in the series will be along in a few months. *Anything Your Heart Desires* is Jo's story and will continue the tale of this wonderful group of friends.

Thanks to all my buddies who beta read, helped find my mistakes, and told me how much they loved the story. Special appreciation to my last minute proofers: Pat, Kay, Christy, and Christie. To my editors, Sue and Lee, and to Desert Palm Press, who took a chance on me last time and now again, thank you.

Last, but never least, thanks to ICL who is my partner in life, my best friend, and biggest cheerleader. I'm so glad it's you.

# Awaiting My Assignment

Chapter 1 .................................................................................... 1
Chapter 2 .................................................................................. 11
Chapter 3 .................................................................................. 27
Chapter 4 .................................................................................. 35
Chapter 5 .................................................................................. 47
Chapter 6 .................................................................................. 61
Chapter 7 .................................................................................. 79
Chapter 8 .................................................................................. 87
Chapter 9 .................................................................................. 97
Chapter 10 .............................................................................. 103
Chapter 11 .............................................................................. 111
Chapter 12 .............................................................................. 127
Chapter 13 .............................................................................. 133
Chapter 14 .............................................................................. 147
Chapter 15 .............................................................................. 157
Chapter 16 .............................................................................. 171
Chapter 17 .............................................................................. 183

| | |
|---|---|
| Chapter 18 | 195 |
| Chapter 19 | 209 |
| Chapter 20 | 217 |
| Chapter 21 | 225 |
| Chapter 22 | 235 |
| Chapter 23 | 243 |
| About AJ Adaire | 257 |
| Sneak Peak Anything Your Heart Desires | 259 |
| Other Books from Desert Palm Press | 285 |

# Awaiting My Assignment

# Awaiting My Assignment

## Chapter 1

Amanda raised both hands to her head and although tempted to use them to cover her ears, she ran her fingers through her dark auburn hair instead. Exhaling a long sigh, she drew herself up to her full height of just over five feet then crossed her arms in front of her chest, her hazel eyes unsympathetic. Bernie was still pleading her case. However, this time, Amanda ignored the excuses and explanations, all of which were achingly familiar.

"Look," Amanda said, her tone measured, her voice more calm than her wrath would indicate, "I told you the last time that if I caught you cheating there would never be a next time or I'd leave you. As you can see, I meant it. There will be no more chances."

"But honey…"

"Don't 'but honey' me." Amanda could feel her anger creeping into her voice. It was time to end this debate.

"Okay sweetie, you're right," Bernie said, trying a new tactic. "It was just a one night stand. You know she doesn't mean anything to me. I love you. With her it was just sex. With you, I make love."

"You're pathetic. Love? You don't even know the meaning of the word. I'm done here." Amanda shook her head in disgust.

It was clear that this pronouncement had no impact because when she turned to head for the bedroom Bernie followed, close on her heels. She strode from the room hoping that would be the end of their discussion. She felt her shoulders slump when she heard Bernie following her down the hallway. Amanda grabbed her matched set of luggage from the hall closet before she entered the bedroom to begin packing. Without making an effort to sort things properly, she grabbed stacks of items she thought she might need for the next few days and jammed them into her suitcase with little care for how wrinkled they would be.

"Where do you think you're going?"

"Away from you. I told you, I'm done here." Amanda repeated her intent as much to convince herself as to convince Bernie she was serious.

Amanda packed her belongings. Recognition of how little there was in the house that reflected her taste compounded her sadness. Their custom built home, not a size or style she particularly liked, was paid for mostly with Bernie's money. Amanda, so enamored with the magnetic woman at the time they built it, would have done anything to make Bernie happy. When Amanda couldn't afford the lavish home Bernie desired, they agreed she'd contribute what she could afford and Bernie would provide the rest. For that reason, Amanda had acquiesced on nearly every decorating decision in their three bedroom home from, in her opinion, the tacky, ornate, and overdone bedroom furniture to the sleek white modern, extremely uncomfortable living room set. None of the artwork was her taste, nor had she picked any of the paint colors, which ranged in shades from eggshell to pale almond. It distressed her to admit how much of herself she had surrendered to be Bernie's partner. She always felt that living in their house was akin to living in a snowstorm.

Amanda's haven was her office. She decorated it with dark green walls, crisp white trim, comfortable leather chairs, a roll top desk, shutter covered windows, and ceiling to floor bookshelves. Books had surrounded her all her adult life. *How was it ever possible for me to establish a relationship with someone who doesn't value the printed word? I'm an author, for God's sake, involved with a woman who hates to read.*

The house was uncharacteristically quiet. Left to her own devices, Bernie would have the television on twenty-four seven. Not in the beginning of their relationship, but for the past few months, Bernie even hated to turn it off when they had sex. *What possessed me? What was I thinking? How could I have been so stupid to have not seen what she was up to?*

"Okay, I'm sorry. Is that what you need to hear?"

Amanda recognized Bernie's statement for what it was, another attempt to deter her, and responded in a voice tight with emotion. "No. You remain completely clueless about what I need to hear."

"Well, then that makes us even, since you're clueless about what I need, too. I need a little excitement in the bedroom, not that bland huggy-kissy, touchy-feely pablum-like, lukewarm sex you prefer. You bore me to death sexually. If you'd spiced things up a little, maybe I wouldn't have strayed."

The education in various sexual techniques and positions that Bernie had provided over their years together gave Amanda confidence and left her with no doubts about her sexual prowess. Amanda knew that Bernie was simply being hurtful. Amanda wanted to say, 'Yeah, *maybe* being the operative word in that sentence,' or perhaps 'So now it's my fault that you cheat?' Amanda's resolve to maintain control steeled her. She managed to clamp her mouth closed and refrain from spitting out either retort. It was important to her that she not allow herself to be pulled into exchanging hurtful barbs with the woman she at one time thought she loved and who, she thought, loved her in return. Unfortunately, their definition of love turned out to be too disparate. Although she had to bite her tongue to keep from tossing a final insult that burned to be released, she managed to remain silent. Instead,

Amanda picked up the overnight bag, slipped the strap over her head, and adjusted its weight on her shoulder.

Bernie grasped Amanda's upper arm with enough pressure to cause Amanda to wince. Pulling Amanda around to face her, while gesturing expansively with her free hand, Bernie assaulted Amanda with her words. "Are you just going to throw all this away? Aren't you even going to fight for our relationship?"

"What for? So you can cheat again? How truly stupid do you think I am?" Amanda shrugged her arm free from Bernie's painful grasp, slid the large suitcase from the bed, and extended the handle. "I'll come back to get the rest of my stuff after you leave on your trip."

"Coward," Bernie uttered. The word was just barely audible as she changed strategy again.

Amanda glanced back at her, noting Bernie's sad expression she didn't for a minute think was genuine. "I can't believe you. You have the balls of life!" In a momentary lapse of control, Amanda allowed herself to be hooked in. "Cheater!" She snapped the word back, her voice strident.

Bernie's eyes flashed. "If you walk out that door, don't think I'll let you come crawling back. I can have that empty spot you'll leave in the bed filled three times over before it's even cold."

Despite the angry and bitter feelings she had yet to express, Amanda replied in a calm and measured tone, "I don't doubt for a minute the veracity of that statement." She was too exhausted to argue.

Although slamming the door might have been more dramatic, Amanda opted to close it quietly behind her, refusing to allow her tears to come until she was alone in the car nearly a block away from the house. She pulled to the side of the road when she no longer could see well enough to drive. *Okay, that was certainly a dramatic exit, but what the hell are you going to do now?* Mentally ticking through her list of friends, she concluded that she had no friends on the west coast that were exclusively her own and didn't want to put their mutual friends in the uncomfortable position of having to take sides. *May as well get a motel room until I figure all this out...*

Her emotions in control and with a destination in mind, Amanda drove as thoughts swirled in her head. She realized she was thankful that, except for the house, they had maintained separate financial accounts, opting not to co-mingle their money. At least she wouldn't have that hassle to deal with on top of everything else.

Amanda settled into her motel room, after a cursory look around the simple but functional room decorated in a combination of green and orange stripes and flowers. Idly, she wondered when designers had begun believing that the different contrasting patterns like stripes, plaids, and floral prints coordinated with each other. "Well, at least it's clean." Spotting the coffee pot on the dresser, "and it has coffee."

Other than the friendships she and Bernie had established as a couple, Amanda had made no new friends of her own since she relocated from her apartment about fifty minutes south of their current home in San Francisco twelve years ago. She moved in with Bernie and pursued her profession as a writer, a solitary endeavor. It wasn't as if she didn't like people or was unlikeable herself, she had simply gotten out of the habit of doing things and placing herself in environments where she might meet people. Bernie's job in hotel management required frequent travel. When Bernie came home for a week off before her next trip to Brazil or across the country somewhere, they would rarely socialize. Sometimes, they might get together with another couple, but more often, they would simply fall into bed or work. Bernie always brought work home with her to do, even on what was considered her down time.

When had their relationship really ended? Certainly it had changed at least a couple of years ago when she'd called Bernie's hotel room early one morning and another woman sleepily answered the phone. She thought back to the confrontation they had upon Bernie's return home. Bernie swore that would be the last time but, of course, it wasn't. Amanda had her suspicions before, but this time there had been proof Bernie couldn't explain away.

Alone, thinking over her earlier dialogue with Bernie, self-doubts began to clamor in her brain. *Were all those cruel things Bernie had said about me true? Am I boring in life and in bed?* It was true that Bernie did most of the talking when she came home. *From my perspective it seemed that Bernie enjoyed the sound of her own voice, so I just let her talk. She was never interested in any project I was working on and had shown absolutely no interest at all in the novel I've been writing.*

Their sex life had changed too, from loving and exciting to something darker and more edgy. Although Bernie had never hurt her, she had become sexually more aggressive, dominating her physically and verbally. At the outset of their relationship, Amanda would miss Bernie when she was gone. Lately she dreaded Bernie's return home from a trip.

*This is a good decision. Although I'm sad, I'm not sorry I ended it.* Amanda exhaled a long sigh and felt some of her tension release. *In all honesty, the primary emotion I'm feeling is relief.* Desiring support and needing to unburden herself, Amanda called her oldest friend Dana in New York.

Dana had obviously checked her caller ID. "Hey girlfriend! What's happening?"

Amanda grinned at her always-upbeat best friend's greeting. Her petite frame, rusty-hair, blue-eyes, and freckle-faced appearance combined with her unflaggingly cheerful and good-natured personality made Dana someone that everyone liked. Born two days later in the month than her own January fifteenth birthday, she was Amanda's closest friend.

Amanda had come out to Dana years ago. Fearing rejection, she'd delayed telling Dana that she was gay. The day she finally worked up the courage her palms were sweaty and her stomach queasy from nerves. However, her concerns were unfounded. Dana's response had been to simply pull Amanda into her arms to give her a hug. "So what," she said. "I still love you."

They became even closer than they were before she'd revealed her secret. Maybe it was because Amanda felt freer to share her thoughts and feelings more openly. Smiling at the pleasant memory, she returned her mind to the phone conversation. "You mean what's new other than the fact that I left Bernie."

"I know this will sound unfeeling, but I'm glad."

"I know. I've pretty much come to the same conclusion."

"So, when did you leave?"

Amanda adjusted her pillow under her head and made herself comfortable on the bed. "About two hours ago."

"Where are you now?"

"Motel."

"Are you okay?"

"Yes."

"So what's your next move? Do you plan to stay in California and get an apartment?"

"I don't know. I haven't really had the chance to process the whole thing yet."

"Are you open to a suggestion?"

"From you, always."

"Okay. Well, less than two weeks from now, I'm leaving for a two and a half to three month assignment in Italy. Why don't you come stay at my place till you figure out what you want to do? Honestly, you'd be doing me a favor." Knowing her diligent and hard working friend all too well, Dana added, "You can work anywhere as long as you have a computer with Internet access and a phone, can't you?"

Amanda smiled as she pictured her friend in her cozy little home. The lovely cape style cabin she owned sat nestled in a small town bordering a large New York State park, a little over an hour from New York City. A mid-sized international pharmaceutical company employed Dana as a certified translator. She was often required to travel with her boss for her assignments. "Yes, I can work anywhere, but let me think about it. I'll call you in the morning and let you know. It's an extremely attractive offer and I appreciate it very much. The best part is that I'd get to spend a few days with you before you leave."

"Okay, let me know. I'll talk to you tomorrow. Call me if you need me. Good night, sweetie."

Amanda gave about five minutes of serious consideration to her friend's suggestion. There was really no down side to it. She checked flight information, booked her flight, and texted Dana her travel plans along with a thank you for the offer.

*** 

Amanda knew her partner's schedule as well as Bernie did. In two days, Bernie was set to fly out on her next trip. Amanda organized her plans then waited patiently for time to pass. Two days later, when she returned to the house she shared with her lover, Bernie had already left for the airport. It took Amanda less than a day to pack up her office, files, a few personal items, and to have her remaining belongings that she wanted or cared about, moved into a storage unit or shipped to Dana's place. The rest, mostly clothes, she decided could be collected once she determined where she would settle.

Amanda only took things she had brought to the relationship, leaving everything they'd bought or accumulated while they were together. She left a note on the kitchen counter for Bernie saying that, after careful consideration, leaving was for the best and that she would be in touch in a week or two to let her know where she decided to settle. After a final look around, she left for the airport.

***

Dana was waiting for Amanda at the arrival gate in Newark. In the car on the way to Dana's cabin, Amanda recalled the wonderful times she'd shared with her friend as they grew up. Dana's grandparents had raised her after her parents died when she was a teenager. Another painful loss struck when her grandfather died just after Dana turned twenty. Dana inherited the cabin when her grandmother passed a few years later and had lived there full-time since graduating from college. Amanda loved the small town's ambiance and its proximity to the park in Harriman, NY.

Amada smiled as they pulled up in front of the house. "I'd almost forgotten how lovely this place is."

While she and Dana grabbed her bags from the trunk, Amanda noticed Dana's neighbor wave in greeting to Dana.

"Mallory, stop over after dinner. I want you to meet my friend," Dana called to the attractive woman with a megawatt smile.

Once inside her house, Dana helped Amanda get settled in the guest bedroom in the loft. "Need anything else?" Dana asked as she turned to leave.

"Do I have time for a quick nap before dinner?" Amanda flopped on the bed.

"Sure. I'm just going to defrost a casserole. We can eat in an hour and a half or so."

"Need any help?"

"No, get some rest. I'll call you when dinner is ready." From the doorway, Dana gave a quick wave before she closed the door and headed downstairs to prepare dinner.

## Chapter 2

Amanda awoke when Dana called up the stairs that dinner was just about ready. Even though she felt more refreshed after her nap, Amanda knew she'd still be able to sleep soundly when she turned in for the night. The emotional strain of the past few days had left her mentally and physically exhausted. Dinner was delicious and the two long time friends chatted easily throughout the meal. Just as they were finishing up, there was a knock at the door and Mallory let herself in.

Dana wrapped her arm around Mallory's shoulder, leading her to where Amanda sat. "Fantastic! I'm glad you're here. You're just in time for coffee and dessert. Mallory, this is my oldest and dearest friend Amanda. She'll be staying here at the house while I'm away."

Mallory flashed her dazzling smile in greeting. "That's great. I'm glad to have someone that I'll know next door."

*Dana's friend is an attractive woman, but when she smiles, she's beautiful.* Her hair was an unusual shade of ash blonde, lightened by the sun on top, with a darker layer underneath. Amanda forced herself to drag her eyes away from the woman's sexy mouth so she could meet her eyes.

"Amanda, this is Mallory Barnes. She's the Director of Nursing at the hospital. Her job there requires her to work some strange hours, but she always lets me know her schedule. That way I don't worry when I hear her come home at some odd hour. Also, when I'm traveling, it's useful to have someone I can text or call at all hours of the day and night, just so someone knows I'm alive and well." Dana gave Mallory's shoulder an affectionate squeeze and a quick wink, for which she received another brilliant smile.

Amanda liked Mallory's warm smile and welcoming demeanor. Mallory was maybe an inch or two taller than Amanda and they had a lean, muscular body type in common. A hint of eyeliner and a light application of mascara emphasized her beautiful sparkly greenish blue eyes. Her hair was streaked with naturally sun-bleached ashy colored highlights that indicated she spent time outdoors. Amanda guessed Mallory's age to be a few years older than her own age of thirty-eight. Her own birthday would occur in four months, leaving her only one year until she turned the dreaded forty.

"It's a pleasure to meet you, Mallory. I hope we'll be good friends. So, a Director of Nursing huh? Do you still do direct care or is your job totally administrative at that level?" Amanda asked.

"For the most part it's administrative, but I'm still able to orient the new nurses, so I get to set standards for my staff. It's true that I still have my fair amount of pure paper pushing as well. There are advantages and disadvantages to any supervisory role, but most days I enjoy my job. What do you do?"

"I'm a writer."

"Have I possibly read any of your work?"

Amanda laughed. "Possibly, I write copy for a direct mail company. So, if you read any of the direct mail fliers, chances are good I've written some of them." She thought for a moment. "I did ghost write a novel that was published last year that you may have heard of."

"Really. Which one?"

"Doctor Jonathan Grandly's book on diet and exercise, *Get Fitter Faster*."

"No kidding. I've more than heard of it. Would you believe that I own it? You did a great job of making an extremely boring man sound interesting." Mallory's engaging grin appeared again and she produced an endearing giggle.

"Oh, you're being too hard on him. He's a genuinely nice man."

Mallory's smirk and raised eyebrow made Amanda laugh in return. "Okay, I'll agree to nice, if you'll give me boring. Plus I'll admit that he really knows his subject. I attended a lecture he gave at my college a few years back."

Amanda liked Mallory's conciliatory efforts. I'll bet she's good at her job. Her warmth is conveyed through her quick smile and obvious willingness to compromise. "It's a deal."

"You know Amanda, like you, Mallory loves to bike ride. You're welcome to use my bike if you want to ride with her sometime," Dana offered.

Both Amanda and Mallory were enthusiastic at the prospect of having someone to ride with them. During the animated conversations over the remainder of the evening, Amanda and Mallory discovered that they had a lot in common. Besides biking, they both enjoyed reading, hiking, photography, and watching old movies. When the evening ended and Mallory hugged Dana before leaving, it seemed perfectly natural for Amanda and Mallory to hug each other good night as well.

"I really like her," Amanda confided after Mallory closed the door. "Being able to have someone to do things with will make my stay here much more enjoyable while you're away. What's her story?"

"Story?"

"Yeah, you know. Who does she date, is she involved? The dirt."

"The dirt, huh?" Dana shook her head and rolled her eyes causing them both to laugh. "Honestly, I don't know who or even if she dates. I've never seen her go out with anybody and she's never mentioned anyone she's been serious about since she moved here about a year ago. She seems to work a lot and her hours are extremely irregular. I'd think it would be difficult for her to have a relationship with anyone who follows a regular work schedule. Maybe she just doesn't have time to date."

"Oh, I was just curious."

"Oh, duh," Dana uttered, just getting it. "If you're asking me about her sexual preference, I honestly don't know. Are you interested?"

"No. Not really. Geez, give me a break here. It's been less than a week since my relationship ended. It's too soon. It's just that she's so darned cute and likable." Amanda refrained from mentioning that Mallory had one of the most kissable mouths she'd ever seen, classifying it as too much information.

"Think about it, Amanda. Your relationship with Bernie has been over since you found out she'd cheated on you the first time, a couple of years ago. You've been pulling back your feelings from her for a long time. Seriously, be honest. How much have you missed your relationship since you ended it?"

"Yes, I guess you're right. I think I've had more of a sense of relief than anything else. Still, I don't know what I'm going to do, where I'm going to end up, or even where I'm headed." Feeling suddenly fatigued and not wanting to talk about Bernie any more, Amanda stood up and hugged her friend. "I'm bushed. I'm heading up to bed. Thanks again, Dana. You're a lifesaver. I'll see you in the morning."

***

Over the next several days, Dana and Amanda spent their time talking and relaxing together as only old friends can. Dana had several things to do to prepare for her trip, so they focused on getting together what she needed. Too soon, the time came for Dana's departure and Amanda drove her to the airport. Each reluctant to say goodbye, they lingered over small talk for a few minutes before she gathered her belongings.

"I'm glad you'll be here to run my car."

"Thanks for letting me use it. I love you, you know. You're the best friend I could ever ask for."

"I know that...and don't you forget it." Dana grinned and winked at her friend before she pulled her close for a final hug. "I'll be in touch when I get settled in. If you need me, text me and I'll call you back as soon as I can. Don't forget, I'm about six hours ahead of you in time." After a final good-bye, she gave a jaunty wave and disappeared into the terminal.

***

The day after Dana left for Italy, Amanda spent time reacquainting herself with the area and buying miscellaneous items that didn't get packed when she'd hastily left home. She shopped for food for the rest of the week, stocking up on staples and buying some snacks in case Mallory dropped by. A brief stop at the video store yielded two of her favorite old movies to rent.

Amanda pulled into Dana's driveway and glanced over towards Mallory's house. The car in the driveway indicated that her neighbor was home. Once inside Dana's house Amanda unpacked her purchases, tidied up the kitchen, and gave some thought to dinner. Suddenly feeling very lonely and a bit panicky with nothing to do, she decided that the safest and most productive thing would be to get back to work. Amanda had set up her computer the previous day and knew some extra hours of work would be required to assure she would get caught up, just not today—she couldn't do it today. Instead, she sat down at her computer and pulled up her novel.

The previous year she'd invested in dictation software that allowed her to speak into a microphone and control the computer with her voice. She'd conquered the training period and, once she'd mastered the program, she found it worked very well. Being able to dictate certainly helped alleviate the typing induced pain in her neck that radiated downward between her shoulder blades. When she had to sit at the keyboard to type her work, she suffered constantly. Now, instead of perching over her keyboard at a desk, she could just sit on the recliner with the computer on her lap and dictate. Amanda hadn't written anything for over a week, making it necessary to go back and reread the last few pages to orient herself to where she was in the story. She checked her notes and was just about to begin dictating when the phone rang.

"Hello?"

"It's Mallory, you know, from next door." The hesitancy in her voice conveyed her nervousness.

"Hey! I almost gave you a call when I got back from dropping off Dana. I didn't because I was afraid I'd wake you up."

"No, I worked midnight to eight a.m. this week. I slept a few hours when I got home. I have some time off before I swap to the four p.m. to midnight shift. It'll take me a day or two to get acclimated. This is the last rotation change I'll have to do for a while. Working midnight to eight a.m., I have fewer interruptions. I use the late night, quieter hours to work on reports and budgeting, and to meet with the night supervisors. Once that's done, I'll go back to covering day and evening shifts. In a couple of weeks, I have new staff coming on board. These two I just hired should be easy, since they're very experienced nurses. I was lucky to get them. I usually stay on schedule with the new folks as much as I can for the first few weeks, just to make sure they get all the training they need. Often those in my position don't have to work shifts. Because I work in a small hospital, I have the flexibility to set up my own schedule to suit my own needs, as long as I'm available for staff and planning meetings. I prefer a hands-on approach to training and supervision. Sometimes, I cover part of one shift then part of another. I find it keeps channels of communication open and makes me more accessible to my staff."

"Our jobs have one thing in common, we both have that unrelenting element. Even though I finish an article or project, there's always another to deal with right away. No breaks from that sense of deadline," said Amanda.

"That's an astute observation. Yes, I do feel that way and, sometimes, I wish I could clone myself so that I could be in more than one place at a time. I know the paperwork is an unavoidable evil of the job, but I'd much rather be working with the staff and the patients. The supervisory position pays better. However lately, I've been feeling like there's more to life than just money." Mallory shrugged, a natural gesture indicating some frustration, even though no one was there to see it. After a brief pause, she revealed, "My work schedule leaves very little time for socialization." She chuckled. "Wow! Where did that come from? I hope that wasn't too much information. You're very easy to talk to, you know...and a good listener."

"Thanks. I feel very comfortable with you also." She hoped that Mallory could feel her smiling through the phone.

"Maybe I'd better hang up now, before I disclose where I've hidden my family jewels."

Several quick comments ran through Amanda's head in response to that straight line, but she settled for the most benign. "Well, in keeping with that sentiment, could I interest you in dinner, another opportunity to discover your secrets, and maybe a video? I was thinking of having grilled hotdogs and a salad."

"That sounds delicious...even if it's not healthy, it's a great suggestion. Think there might be enough time before dinner for us to take a walk?"

"Sure, that sounds wonderful. It'll help me wake up. Shall I come collect you, or do you want to come here?"

"I'll come to you. See you in a few minutes."

Amanda realized that her heart was beating a bit faster than usual, and she recognized that she was excited by the prospect of spending time alone with Mallory. A few moments later as they left the house, Amanda gestured for Mallory to lead the way. "I'm not sure where to go from here. I'm sure you have a trail you like."

"How much time do we have?" Mallory glanced at her watch.

"Until about a half hour before you reach famished. We just have to grill up the hotdogs. I have potato salad, coleslaw, and some tomatoes to slice. Easy as can be."

"There's about a two mile walk I like a little ways up the road here." Mallory indicated a path a short distance away. "Will that be okay with you?"

"Perfect."

The first few minutes were quiet as they adjusted their strides to one that was comfortable for each of them. They were well matched in height, so it wasn't much of an issue. They fell into an easy, ground-consuming pace and before they knew it, they were deep into the shaded woods. They walked for about thirty-five minutes before pausing to rest on a fieldstone wall overlooking a small creek.

"What a beautiful spot," said Amanda glancing around. "Just gorgeous."

They sat in companionable silence for a while until Mallory nudged Amanda and gestured with her head upstream. A deer emerged from the brush and lowered her head to drink from the water.

"Wish I had my camera with me," Amanda whispered.

The deer looked up, noticed them, and melted back into the undergrowth.

"Isn't it amazing that a large animal like a deer can disappear into the brush like that with hardly a sound?"

"Absolutely," agreed Amanda.

"So, tell me a little about yourself." Amanda propped her chin on her hand and waited for Mallory's response.

"I finished my degree by attending college in New York City, after which I returned home to Philly. I moved back to New York State a little more than a year ago to take the supervisory position at the hospital. I fell in love with this area while I was in school because of its rural nature. I wanted to advance in my profession, which was something this supervisory role at the hospital offered me. It didn't take long for me to discover that the grass is not always greener on the other side of the fence."

"What do you mean?"

Mallory shrugged. "Don't get me wrong. Although there are numerous aspects of the job that I like, there are just as many that I don't. Once I began working in the supervisory role, I discovered that I missed providing direct care to the patients, and I hate the report writing and the politics of the budgetary process. In the plus column, I do enjoy helping to decide hospital policy and training the new employees. So there are tradeoffs in everything and since I don't hate the job, I've made myself contented."

"Does the shift work bother you?"

"Not any more. I've adjusted to it I think. It makes socialization difficult. It's sometimes hard for me to find people to do things with. It's nice that you're able to join me today." Mallory smiled and turned toward her right. Pointing she said, "See that path there? That's a loop I usually add onto the shorter trail if I take this route with my bike."

"I can't wait to do that. If we walk or bike again tomorrow, I want to bring my camera." We should be getting back. I'm starting to get hungry. How about you?"

\*\*\*

They retraced their path back to the house. Amanda opened the fridge and gathered the ingredients for a salad. "I'll start the grill if you'll make the salad,"

"Deal. You want onions in yours?"

"Sure, why not. Throw whatever you have in there, I'll eat anything."

They ate at the counter in the kitchen. Mallory pushed her plate back then wiped her mouth with her napkin. "That was great. I'm stuffed."

"In my one concession to good nutrition, I have fruit for dessert."

Mallory laughed. "You might need more than that to make amends for those hotdogs."

"Would you like to stay and watch a movie with me? I picked up a couple of movies earlier." Amanda retrieved the DVDs and slid them across the table.

Mallory assessed her choices. *"You've Got Mail* is one of my favorites. However, since I've never seen *Overboard*, let's watch that one,"

They cleaned up the dishes and finished dessert. Amanda set up the DVD. The light and funny movie had them sharing laughter as they watched.

"That was wonderful. Any movie that makes me laugh out loud gets five stars in my book." Mallory stood and stretched. "Thank you so much for dinner and the video."

Amanda walked her guest to the door to bid her good night. "I mentioned to you that I finally have a couple of days off. Would you be interested in taking a bike ride tomorrow? We could go a bit farther since we'll have more time, see some new scenery, and maybe take a ride around the lake. I'll pack us a lunch and we can make a day of it."

Amanda didn't hesitate at all. She could write at night, or in the morning before they left for their ride. "That sounds great. Would it be okay to leave around ten? If I get up early, I can get some writing done before we take off. What do you think?"

"Sounds like a plan to me. Okay, it's a date then." Mallory gave Amanda a quick hug and left without looking back.

*Hmm, date. Did she mean 'date' as in a friendly get together or date as in 'date date?' Which do I want it to be?* She wasn't even sure if Mallory was gay or straight. Since she'd recognized and accepted her own attraction to women, Amanda had made it a policy to only date other lesbians because she didn't want to bring a straight woman out. She'd seen too many of those relationships end in heartbreak when reality faced them. The pressures of coming out to parents, family, and friends too often sent them running back into the folds of heterosexuality, leaving a wake of pain behind. Amanda's own coming out had been painful enough. She told three of her closest friends about her 'secret' only to have two of them cut her from their lives. Only Dana had stood by her. Telling her family had brought additional heartbreak.

*\*\*\**

Amanda locked up the house before she went upstairs. There was ample time to get in a couple of good hours of work before she went to bed. She logged into her email to see if the new assignment from her boss had arrived. In addition to the standard batch of spam she didn't need to bother with, there was an email from Bernie. She ignored it not wanting to ruin the good mood she was in after her evening with Mallory, by reading what she expected would be a poison pen note from Bernie. She had closed that door and was happy leaving things as they were.

Before snapping the lid closed on her laptop, Amanda noticed that it was just after one o'clock. She was pleased with her accomplishment of finishing another chapter in her book plus a short article that she'd been putting off writing since arriving at Dana's. It was a relief to finish it and email her submission. After setting the alarm for nine, she slid into bed between the soft sheets and fell asleep almost immediately.

*\*\*\**

Refreshed after a solid night's sleep, Amanda lingered in the shower then ate a breakfast of cereal and fruit. She was just finishing a cup of tea when Mallory knocked at the door.

"Good morning." Mallory's greeting was as cheerful as she looked. Dressed in a bright red jersey and black body conforming biking shorts, she entered the kitchen and took a seat next to Amanda at the breakfast bar, but not before Amanda got to check out Mallory's tight body in the outfit that fit her like a second skin.

"Want some breakfast or some tea? The water is still hot," Amanda pointed to the kettle on the stove.

"No, thanks, I ate already, but I'm out of juice. Do you have any?"

"There's some OJ in the fridge. Help yourself." Amanda allowed herself to appreciate the view as Mallory leaned over to get the juice from the fridge. *There's no doubt about it—I find Mallory's sporty good looks and tight body very attractive.* Her eyes, an interesting blue-green, appeared greener in the morning sunlight streaming through the kitchen window. Her lashes were darker than her paler hair color, almost black in fact, giving the appearance that she was wearing mascara although she was not. *Mallory is cute, for sure, but her smile transforms her face from cute into lovely. She has a very kissable mouth, especially the way her lips turn up at the corners giving the impression that she is always just about to smile.*

After finishing their beverages, Amanda rolled Dana's mountain bike out of the garage and they set off following the path they had taken the previous day. They took a trail that headed north at the first intersection and rode for about an hour before stopping for a break. Mallory produced some nuts and raisins from her seat bag. She shared them with Amanda who, in her pack, was carrying bottles of water, one of which she shared with Mallory.

Amanda wiped her brow. "This is a great ride. Not too steep, but it still presents enough of a challenge for someone like me who's out of practice. You're definitely a much better rider than I am."

"You have to be patient with yourself. When was the last time you rode?"

"At least a year or more ago. I got focused on working and really didn't pay attention to my health as much as I should have. I'm glad you're here to encourage me to not just sit around and veg out."

Mallory let her eyes travel the length of Amanda's body, boldly assessing without appearing the least bit self-conscious. "You look to be in good shape. You must have done something, because you're still fit."

"I used to jog or walk, but not often enough. We had a gym in the basement of the house, so I could go there and work out occasionally." *What was that look that flashed across Mallory's face? What did I say?*

"Maybe we should get on with it. Think you can manage another twenty-five minutes or so? There's a wonderful place to stop up the trail a bit further. We can eat lunch and have a rest before we head back."

They rode to the spot Mallory had described and stopped for lunch. Amanda was tired. She hoped she'd be able to make it back and that she wouldn't embarrass herself by having to ask Mallory to stop too frequently. "So, do you ride often, then?"

"As often as I can. When I work the day shift, I try to ride to work if my schedule allows and the weather permits it. Other than that, I do try to ride at least five miles two or three times a week. Time is always an issue though, isn't it? Do you find that you generally seem to find time for everyone but yourself?"

Amanda nodded her agreement.

"My mom always told me, 'Pay yourself first.' Of course, she was talking about saving money. She tutored me to think of myself as a bill that I owed and to be sure that I paid myself every pay period just like the telephone, electric and gas bills. I maintain that habit to this day. In the past, I've always been reasonably well disciplined financially, but not always personally, especially as it relates to exercise. When I moved up here I decided to generalize my mom's rule to include health. So, now I follow my mom's advice and pay myself first by taking time to exercise. Now I'm doing better about putting my health and fitness at the top of my daily list of things to do."

"Sounds like a good policy. Maybe I'll try to emulate your good example. I mean, I always enjoy myself when I'm getting exercise, but left to my own devices, I often just can't muster up the initiative," Amanda finished up her sandwich and took a long swig from her water bottle.

"Well, then, I'm glad you're here. We can motivate each other. Besides its more fun doing it with someone, isn't it?"

"So you're close to your mom?" Amanda asked.

"Yes. I'm especially close to my mother. My dad and I don't always see eye to eye about all things, but we still get along. I think they gave me a good start in life and I love them both. I wish we lived closer sometimes, but I haven't helped that by moving too far away for them to pop over. I was thinking of inviting them up for either Thanksgiving or Christmas. I haven't made a final decision yet. My family usually tries to get together for at least one of the holidays, but it's getting to be a bit labor intensive for them the older they get."

They sat quietly together enjoying the scenery. Mallory nodded toward the clearing. "Look, a chipmunk."

Amanda followed the progress of the cute little creature as it scurried furtively from the sanctuary of one form of vegetation or shrub to another, darting quickly from beneath a leaf of some plant to another place of safety. Suddenly, he slipped into a hole that would have been virtually invisible had they not been watching so intently.

Amanda furrowed her brow. "Wonder if he has a family in his little burrow."

"Don't know," Mallory replied. "Maybe we'll see if we watch a little longer. What about you, Amanda? Tell me about your family. You have sisters, brothers?"

"My parents are both deceased. They were smokers and ended up going long before they should have. Dad had lung cancer and mom had breast cancer. I have one brother."

"You must be close, since it's just the two of you now."

Amanda shrugged. "We used to be." She paused. Amanda assumed that Dana would have told Mallory that she was a lesbian. "Um...when I came out, not only did I lose some of my friends, but my parents also disowned me and my older brother stopped speaking to me. The worst part is that he refused to allow me to visit with my nieces and nephew, a punishment that I still can't forgive him for to this day. Despite his refusal to allow me to see the kids, I continued to send the kids cards and gifts on their birthdays and other holidays, but never receive any indication from my brother or the kids that they arrived at their proper destination. On the QT, my sister-in-law sends me a picture of the kids each year along with a note and an update on the highlights of their lives. When she sent the first photo, she begged me not to let him know."

"Thank God for your sister-in-law. At least she has sense, in addition to being kind. But never hearing from your brother must be a heartbreaking dismissal, especially since you said you were close before you revealed your sexual orientation."

"Yes. Initially it was devastating. Now, it's just painful." Amanda looked away.

The play of emotions across Amanda's face hinted that, obviously, there was more to the story, but Amanda wasn't ready to share the depth of hurt her brother's dismissal had inflicted. After such a wonderful day, she didn't want to bring down her spirits by digging up how deeply his rejection hurt her. Amanda was grateful that Mallory was willing to allow her to reveal things at her own pace and to not push by asking questions. The silence between them was comfortable.

Referring to the chipmunk, Mallory said, "Well, I suppose the little guy is tucked in for now. You feel rested enough to start back?"

"Ready when you are, I guess." Amanda wanted to ask Mallory more about her family, but Mallory was already packing up the remnants of their lunch and seemed eager to get under way. *There's plenty of time, I guess, maybe tonight when we have dinner.*

Before she swung her leg over the seat of her bike Mallory said, "You'll probably be glad to hear that the path home is much less strenuous and the ride goes much more quickly than the ride up...I know I sure am."

Standing together next to their bikes, they took a few minutes to appreciate and comment on the beauty around them. It won't be too many weeks before the leaves begin to change,"

"I know. The fall colors of the forest will only add to the beauty of the mountains in the background."

The comfortable, sunny weather contributed to a wonderful day that the new friends were sharing. The path that Mallory selected for the ride home was exactly as promised, easier than the earlier ride out, because it varied between being flat or, in places, slightly downhill.

"There's only one steep part that can be difficult. When I signal you to be careful, either get off and walk your bike or take it very carefully. That one curve up ahead can be tricky."

They had ridden a short distance down the trail when Mallory signaled with a downward motion of her hand and they dismounted to survey the difficult part of trail ahead. With Mallory's guidance, they both navigated the trickiest bit of trail. Things were easier after that for both riders. They stopped to rest twice before taking on the final leg of their ride that brought them back home.

"I don't know about you, but I need a shower," Amanda said as she toed the kickstand into place.

"I know what you mean." Mallory stretched out her legs before she turned toward Amanda. "That was a great workout, though. I think I might add a soak in my hot tub to my agenda as well. Want to join me? I bet it would make you less sore tomorrow."

"I definitely can't decline that offer. Let me wash up, get my suit, and I'll meet you at your place as quickly as I can."

Mallory gave a wave as she pedaled towards her garage.

## Chapter 3

Amanda washed off, before going in search of her suit. Unable to find it quickly and knowing that Mallory was waiting for her, she gave up searching and settled for a pair of lightweight jogging shorts and an old sleeveless T-shirt that she threw on.

"Well, at least they're clean. Can't wear what I don't have with me. Hopefully, she'll understand," she mumbled.

After gathering a towel and a comb, Amanda cut across the back yard to Mallory's house. The hot tub was recessed into the deck and Mallory was already in it, submerged to her chin in the furiously bubbling water. The air had already grown cooler since they returned from their ride causing steam to rise from the water.

"I'm sorry I took so long. I couldn't find my suit. Hope what I have on will be okay." Amanda tugged at the shoulder of her T-shirt.

"You don't need anything but your skin. Get out of those clothes and climb in. You'll feel one hundred per cent better."

"You sure?"

"Yes, come on. We're not getting any younger." Mallory softened the words with a smile and a wink.

Since high school, Amanda couldn't remember a time when she didn't feel shy about being naked in front of anyone who was not her lover. The little voice inside the left side of her head said, "*Grow up, she's a nurse, for God's sake. It's not anything she hasn't seen before.*" To which the voice on the other side of her head replied, "*Yeah, but she hasn't seen mine before.*" Amanda looked around for a sheltered spot where she could remove her clothes and found none. She also noted the neighbors wouldn't have a view of the deck area.

A devilish grin accompanied Mallory's giggle and amused, twinkling eyes. "Come on, nobody can see you but me."

Amanda slipped out of the shorts and took off her T-shirt, leaving the final bastion of modesty for last. Finally, in one quick motion, she bent and stripped off her underwear. As she stepped down into the hot tub, Mallory appreciatively swept her eyes over Amanda's body from head to toe. It was obvious that she didn't miss anything in her quick perusal. "So what's the significance of the tattoo?"

Amanda had a bar code tattoo just below her navel done in rainbow colors. Ignoring the rainbow coloration, she replied, "Just my date of birth. The tattoo seemed like a good idea at the time. I've never had any doubts about my sexuality and have always described myself as 'gay from the day I was born.' So in my drunken state one night, I thought the tattoo expressed that sentiment perfectly. It wasn't anything I've ever regretted doing exactly. Given a second chance to make the decision, I might have considered locating it in a less public place." Amanda hadn't noticed any change in Mallory's attitude when she mentioned coming out before, but she still waited to see if Mallory's attitude toward her would change.

"What a neat idea. I like it a lot and there's nothing wrong with the location you chose. I don't have any tattoos…I'm too cowardly."

"Ha! You can dish those needles out, but can't take them, eh?"

"Busted!" Mallory chuckled at the reference.

Amanda felt herself respond to Mallory's endearing laugh and warm smile. Once Amanda settled into the water, the two women enjoyed the relaxing heat of the water in shared silence. They soaked in the hot tub together for about ten minutes until the timer chimed.

"I'm cooked. I think I need to get out, but you can probably do another ten minutes or so. I was in for a while before you arrived. How about I go start some dinner? You'll join me, won't you?"

Amanda nodded her agreement and Mallory reset the timer for an additional ten minutes, stood up and walked to the steps providing Amanda an opportunity to appreciate the woman's well-toned body. She felt herself warm in response and was amazed that she could be so attracted to someone so soon after she had ended her relationship with Bernie. After Mallory's departure, as she soaked alone in the tub, she realized that Dana was right about the fact that she'd emotionally left her relationship with Bernie long ago when she'd learned that Bernie had been unfaithful the first time, or at least the first time she had caught her. She suspected there might have been many others she didn't know about.

The timer turned off the jets in the hot tub. Amanda stepped out and dried off. She still felt awkward standing outside completely nude, even though she was alone and knew no one was able to see her. From the corner, where the hot tub was tucked, to the sliding door was nearly the whole length of the house. She didn't feature making the dash naked, so she got out of the tub, hid in the shadows as best she could before drying off. Quickly throwing on her clothes, she scooted across the length of the deck. Her soft tap at the window drew an invitation to come in from Mallory. Amanda entered the living room of the cozy cottage and appreciatively absorbed the welcoming room. Decorations were in warm earthy colors with splashes of red as the accent color. Two rich reddish brown leather recliners, facing each other, were placed strategically on either side of the fireplace. A leather sofa in the same shade appeared soft and inviting. It sat opposite the fire, providing a straight on view of the flames through the glass doors that covered the hearth.

"I'm in here, around the corner," Mallory called.

Amanda, moving in the general direction of Mallory's voice, made her way into the modern kitchen. The cherry cabinets and granite countertops with swirls of deep burgundy accents complimented each other and made for a pleasing combination. "Do you want to eat in here at the counter or in the dining room?" Mallory held two plates, napkins, and silverware in her hands.

"Let's eat in here. We don't have to be fancy. What's for dinner?"

Mallory smiled. "Hungry?"

"You bet. It's probably a good idea that we're not going to the dining room. I might gnaw at the table leg and ruin the good table."

Mallory chuckled. "Well, then it's good we're staying here. I defrosted some sauce I made a couple of weeks ago. We're having pasta, my special recipe meatballs, and a huge salad. Oh yeah, and some garlic bread." She gestured between the sink and the wine rack. "Water or wine?

"Wine. Want me to open it?"

Mallory handed the dishes and silverware to Amanda. "How about you set the table and I'll finish up everything else in here." When the meal was ready, the two women sat down to their dinner. Mallory held up her glass and offered a toast. "To a wonderful new friendship."

"Absolutely," replied Amanda. "Cheers!"

"I've really enjoyed the time we've spent together the last two days. I love having company for dinner and having someone to enjoy hiking and biking with has been a gift. There have been many times that I've been lonely since I moved here," Mallory admitted with characteristic candor.

"I can understand that. It must be difficult meeting people when you work such irregular hours. How do you even begin to establish friendships, let alone find anyone to date?"

Mallory shrugged. "Yes, it's tough. Even tougher now that I'm in a supervisory role, which eliminates most of the people I know at the hospital from the friendship pool. It would be too awkward to be friends outside of work with people I supervise and impossible to date anyone from there. I just wouldn't be comfortable. A few months ago, I met a police officer named Jo, who is someone I like a lot. She was on duty at the hospital guarding a prisoner. Because we both work shift work, we've only managed to get together sporadically. I played cards with her and a couple of her friends a few times. So, honestly, the closest friend I have here is Dana and unfortunately, between her schedule and mine, we don't see each other all that often."

"So how do you go about meeting people?"

Mallory paused before she responded, giving thought to her answer. "It seems that I just wait patiently for my neighbor to invite a lovely woman friend of hers to stay at her house—someone with whom I immensely enjoy spending time.. Problem solved." Mallory winked at Amanda and flashed a wide grin, displaying perfect teeth. "We really have to thank Dana when we talk to her. She's done well by both of us."

The two women cleaned up the remnants of dinner, storing the leftovers, before they carried their wine into the living room. "Think we need a fire?" Mallory asked.

"Not unless you want one. I'm going to have to be going soon, anyway. I have to check my email to make sure everything was okay with the article I just submitted, and I wanted to write a quick email to Dana."

"If you'd like, you can log into your email account from here. You could check your mail and we could write a note to Dana together."

"Great idea. That would be fun, wouldn't it?"

The email to Dana was great fodder for laughter for both women. They commented on Dana's great choice in friends and wrote a breezy, lighthearted account of their day together. Without discussion, neither seemed to feel that it was necessary to describe their soak in the hot tub to their friend, but they mentioned the delicious dinners and how much they both enjoyed sharing meals the past two days.

Amanda reread the letter aloud one final time to allow for edits and corrections. "Okay?"

"It sounds good to me. Hit the send button." Mallory stood and stretched. "I think, after our workout today, we both may be a bit too sore tomorrow for another ride. If that turns out to be true, I wouldn't mind going into town for a leisurely lunch and a movie. I'd love to have some company. Are you up for it?"

"Sure, that sounds great, but I have to do a few hours of work sometime tomorrow. Could we do lunch after 12:30? Maybe we should check what time the movies start, decide what we want to see first, and then let the movie time dictate when we eat."

Mallory nodded her agreement. "Works for me. I'm going to use the facilities. Do you mind looking up the movies for us?"

"Sure. Not a problem."

"I'll be right back."

Amanda reached for the laptop and turned the screen to face her. The screensaver was rotating through several pictures. Each picture showed Mallory with a very attractive blonde woman. They were touching in each picture, either clowning for the camera or standing with their arms linked or one behind the other with their hands on the other's shoulders. The next photo was a picture of the two women close, face-to-face, looking into each other's eyes. Mallory was kissing the other woman on the nose. The lovely, fun photo revealed a deep intimacy between the pair. The meaning left little, if any, doubt in Amanda's mind that Mallory and this woman had a romantic relationship with each other.

When she heard the toilet flush she quickly looked up the local movie theater. By the time Mallory returned, she had the current show times up on the screen. She didn't know if she should address the information that she'd just learned about Mallory or wait for her to disclose the relationship on her own. She decided not to mention anything right away, but before she allowed herself to become too attached to Mallory, she needed to know something about the status of her relationship with the attractive blonde. Perhaps they still had a long distance involvement.

"So, did you pick out a movie?" Mallory asked as she returned to the living room.

"No," Amanda smiled. "Thought I'd wait for you so we can pick it together. I have the list here."

They selected a movie that began at two-fifteen and agreed to hold lunch until one o'clock.

"Do you have a favorite place for lunch?" Amanda asked.

"Yes, I do, and I think you'll like it too." Mallory quickly pulled up the restaurant's website and clicked on their lunch menu.

"Umm, I'm sure I can find about ten things I'd love to eat on this menu," Amanda exclaimed. "Okay, I'd better get back home so I can get up and do what I have to do tomorrow before we meet. Thank you, Mallory, for a very enjoyable day and an amazing dinner. Shall I pick you up tomorrow at what...twelve-thirty or so?"

"That would be perfect." Mallory walked Amanda to the door. "I had a great time today and am really looking forward to another day with you tomorrow." She gave Amanda's hand a quick squeeze as Amanda slipped out the door and headed home.

Before stepping off the deck, Amanda glanced back to find Mallory watching her departure, a sad expression on her face. Amanda gave a quick wave, which Mallory rewarded with a sweet smile.

## Chapter 4

Amanda pulled up in front of Mallory's house at exactly 12:30 and tooted the horn.

"So what did you get accomplished this morning?" Mallory asked as she slid into the front seat of Dana's car and buckled her seatbelt.

"I started on some copy for a new marketing campaign. That'll keep me busy for a while."

"Can you do all your work from here?"

Amanda nodded. "I think so. If it becomes necessary, I can be there virtually. My boss is flexible. In the event of some sort of disaster that requires my personal appearance, I can fly back if I have to, but that won't be for a while, till we're deeper into the ad campaign. Everyone on the team I work with has done this long enough that we can read each other's minds. The need for face-to-face meetings is extremely rare and most issues can be resolved by Internet or phone conference."

After navigating the turn at the end of the street, Amanda pulled smoothly into the light traffic, and headed for town. They easily found a parking spot near the restaurant, a small, intimate place with a glistening tan counter running down one side. There were individual color-coordinated stools on the customers' side of the counter with the food prep area opposite. On the remaining wall, there were deep chocolate brown booths with a few tables scattered between the two areas. Natural wood frames, displaying old pictures of the town taken thirty or forty years ago, decorated the freshly painted cream-colored walls. Amanda liked Mallory's choice of restaurants. There was a homey and welcoming feel to the place. The cheery hostess greeted them warmly before she seated them in one of the booths. They quickly settled and ordered their drinks.

As Mallory looked up from the menu, Amanda was waiting for her to make eye contact. With Mallory's attention now focused on her, she asked, "How about you? What did you get accomplished this morning?"

There was a brief lull in their conversation as the waitress took their order. The waitress turned and hurried towards the kitchen and Mallory clasped her hands in front of her and sought Amanda's eyes. "I got a lot accomplished. I did my laundry, then went through my laptop, and cleaned up my hard drive. I burned some old pictures to disk and just did odds and ends."

Amanda suspected that Mallory might have been reviewing some of the pictures of herself with the blonde. Amanda could see Mallory's muscles in her cheek work as she clenched her teeth together while she studiously studied the saltshaker she was playing with. Her struggle was visible.

"Mal?"

Mallory's eyes snapped up, her attention focused. Amanda wondered why she had reacted that way. "Do you not like that nickname?"

"No, it's fine. It's just that nobody around here ever calls me that. No one since...well, no one has called me that for a while."

Amanda decided it was time they quit dancing around the elephant in the room and answer the unanswered questions they probably both had. She decided to just get it over with by addressing the issue head on. "Do you want to tell me about her?" Amanda's voice was soft, her expression kind.

Mallory adjusted her position in the booth and looked away. Her eyes glinted with tears that suddenly flooded them, before she quickly blinked them away.

"How did you know?"

"I saw your screensaver last night. It's obvious you two are in love."

"Were...were in love." Her voice was nearly a whisper. "She died." Mallory expelled a deep sigh.

"I'm sorry." When Mallory didn't offer any more, Amanda waited patiently for her to continue and when she didn't Amanda asked, "When?"

Mallory exhaled another long sigh. "A little over two years ago." Mallory shifted her position in the booth, and with her eyes closed, leaned her head back against the wall. A few seconds passed before she turned toward Amanda with an open expression on her face. "Look, I know we need to talk...that I need to..." She stopped, "No, need is the wrong word. I want to tell you about her, but do you mind if we wait until we're somewhere else a bit more private?"

"Sure thing. I didn't know it would be painful or I wouldn't have brought it up. I didn't mean to make you uncomfortable."

"It's not that. It's just that sometimes talking about her makes me cry and I don't want to do that here."

"Sure." Amanda reached across the table and gave her companion's hand a squeeze. A wan smile flickered across Mallory's face. "So what do you want to talk about instead?"

"Is it a safer topic to talk about you, Amanda? What's your story? Trouble on the home front?"

"I think it's safe." She smiled. "I'm not sure how to answer that, exactly." There was a lull in the conversation while the waitress delivered their lunch and they took the first bites of their sandwiches.

"Can I ask you why you're here and not back in California?"

"Let's just say I don't like to share. Bernie felt differently. That probably sums it up reasonably well."

"How long were you together?"

"Twelve years or so."

"For how many of those years was Bernie faithful?"

"I don't know for sure...definitely not for the past two years and probably for several years before and even after that. It took me a little while to catch on. I was too trusting...too stupid, I guess."

"Don't blame yourself. Don't assume responsibility for her infidelity. I assume that since you're here at Dana's it's over. How long ago did you end your relationship?"

"I guess if I were honest, I'd admit it ended two years ago or more. I hung on longer than I should have, unwilling to give up on the twelve years I'd invested in our relationship. I just left her before I moved here."

"You seem surprisingly calm about it."

Amanda shrugged. "No choice, really. As I told Dana, I'm sad that my relationship with Bernie ended, but not sorry, if that makes sense to you. Honestly, I've had more fun with you in the past few days that I've known you than Bernie and I had in the past couple of years."

"Well, I've enjoyed our time together too, Amanda. I'm sorry about your relationship ending. Twelve years is a long time. I'm sure it was difficult to call it quits." Mallory took a bite of her sandwich. "Let's talk about something cheerful. I do want to hear more, but maybe it would be better to do it in a more private place. Besides, this is a day off. We should be having fun. We're spending too much time with sadness today. Let's try to lighten the mood and enjoy our day together."

"I agree." Amanda's enthusiasm for Mallory's suggestion was evident in her voice. Easily changing the subject, she asked, "So, what have you heard about this movie?"

They chatted about inconsequential things throughout the rest of the meal, even managing to laugh a few times as they exchanged humorous anecdotes about their favorite movies. After lunch, they gathered their belongings and walked the two blocks to the theater, happy that they had chosen to see a comedy.

They were both smiling as they exited the theater, having thoroughly enjoyed the lighthearted tale. As they walked back to the car, Amanda asked, "So, are you terribly sore today? I mean too sore to walk a bit?"

Mallory shook her head.

"Good! I rarely have anyone with whom I can enjoy shopping, so I'd like to take advantage of your presence today. I need to buy a bathing suit. Think we can find a place that would still have some left and maybe do a little window shopping along the way?"

"You don't really need a bathing suit on my account." One raised eyebrow emphasized Mallory's suggestive tone, while a slight smile played at the corners of her mouth. "Let's head over to the outlets, I'm sure you can find something there."

True to Mallory's prediction, one of the stores still had a substantial number of bathing suits left. Amanda flipped through the selection but only found two-piece suits. The sales woman approached. "Can I help you with anything?"

Amanda nodded. "Yes. Everything here is two-piece. Don't you have any one-piece suits?"

"No. Just the two-piece ones." The saleswoman made a quick scan of Amanda's body and with a demeaning tone and a decidedly superior manner, she replied, "They are in style, you know. Everyone is wearing them. We could probably even find one that would fit you."

Mallory turned away to hide her smile, while Amanda, who couldn't believe the young woman's attitude, fixed the woman with a straight face and a direct gaze. "Yes, I'm sure that's true. However the beauty pageant I'm participating in only allows one piece suits. Thanks anyway."

Mallory covered her laugh with a cough, and the pair left the store. Once outside they burst into laughter. "Did you see her face?" She brushed moisture from her eye caused by laughing so hard. "You're so quick. She's still trying to process that little nugget of information you hit her with!" She chuckled again, her spirits lifted between the humorous movie and the fun she was having with Amanda.

On the way home, Mallory broached the subject of dinner. "Interested in some left over pasta for dinner?"

Her enthusiasm evident in her tone, Amanda replied. "Oh, yum! I've got all the ingredients for a big salad. I'll make it and bring it over after I finish checking my email."

Forty-five minutes later, Mallory responded to the knock on her door and greeted Amanda with a smile.

"Did you miss me?" Amanda asked, smiling in return.

"I most assuredly did." Mallory pulled Amanda into a quick embrace. "Come on, dinner's almost ready."

Mallory finished heating the pasta in a skillet with a little butter while Amanda set the table and poured the wine. As Mallory took the first bite of the pasta, she sighed in contentment. "Mmm. I love leftover pasta. It's probably even better heated up the second day."

Amanda agreed with her. She paused to wipe the evidence of the pasta from her lips with her napkin. "So tomorrow you start four to midnight, right?"

"Yes, I have to get into the swing of that shift. I'll go to bed regular time tonight and will take a short nap tomorrow afternoon." Mallory's brows furrowed. "I don't want to take up your time tomorrow, if you have work to do. However, we've been having such a good time, I wonder if you have any free time tomorrow to do something together?"

Amanda thought for a minute. "Work? Oh, didn't I tell you? I've been moved to the four p.m. to midnight shift." She winked. It took Mallory a few seconds to absorb the implication of the statement. "I can work anytime. It's one of the joys of being self-employed. So, until you get sick of me, I'll just work when you work. That'll allow us to play together during our off hours. If you want, during the days when you're working, I can make dinner for us and you can cook or we'll eat out on our days off."

"That's a good deal for me. It'll be like having a wife." She immediately realized the implication implied by her statement.

"Or a housekeeper," she corrected, a sentiment that was even worse. She couldn't seem to extricate herself gracefully from the hole she was digging.

Amanda finally let her off the hook. "I'd say you'd better quit while you're behind. She patted Mallory on the back. "It's okay, I know what you mean. It'll work to the benefit of both of us, I think." There was nothing but kindness in her expression.

They tidied the kitchen before moving to the living room. Mallory struck a match and lit the logs in the fireplace. The weather had become quite chilly since the sun went down, so the warmth from the blaze felt good. Sitting in companionable silence watching the fire was pleasant to both women. Their silences were comfortable and each enjoyed sharing the quiet times as much as they did their animated conversations.

Mallory broke the silence first. "Thanks for letting me off the hook this afternoon at the restaurant. I didn't want to tell you my story there, because I can't always make it through without crying." Mallory began her story by extracting two tissues from her pocket. "Her name was Piper. Really, her first name was Adeline, Adeline Piper McGraw to be exact. However, she hated her first name and never used it. She was Piper to everyone except her parents who called her Addy. We knew each other over twenty years and were together nearly that long. I met her my first day in nursing school. We started out as friends. It took us almost two years to figure it out." She smiled, her eyes bright with happy memories.

"I had never met anyone like her before. She lit up any room she entered and I couldn't understand why she chose me to be her best friend." Mallory placed her palm on her chest, fingers spread wide. "Me, a boring little nobody from a small town near Philadelphia. Everyone wanted her friendship and she was genuinely friendly with everybody in our class. Me, however...she treated me special. She came from a very wealthy family in Philadelphia. They wanted her to go into the family business. She wanted to be a nurse, much to their disappointment." Mallory hesitated, thinking back. "Piper wouldn't have been happy in the business world. She had the most loving and giving heart of anyone I ever knew and I swear the patients healed better under her care simply because they drew from her strength of spirit."

Amanda smiled. "She sounds like she was a wonderful person."

"She was amazing," replied Mallory, also smiling, her voice reverent. "We laughed all the time when we were together. That's not to say we didn't work hard on our coursework, though. She was a diligent student and together we excelled in school. We were top of the class the whole four years of college. The two of us were naturally competitive and that spurred us both on in our studies. She got her BSN with a four point zero average" She shrugged, a smile on her lips. "Unfortunately, I only finished with a three point nine five—a fact she never let me forget."

After pausing to take a sip of wine, Mallory drank and settled back into her chair. "During our second year of school, Piper suggested that we get an apartment together. We found this little hole-in-the-wall place. It was so small. We couldn't figure out how to fit two single beds in the bedroom, so we agreed to share a double. We scrounged furniture from our families and the unit ended up being an extremely cozy little place to live. We were happy there. At first we were just roommates who slept together for convenience, because we couldn't fit two beds in the bedroom. Eventually, we figured it out." Mallory grinned.

"Piper made the first move." Mallory looked away, remembering. "I tend to be warm blooded—rarely feel the cold. I always accused her of having no blood. She was always chilly. At night in bed we'd spoon. I'd wrap around her to warm her up. I grew up with a sister, Sandy, who is only ten months older than me. We shared a bed throughout our childhood, so it didn't seem a big deal for me to warm Piper. I'd done it all my life for Sandy and I didn't think anything about it. I know it sounds naive of me to say this, but I never thought of her sexually until the first time she kissed me. I mean I knew I loved her, but there was a purity, a chasteness to that emotion." Mallory paused as if checking what she'd said could really be true.

Amanda waited patiently for her to continue and when she didn't, she prompted her. "Until she kissed you."

"Yes, it was a few weeks before school ended for the term. We were spooned together with me holding her. She said my name softly as if to see if I was still awake, though I'm sure she knew I was. When I responded, she said, 'I love you, you know.' I told her I loved her too. She rolled over to face me and kissed me on the lips. 'No, I mean I *love*, love you.' She kissed me a second time, pressing her body to mine. She took her time this time and started to use her tongue. I thought I'd explode. The dam burst and I kissed her back with all I was worth. I never thought, 'My God, I'm a lesbian,' or even, 'This is wrong.' It just felt like the most natural thing in the world. We didn't have sex that night. It took us a few days to get to that, but we kissed and touched, eventually progressing to being naked together when we did. The first time we made love, I came the minute she touched me. I thought that would be it, but when she slipped inside me, and it happened again, it was pure rapture. We only had a few weeks together when the semester finished, and we had to go home for the summer. Her parents were sending her to visit family in Scotland and I had a job at a summer camp. I thought I'd die of loneliness until we went back to school in September. I missed her so much."

"New love is always exciting, isn't it? All those wonderful feelings—like you'll die if you don't see your special person and then that euphoria when you do."

Mallory smiled. "Yes, I know it sounds corny, but we had a perfect relationship. I can't recall once in the whole time we were together, that we ever had a cross word or an argument. It is probably hard to accept, to believe that, but it's true. She was truly my soul mate."

"It's a beautiful story, Mallory. You were blessed to have enjoyed a relationship like that."

"I know. I think it's because it was so perfect that I miss her all the more." Mallory's eyes slowly filled with tears. "Sorry. I haven't cried about losing her for months now. I guess it's just churning up all the old memories. Know what I mean?" Mallory blotted her eyes with the now soggy tissue.

"Yes, I do. Don't be sorry...you lost something very special. I'm sure it hurts." Amanda's eyes filled in sympathy for her friend.

Smiling at the gesture, Mallory handed Amanda a tissue. They laughed as they blotted at their eyes.

"What a pair we are," Mallory's laughter broke the sad mood. "We both finished school and then went on for our Masters degrees in New York. Once we'd finished our degrees, we went back to Philly and got jobs working at the same hospital. After several years, Piper wanted to get her PhD. I agreed to support us while she finished up her degree. Then, she got a job and I went back to school."

"So, you're Doctor Barnes?"

Color crept up her face and Mallory smiled self-consciously. "Yes, hard to believe, isn't it?" She chuckled, a sound that carried no mirth. "You'd think that two people in the medical profession, like us, would have recognized it when she got sick. She was diagnosed with breast cancer that wouldn't respond to any of the treatments they tried. Before we knew it, she was in hospice. It seems we hardly had time to say good-bye." Her tears were coming freely again.

Amanda stood and moved next to Mallory on the sofa. She pulled the unresisting woman into her arms and held her as she cried, her own tears brimming in her eyes. The sobs gradually turned to whimpers. Mallory sat up, wiped her eyes, and blew her nose. She brushed her hand across the tear stains on Amanda's shoulder.

"Thanks. It was good to remember all the good things instead of just the illness. We had an amazing run and despite my sadness about her death, I do recognize how lucky we were."

Amanda nodded and waited for Mallory to quiet.

Mallory looked Amanda in the eyes, seeking something. "It's just that sometimes I'm so lonely. I miss her so much."

"I'm sure. I know how you feel. I was lonely even though I had a partner."

"Will you tell me about your life with Bernie?"

"Yes, but not tonight. Tonight was for your story. We'll get to mine next time, okay?"

"Sure. How about a cup of tea? Tea mends all hurts."

"Let me make it for you." Amanda rose from the couch and went into the kitchen to brew the tea. Tea in hand, they sat across from each other at the breakfast bar talking about nothing and everything. When the cups were empty, Amanda stood. "I think it's time for me to be heading home."

"I'm going horseback riding tomorrow morning. Want to join me?" Mallory asked.

"Horseback riding? I've never done it. Do you ride often?"

"As often as I can. I love it."

"Maybe I'll slow you down."

Mallory laughed. "It's not a race." She put her hand on Amanda's shoulder and shook her gently. "Relax, it'll be fun."

"Okay, when do you want me to be ready?"

"Well, I want a nap before I report to the hospital, so how about nine? Is that too early?"

"No, that'll be fine. I'll see you then." Amanda stood to leave.

At the door, Mallory pulled Amanda close and hugged her hard, not releasing her for a few seconds. Amanda knew she was appreciating a new sense of closeness between them. She felt it, too. She felt that she could tell Mallory anything.

## Chapter 5

Mallory picked Amanda up at her doorstep at nine and drove to the stables where they selected their mounts and paid the rental. Mallory gave Amanda a crash course in how to mount and control her horse. Together they rode for over two hours, exploring the trails Mallory selected. The scenery was beautiful, and seeing the area from the back of a horse provided a completely different perspective. It was with a shared reluctance that they turned the horses back toward the stable.

Amanda was sore by the time they got back home, a fact she demonstrated as she slowly climbed out of the car.

Noticing her obvious discomfort, Mallory offered, "How about a quick dip into the hot tub?"

"Is there time?"

"There's always time if it involves getting to see you naked." Mallory teased, adding a wink.

"Suave, Mallory. You really know how to relax a shy woman such as myself," Amanda smirked, tongue firmly in cheek. Truth was, the teasing made her feel more relaxed. They headed for the back deck. While Mallory veered to the linen closet to get them towels, Amanda took advantage of her departure to strip quickly. She was already sitting in the tub when Mallory came back outside.

"Oh, I see. Turnabout is fair play in your book, huh? Okay, fair is fair." She locked her eyes on Amanda's and reached for the first button on her shirt. She loosened it slowly, and moved to the next. With each button she opened, Mallory separated the blouse slightly, giving Amanda a quick flash of the soft, tan skin beneath. Seeing the look of shock, accompanied by possibly the beginning of desire, Mallory laughed. "You're so easy."

Mallory quickly stripped off her clothes and stepped into the hot tub. She was aware of Amanda's eyes traveling the length of her body as she entered the water. A mirror wasn't necessary to tell her she was blushing. They soaked some of the soreness out of their muscles as they relaxed in the bubbling water.

"So what's on your agenda for the rest of today?" Mallory asked.

"Same as your day…work, work, and more work. When I'm tapped out with that, I'll probably work on my novel."

"What are you writing about?"

"It's a lesbian love story—a classic girl meets girl, girl and girl struggle, girl gets girl story…what else?" They both laughed.

After adjusting her position so the jet hit her lower back, Mallory asked, "Will you let me read it?"

"It's not finished yet. Not even close really. However, if you're willing to run the risk that you'll never know how it ends, I could use a first reader."

"Why won't I get to read the end, you planning on going somewhere?"

"No, of course not, but I've sort of reached a dry spell. I sit and stare at the screen and the going is tough. I've rewritten this same chapter several times and just can't seem to make myself happy with it. Maybe you'll have an idea for me after you read what I have so far."

The timer on the hot tub turned off the bubbles. "You first," Mallory said, a wide grin lighting her face.

Amanda stood up, raising an eyebrow as if to say, 'So there!' She climbed the stairs and wrapped up in a towel, unsure if she should put her clothes on there or make a dash across the yard to Dana's place. As if reading her mind, Mallory offered her the shower in her house.

"I think I'll just put my clothes on and make a run for home. Thanks anyway for the offer."

"At least come in and dry off first," said Mallory.

Inside, Amanda dressed quickly. When she emerged from the bathroom, she noticed that Mallory had wrapped herself in a robe. The realization struck Amanda, as she strolled across the living room, that she would miss Mallory when she returned to Dana's place.

"I know this is ridiculous after knowing you for such a short time," Mallory said, as if reading Amanda's mind. "I'm growing used to your presence in my life. You're such easy company. These last few days have been more fun than I've had the whole time I've lived here."

Amanda smiled. "I know what you mean. I'll miss you, too. We have to be reasonable. You need some rest before you go to the hospital and I have work to do as well. Call me when you get home later, okay?"

Mallory shrugged. "Are you sure? It'll be late, probably twelve thirty or twelve forty-five. Won't you be asleep?"

"No. Like I told you, I've decided that in order to allow us to spend an optimal amount of time with each other, whenever I can, I'll work the same hours you do. So, if you want to do something in your off time I'll be available."

"You'd do that for me?" Mallory shook her head in disbelief. "Because of my crazy schedule, I find it almost impossible to get together with friends, even those I've known for a long time. Thank you, I really appreciate that. I look forward to our having fun and being great friends."

"Okay then...catch you later?"

"Right." Mallory reached for Amanda and pulled her into a close embrace.

Amanda could feel Mallory's tight body through the thin material of her robe. She pulled away when she felt that familiar tingle start between her legs. The thought flashed through her mind that neither she nor Mallory was emotionally ready to move their friendship to that next physical level, despite what her body wanted.

"I'd better get going so you can get some rest." Reluctantly she pulled away and turned toward home.

\*\*\*

Her shower completed, Amanda dressed in jeans and a long sleeved T-shirt and headed for her laptop. She decided that today would be the day she finally read Bernie's emails. She clicked on the first in the list and began to read.

*My Dearest Amanda:*

*The house is so empty without you here. I came home from my trip expecting that you would have changed your mind and I would find you here waiting for me. Don't get me wrong. I fully expected you'd be here waiting to give me hell. I know I deserve it. I admit that I've treated you shabbily and I apologize to you sincerely. Can you find it in your heart to forgive me? I miss you baby. Please come home to me. I love you and I know you still love me.*

*Bernie*

Amanda couldn't believe it. Bernie honestly thought she'd be there waiting for her to come home? She shook her head struggling to believe what she read. She didn't even know how to respond to Bernie's note and the sentiments expressed there. She scrolled down the list of her emails and found a second note from Bernie. Realizing she was holding her breath as she read the first email, she sighed, exhaling fully through pursed lips. She clicked and read the next.

*Dear Amanda:*

*I wonder why I haven't heard from you. Where are you? I hope you are okay and that nothing has happened to you. I'm worried. Please call me or email me to let me know you are all right. I love and miss you.*

*Bernie*

It amazed Amanda that Bernie was acting like nothing was wrong between them. She didn't want to call her, so she decided to write back to her instead. She gave a great deal of thought to what she wanted to say and just as she was ready to write to Bernie, an Instant Message from her appeared on the computer screen.

**Roomwithaview:** There you are. Finally. Where are you and why didn't you respond to me?

**Hazeleyes4u:** Yes, I'm here…was just about to write to you.

**Roomwithaview:** About time, too…I've been worried. Where are you?

**Hazeleyes4u:** It is really of no concern to you. I told you that I was done, Bernie. Let it go. Let me go. Go hook up with one of your little floozies if you're lonely.

**Roomwithaview:** That's so unlike you. You're rarely intentionally unkind.

**Hazeleyes4u:** What do you want from me Bernie?

**Roomwithaview:** I want you to come home.

**Hazeleyes4u:** Well, it's no longer about what you want, is it? I'm happier not being there.

**Roomwithaview:** That's too bad, because I'm happier with you here. I said I was sorry. What else can I do? Can I buy you something pretty? If I knew where you were, I'd send flowers.

**Hazeleyes4u:** Do you really expect me to forgive your infidelity if you send me some posies? God, Bernie. You really just don't get it. I loved you once. Couldn't get enough of you or do enough for you. Anything that would make you happy...but you threw it away. I hope that little piece you had on the side was worth it, because your cheating cost us our relationship.

**Roomwithaview:** So it's entirely my fault then?

**Hazeleyes4u:** What? Now I'm guilty of making you cheat?

**Roomwithaview:** Well, it can't be all one sided. I wanted things in bed that you wouldn't give me. So, I had to find them elsewhere. I never cheated when I was close to home. I respected our relationship too much.

**Hazeleyes4u:** Bernie, I never denied you anything in bed and you know it. Well, despite what you think, only cheating when you are away is not being respectful...it's being sneaky and it still counts as infidelity. Unfortunately, you were not clever enough to do it without getting caught or you just didn't care.

**Roomwithaview:** You're the only important one. None of them meant anything to me.

**Hazeleyes4u:** That's too bad. They meant something to me. The fact you would be with them meant something to me.

**Roomwithaview:** We've had twelve good years, Amanda. Don't throw it away.

**Hazeleyes4u:** Throw it away...me? You need to remember I wasn't the one who threw it away.

**Roomwithaview:** Yes, I know that. I don't know how to say I'm sorry any other way. I guess I'll just have to keep saying it until you forgive me.

**Hazeleyes4u:** Okay, if it helps you any, I accept your apology. Thank you for that. But it doesn't change anything. I'm not coming back.

**Roomwithaview:** I hear you. You've said that before. I'll just have to try to make you change your mind. I love you Amanda. If you come back to me, I'll go to counseling or do anything you want, if you'll just forgive me and come home. Won't you at least tell me where you are? I'm worried about you.

**Hazeleyes4u:** No need to worry, I'm fine. I'm at Dana's place in New York. She's away for a few months.

Roomwithaview: Thank you.

**Hazeleyes4u:** I'm signing off now, B. take care of yourself.

Roomwithaview: I love you.

Amanda didn't respond to Bernie's last comment, she simply closed her IM program. The first thought she had was that her conversation with Bernie was less painful than she had expected. The anticipation had been far worse than the reality. Her second thought was that despite Bernie's profession of her love and seemingly genuine admission of sorrow, Amanda remained unmoved and ever more convinced that her decision to leave Bernie was the best resolution for her. She didn't doubt that Bernie loved her, or at least thought she did. In her heart, she knew that Bernie would never change. She was too good-looking, too charming, and too suave for her own good. Women were drawn to her like bees to honey, and she obviously couldn't bring herself to disappoint any number of them who desired her company.

Bernie's willingness to go to counseling was a new wrinkle though. It puzzled Amanda, since Bernie had never been willing to go for help before, despite the many times she'd asked her to. Regardless, there was not one doubt in Amanda's mind that she'd made a good decision to leave the relationship, and she did not intend to change her mind despite her twelve year investment in the failed partnership.

Over the next few hours, Amanda worked on her current project. She wrote and submitted the completed copy, ate dinner, finally finished the problematic chapter in her book, then watched the news. She was eager for Mallory to get home. Restless, she paced around the living room, repeatedly peering out of the window, knowing it was a futile activity since Mallory wasn't due to be home for some time yet.

*Get a grip—she's only been gone a few hours. You act like she's been gone weeks.* Amanda put on some classical music, poured herself a small glass of wine, and settled into a comfortable, oversized chair. She kicked off her shoes and put her feet up on the ottoman determined to relax until Mallory showed up. Dana had made few changes to the cozy room over the years other than to paint the walls a soft, restful shade of sage green. The dark bookshelves on either side of the fireplace contrasted nicely with her color choice.

Amanda's mind traveled back through her conversation with Bernie. She wondered if the reason she was no longer willing to work on her relationship with Bernie was because she was attracted to Mallory. She had to admit she enjoyed Mallory's company and she was certainly pleasing to look at. Was she falling in love with her? No, not yet...but she definitely was in like. Mallory was easy to be with and after all, she was the only person she knew in this area. It was natural that she'd want to spend time with her, wasn't it? While she was pondering that question, she heard a knock at the door. A quick glance at the clock told her it was only twelve o'clock. It was too early for Mallory who wasn't due for another half hour. *Who would be at the door at this hour?*

Amanda peered through the peephole in the door. A smile came immediately to her face, as she pulled open the door to be greeted by an equally big grin on Mallory's face. It seemed totally natural when Mallory easily moved into Amanda's arms for a welcoming hug.

Mallory placed a quick kiss on Amanda's cheek. "I was finished with everything I had to do by eleven thirty, so I left early. I saw your light. It's okay that I stopped by?"

Amanda stepped aside to allow Mallory entrance into the living room where they sat down. "Of course it's okay for you to stop in. Honestly I was just thinking about you."

Mallory smiled. "Good thoughts, I hope?"

"Without a doubt. I was wondering when you'd be getting home. I know this will sound strange, but I missed you while you were gone."

"No, not strange at all. I missed you too." Mallory graced Amanda with a warm smile. "You're the first person I've met since moving here that I've really had an opportunity to spend down time with, other than Dana of course. The two of us, well…we were just always so busy, we didn't get to do that much together."

"I'd love to see her settle down with someone. I don't know that she's even dated anybody for a very long time."

"Can I ask a personal question?"

Amanda nodded yes.

"Have you and she ever, you know, had anything between you?"

"Other than friendship?" Amanda shook her head. "No, never. She's simply my oldest and closest friend and I love her to bits. For as long as I've known her, she's been straight and has only dated men. Why, have you?"

"No, although I admit that at first, I definitely found her attractive. I didn't get any specific vibes that she was gay when we initially met. Besides, I was still completely broken up, mourning Piper's death. So we became friends and that was all there was. Does Dana date, though? I've never seen her have anyone around, and she never mentions anyone."

"She's dated in the past." Amanda looked up calculating time. "Last time Dana dated anyone for any sustained time was quite a while ago. She briefly dated a guy about six years ago, but I think it ended badly. She didn't talk about it much, just said she was over him, and that she didn't consider herself good relationship material. I've not known her to date anyone since. If she has, it must have only been casual, because she never mentioned anybody specific. If I raised the issue with her, she'd always say she was too busy to get involved."

"I wish she'd find someone, too. It's lonely facing the world on your own."

"Yes, so true. Speaking of not wanting to face the world alone, what time do you want to get together tomorrow...well today, rather." Amanda asked.

"Want to have breakfast together? Afterwards, I need to go to town and do some food shopping."

"Oh, great idea. I need some provisions too. Expecting she'd be away, Dana didn't leave much here in the way of food. I've used up some of her staples that I want to replace and I need food for the week. Since you and I have been eating together almost every day, want to just plan our menus for the week and split the bill?" Amanda hoped she wasn't being too presumptuous.

"That's a wonderful suggestion. Why don't you decide our menu on the odd numbered days and I'll plan them for the even numbered ones? Then we'll combine the list and get all the stuff we need."

Amanda liked that idea but made one suggestion. "You've been supplying all the wine. Let me supply it this week."

"Agreed."

The two women got busy making their shopping lists. They compared them and combined the lists into one that included everything they'd need to prepare their meals for the week.

Mallory suggested, "How about we go out for breakfast tomorrow morning, or should that be this morning, and then do our shopping. It's supposed to start raining late in the morning, so should we get an early start around eight?"

"Sounds great, Mallory, I'll pick you up."

"I'd better get out of here then, so we can both get some sleep. Since it's going to rain, want to have a 'reading day' after we do our chores?"

"Yes, absolutely. That sounds perfect."

\*\*\*

The next morning with their shopping and other chores completed, Mallory and Amanda settled into the recliners in Mallory's living room after they started a fire in the fireplace. They spent the afternoon reading and talking about their favorite books and other things they enjoyed.

The remainder of the week followed a similar pattern. The two women continued to work and play together. They biked, walked, or chose something active to do in the morning after breakfast, before they returned to their individual houses to rest in the afternoon. They rented the horses again and because Amanda was less nervous this time, they took a different, slightly more challenging trail. Amanda was no less sore at the end of the ride.

The new friends took turns cooking and soon discovered that they were both good cooks. A natural rhythm seemed to exist for them when they were in the kitchen, like a wordless and tuneless dance. It seemed that neither was in charge or ordered the other around. Each would volunteer to do specific chores. Rarely did they have to say any more to each other than 'I'll do the salad,' or 'Let me peel the potatoes,' before the meal seemed to magically come together.

"Umm, this is good." Amanda complimented Mallory on the lunch she'd prepared.

"Just pork chops on the grill."

"Yeah, I know, but that marinade you made is really good," said Amanda after licking her fingers. "Yum!" She grinned.

It was Mallory's first day off, meaning that she started a new shift in two days "You start eight to four next, right?" Amanda asked.

"Yep! We'll be back on normal hours. Before I used to hate changing shifts, but I guess I have sort of gotten used to it by now. It helps that you work shift work, too." She winked at Amanda and the two chuckled.

Mallory said, "Want to see if we can get in touch with Dana? It'll be harder for us to reach her next week due to the shift I'm working."

Amanda readily agreed to the suggestion as they quickly booted up Mallory's computer. A few seconds, Dana's face appeared on the screen.

"So how are my two favorite people?" Dana asked.

The three women chatted as though they were in the same room. "I can't talk long," Dana cautioned them. "I'm meeting some of my team from work for dinner later and I have a ton of work to do before that." She told them about the group of people she was collaborating with on her assignment. "I'm working closely with a team member who is an American born Italian named Nic. Italian is the native language spoken in their home. I thought my Italian was good, but Nic's is wonderful—very idiomatic. I've learned so much while we've been working on some of the translations and it's been great collaborating with Nic and the other members of the team."

"It's wonderful to hear that you're enjoying your time there," said Mallory when she could get a word in edgewise.

"Yeah, definitely. We've all been hanging out together when we're off duty so it's the most fun I've ever had on an assignment. Mostly I'm doing the touristy things. Nic has visited here many times and volunteered to be my escort. We've been going to some very interesting places. I'm thoroughly enjoying this assignment and spending my time here."

"It's good to see you so happy and to hear you're having fun. It almost sounds like more of a vacation than a job this trip," said Amanda.

"True, so true." Dana grinned at her friends. "Oh, Amanda, remember my friend Tony? He's working on the project with us. In a couple of weeks, Nic and I are going to a party at Tony and his partner Bruno's place. They live on a lake a short distance from the city. That should be a fun, weekend long event."

"Sounds like you're having a good time. We've been enjoying ourselves too." Amanda elaborated on some of the activities she and Mallory had been enjoying since Dana left on her trip.

They chatted for a few more moments until Mallory said, "I know you have to get to work, so we'll let you go. Give us a buzz when you have time to chat some more. We're both working eight to four this coming week."

Amanda and Mallory smiled at each other when Dana asked, "Both of you? You too Amanda?"

"Yeah, I decided to work Mallory's hours when I can, so it'll make it easier for us to eat together. We're pooling our resources and our cooking talents as well."

"It's good to see that you're both getting along so well. From what you've told me you seem to be so compatible. It's good to have company. It can be lonely when you're by yourself all the time. Take it from me, I know how it is because I travel so much."

"Well, it's good you found someone to have fun with this trip. You usually work too hard," Amanda replied.

"Not this trip, it seems. Okay, I've got to run. It was great seeing both of you." Dana made quote marks with her fingers and grinned as she said the word seeing. "I'll try to catch you next weekend, if I have any time to chat. The team has been extremely busy and doing the touristy things is taking up most of my spare time. If I can't call, I'll write the minute I have time. Don't worry if you don't hear from me regularly. I'm busy...it's a good busy, though." She gave them a big grin and wiggled her fingers in the traditional farewell gesture. "Bye."

As she switched off the computer, Mallory commented, "It was good to see and speak to Dana. I thought she was in good spirits, didn't you?"

"Yes, absolutely. I love it that we can see her as well as talk to her. It's been hard for us to connect with her due to the time difference and everyone's schedule. From everything we just heard she's really been enjoying this assignment. At least she's having some fun on this trip, especially since she's in Rome. She seems excited about Bruno and Tony's upcoming party and about this guy Nic she's been seeing so much of." In awe of the technology that made it possible for them to see and talk to Dana in Italy, Amanda added, "Who would have thought that some of the gadgets we read in comic books when we were kids would ever be a reality in our lifetime?"

"I know. Wow! Look at the time, Amanda. I'd better get out of here."

"This was fun."

The smile Mallory returned lit up the room.

## Chapter 6

Dana clicked quit and closed the program. She was expecting Nic at any moment. They wanted to spend a couple of hours translating one of the contracts they were working on before meeting Tony for a drink. Tony was their counterpart on the Italian company's team with whom their employer was negotiating a huge deal. Several smaller sized international companies were involved in the merger. Each one had one or two translators or interpreters with them to translate the stacks of extremely difficult negotiations and contract agreements. Dana and Tony had worked together before and formed a close friendship. She was glad he was assigned on this contract. She trusted him and found him very agreeable to work with, along with enjoying his company outside of the workplace.

Tony's partner Bruno, a hair stylist, was always after Dana to let him color her hair. She had never been fond of her rusty shade and had finally agreed to allow him to work on her. His salon was in a caretaker's cottage behind their home. They lived in Bracciano, a resort town on Lago di Bracciano, a roughly forty minute ride from Rome, depending on traffic. Dana had visited them the last time she worked in Rome and had spent the day with them at their lake house. During her previous visit, they'd toured the scenic resort area, visiting a beautiful church and the castle there. Because tourists filled the town the day she went to visit, she especially appreciated having her own personal tour guides. It was that day that Bruno persuaded her to let him work on her hair. She made the promise 'next time I'm in Rome' and he was holding her to the promise.

She was pleased to accept the invitation to visit Tony and Bruno for the weekend, two weeks hence, when they were having a small party on Saturday evening. Nic was invited, too, and they had already agreed to go together. There was a soft knock on the door. Her pulse picked up its tempo in anticipation as she opened the door. After a quick embrace, Nic smiled down at Dana. "Hi. Ready to get to work?"

"Yes," she said, for once not minding having to put in extra hours.

***

The next two weeks flew by. Dana and Nic worked together every day. When not at work, they toured Rome, visiting all the well-known places including the museums, historical sites, many of the churches and, of course, the Vatican. Each of them tossed coins over their shoulders into the water on their visit to the Trevi fountain. At the end of several weeks of work, they were both exhausted and ready for a break.

The weekend of the party, Dana and Nic met at the train station for their trip to Tony and Bruno's. Nic took Dana's bag and, after they found a seat, placed it in the overhead storage area. An hour later, after climbing into Bruno and Tony's car, they wound their way through some narrow streets before skirting over to the lake. The view was breathtaking. Towering mountains and hills cast their long shadows across the clear, refreshing looking water. Seafowl floated in the lake, while humans shared the peaceful location.

Bruno navigated the traffic like a pro and before too many minutes passed, they were unloading the luggage. Bruno handed both of the guests' bags to Tony. Grasping Dana's hand in his own, he winked at Nic. "Mi dispiace–oggi lei viene con me. Più tardi sarà vostra." (I'm sorry–today she comes with me. Tonight she will be yours.)

As Bruno led Dana away, Tony invited Nic inside. "Come. Some friends are already here for the party. Obviously Bruno has plans for Dana. He's been eager to get his hands on her hair for over two years. We'll see her in a few hours and, if I know Bruno, we'll be lucky if we recognize her."

By cocktail hour, Dana hadn't returned from her session with Bruno so Nic used the time alone to shower and dress before heading downstairs to meet some of the other guests for drinks and hors d'oeuvres.

\*\*\*

Bruno was busy making the final changes to Dana's new hairstyle. He began, two hours earlier, by styling her hair in a very short cut, which swept back from her face and accented her beautiful pale blue eyes. He highlighted her naturally rust colored hair with lighter tones, softening and lightening the overall color by a couple of shades. With her back facing the mirror, he shaped her eyebrows and applied makeup. Finally finished, he bent and kissed her lightly on the lips. "Beautiful," he declared. "If I were a lesbian or a straight man, tonight I would be begging for your attention. More to the point, I don't think Nic will be able to resist your charms tonight."

Dana blushed. "I'm not so sure that's a good thing for all the reasons we've discussed."

While Bruno worked on her hair, she had explained her nervousness about her new relationship. "I've never been involved in such an intense relationship before, and then there is the fact that we work together. Things could get complicated."

"Sometimes complications can be very enjoyable. Go, Dana, drink some wine and live a little on the wild side tonight. You never know, sometimes where there is a little smoke, there smolders a hot fire beneath. Have fun tonight, my friend."

Bruno showed her to her room. Once inside, she noticed her untouched suitcase was on the bed, and that her companion's bag was already unpacked, as was her own suit bag. Her dress was hanging in the closet next to Nic's clothes. She walked over to the closet to get her dress off the hanger. She put her nose against the jacket hanging there and inhaled, immediately feeling the flush overtake her body at the familiar scent.

*What's wrong with me? I never respond to anyone like this.* She was puzzled and a bit frightened by her emotions, and wished she had time to talk to Amanda about what she was feeling. However, there wasn't time because she was late already. Earlier, after he finished her hair, Bruno had done her makeup. Because she'd already showered that morning, she opted just to wash and quickly dress. The slinky emerald green silk sheath fit her trim figure like a second skin. She hardly recognized herself when she looked into the mirror. The quiet knock at the door caused her to nervously run her hands down the front of the dress to smooth out any imaginary wrinkles.

Bruno expelled a long, slow whistle as Dana opened the door. "Sei bellissima. Se non sto attento mi ruberà il cuore. Antonio sarebbe molto scontento."

"Bruno, you know I couldn't steal your heart from Antonio if I tried. You're such a flirt... thank you. I love the new hairdo...especially the color. You outdid yourself."

"Shall we go down and join the others?"

They descended the stairs together entering the large, ornate living room already filled with guests. As she scanned the room, she spied her date leaning casually against the far wall speaking with a middle-aged woman. Dressed in a well-tailored navy jacket, white shirt open at the collar, and tan well cut slacks—height was not the only attribute that made Nic a standout in the crowd.

Their eyes met and it was as if their bodies were magnetic, pulled naturally towards each other. The tall, slender frame and dark good looks drew Dana in, and they met somewhere in the middle of the room. Nic grasped Dana's hands, leaned down, and whispered into her ear, "You look especially beautiful tonight. I love your hair short like that. Can I get you a drink?"

"Thank you, yes. Some wine I think."

Drinks in hand, they circulated, socializing with each of the guests in turn. Eventually, after speaking with everyone in the room they finally found themselves alone. Dana thanked her companion for hanging her dress. "That was so considerate of you. I really appreciate it."

Noticing that Dana seemed a little nervous, Nic leaned closer to keep their conversation between the two of them. "I hope you don't mind. More guests than they anticipated asked to stay and they were short of bedrooms. I guess he assumed that since we came together, we wouldn't mind sharing a room. He asked me and I told him it would be all right. I hope I wasn't wrong."

Dana smiled. "We're both adults, I'm sure we can manage a night together."

Nic, in a voice so low that Dana had to lean closer to hear, whispered, "Relax, sweetheart. I've made it very clear to you that I want a more intimate relationship with you. Don't forget that I promised I wouldn't push you into anything that you're not comfortable with, and I'll keep my word. I meant it when I told you that I wouldn't be the one to make the first move. If your answer is 'no' and you decide that you don't want me the same way I want you, we can simply stay friends. I swear it won't interfere with our ability to work together either way. Let's be honest about this, you wouldn't be the first woman to turn me down." Nic grinned before leaning closer again to whisper into Dana's ear, "But I hope you're smarter than they were."

Dana laughed in spite of her concerns and visibly relaxed. Intellect, wit, charm, a good sense of humor—all those attributes were wrapped in a physically enticing package of dark hair and eyes, and a sensuous mouth that drew Dana's focus. She didn't know how she, or anyone else, could resist the many charms of Nic Bianchi.

They sat across from each other at the dinner table. Despite the spirited conversation from the people sitting on either side of her, Dana's eyes kept being drawn back to those long-lashed dark eyes and sensuous mouth. She didn't know what possessed her, but she couldn't refrain from winking when she caught Nic looking at her. She smiled when Nic's only response was a slight nod and a raised eyebrow.

Finally, dessert arrived. Dana couldn't stop herself from feeling that she had been away from her companion for too long. She looked over and smiled when their eyes met. She noted that each of the women on either side of Nic was speaking simultaneously trying unsuccessfully to obtain undivided attention. Dana felt a shiver run up her spine when warm chocolate brown eyes met hers and dipped to sweep across her breasts lingering longer than was appropriate. Dana felt her nipples tighten. She glanced down to check that they were not visible through the soft material of her dress. She slid her hand down from the base of her neck, stopping to rest it over her pounding heart, telegraphing her response. She reached for her wine glass and took a sip, which did nothing to cool her racing pulse.

Dana still didn't understand this heightened physical response she was feeling. She had never experienced this elevated level of attraction for anyone before. She wondered, why now, why never before this, and why Nic? Did it really matter—the reason why? Perhaps it was just the right place, the right time, and the right person. Regardless of what was generating the impact to her libido, she vowed that she was not going to allow herself to miss out on something that she hoped would have a better outcome than her past sexual experiences. She'd been celibate now for six long and lonely years. Maybe it was time to try again, to accept that it was meant to be.

Following dinner, Dana was detained by one of the other dinner guests as the group filtered out back for dancing. Finally freeing herself, she found Nic waiting outside for her. When the musicians began to play, it didn't take long for the DJ to get the group back on their feet and dancing. Nic was a wonderful fast dancer. Despite the differences in their height, they seemed to move with each other as though they had been dancing together all their lives. She was beginning to warm to the idea that they would sleep together later and hoped that the old adage that one's dancing prowess was a predictor of how skilled the person was in bed.

The music slowed and Nic pulled Dana tight before leaning down to whisper seductively in her ear. "I know we will be sleeping together in the same room tonight, but are you going to make love with me?"

The soft words and warm breath against her ear sent another set of shivers down her spine and she felt an unfamiliar warmth and moisture between her legs. Dana leaned back and looked up, pinning their eyes together. With a coy smile, she replied, "The jury is still out on that."

"What was the last vote, if I may inquire?"

"Ten-two."

"In favor or opposed?"

Dana slipped her hands beneath Nic's jacket and slid them slowly up and down the lean but muscular torso. She leaned into the body she wanted, the body that had excited an interest from her like no one ever had before. She closed her eyes and inhaled deeply. After she inhaled her fill, she reached up to whisper, "What do you think?"

"Oh God! You're killing me here, and you know it too, don't you? I've been turned on for weeks, ever since I met you. You have no idea what you do to me." Nic placed a quick kiss on the top of Dana's head. "I want you so much. You're making me crazy. Is it possible, in any way, for me to bribe those last two holdout jurors?"

The unexpected response made Dana laugh. "Perhaps one of them could be convinced by a glass of wine," she teased. Dana slid her hands out from under the jacket, allowing them to linger seductively as they drew around the front to toy with the buttons of Nic's shirt before she dropped her hands. *What's wrong with me? Who is this person? Bruno must have done more than just bleach pieces of my hair—he must have bleached my brain as well.*

They had a wonderful evening together as they enjoyed dancing and spending time with the other guests both singly and together as a couple. Dana was talking with Bruno when Nic came up behind her and whispered in her ear. "I'm going to head up. I have a call to make. Take your time. I'll wait up for you."

"You make a very attractive couple, you know," Bruno said when they were alone.

"Thank you."

"Have you made a decision yet?"

Dana looked at Bruno and nodded.

He studied her face for a moment before he said, "Then what are you doing hanging around here?"

"I'm nervous. It's been a long time for me, and this feels so different."

"Don't be nervous. Sex is as old as time. Tab A/Slot B. Even those of us who end up with two tabs or two slots seem to figure out how to make things work," he said, his eyes twinkling. "Not to worry...you'll be fine." He gave her a hug of encouragement before sending her on her way.

Dana climbed the stairs. Butterflies fluttered in her stomach. She rapped softly at the door then entered the bedroom. Nic was seated across the room reading. Undisguised desire burned in the eyes that traveled the length of Dana's body then slowly returned to meet her eyes.

"Jury's in." Dana said with a smile, as she slipped off her shoes and started to slowly cross the room.

"So, what was the verdict?"

Dana slid into Nic's lap and nestled easily into welcoming arms. "Well, I think the decision was unanimous in the end."

Nic didn't move, keeping her word till the last minute that it would have to be Dana who made the first move. She wasted no time, however, pulling Dana against her when Dana's lips closed over her own. They sat on the chair kissing and cuddling. They were both breathing heavily when Dana pulled back. She kissed Nic on each cheek and then kissed her softly on the mouth.

"I'm sure I've never told you before what an incredibly sexy woman you are. I'm not sure why it is, but I find you simply irresistible." Dana's finger traced from the bridge of Nic's nose down to the tip, then circled the outline of her lips.

Nic grasped Dana's hand drawing her finger into her mouth, teasing it with her tongue. She watched with pleasure as Dana's eyes clouded over before closing half way. Nic slid her hand up Dana's thigh under her dress, an action that was rewarded with a soft moan. She stroked Dana's thigh using her nails alternately with her fingertips.

"Umm."

"So, is the jury rethinking its decision?"

"No, Nic, not at all."

"What are you thinking then?"

"I'm thinking that you do things to me and make me have feelings that no one else has ever made me feel. I'm thinking that I want to get out of these clothes and make love with you. I'm also thinking that I need to take a shower first. It's been a long day."

"Well, it's been a long day for me too." Nic raised her eyebrows, fighting to maintain a serious look. "Perhaps we should be considerate of Bruno and Tony's water supply and save some water by showering together?"

"I've always admired how environmentally conscious you are," Dana nuzzled Nic's neck, placing a kiss just below her ear.

They stood and Nic turned Dana around, encircling her in her arms from behind. She ran her hands from Dana's waist up her body over her breasts as she kissed Dana's neck where her hairline ended. Feeling Dana's response, she allowed her hands to again make the slow and sensuous trip down and back up Dana's body.

"I thought to myself, when we were dancing, how much I loved the feel of this dress. Now that I'm able to feel what's under the dress, I love it even more."

Nic stepped away to allow enough room to slide her hands around to the zipper on the back of the dress. Slowly, an inch at a time, she exposed and kissed her way down Dana's back. When Nic finished opening the dress fully, she slipped it down Dana's arms and helped her step from the sheath.

"My turn," said Dana sliding her hands under Nic's jacket then across the tops of her breasts to slip the jacket down Nic's arms. She burrowed her nose in Nic's neck. "This is something I've wanted to do from nearly the first moment I met you. I love the way you smell."

Dana reached for the buttons on Nic's shirt and undid them one by one. She pulled the two front pieces apart and paused, surprised to find that Nic wasn't wearing a bra and she was tall enough that her nipples were exactly in line with Dana's mouth.

Nic held her breath waiting to see if Dana was going to change her mind. "It would kill me if you wanted to stop now. I need to be sure, Dana. Sure that this is what you really need, that I'm what you really want." She stood passively waiting for Dana to decide.

Dana looked up and swallowed hard. "You're beautiful," she said softly then deliberately licked first one nipple then the other before she fastened onto one of them pulling it into her mouth. In unison, they groaned with pleasure. She leaned back and looked up at Nic, a look of surprise in her eyes. "How can doing that to you get me so excited? It just doesn't make sense to me."

Forcing herself to keep control, Nic inhaled a sharp breath. "Believe me when I tell you, it does. That's exactly how it's supposed to work." She kissed Dana deeply, unhooked her bra and slid it off. She pulled Dana's nipple into her mouth and sucked, teasing it with her tongue as she pinched and stroked the other breast. "Are you ready to get out of the rest of these clothes and into the shower?"

"Yes, although I'm sorry you'll have to stop what you're doing, I want to feel your skin pressed against me. " Dana stepped back and slid off her underwear finally standing nude before the woman who was capable of making her weak in the knees. Nic slipped out of the last of her clothes. Dana stepped back to allow herself the pleasure of absorbing the sight of Nic's beautiful body. She was tall, and slender but well toned. Her small round breasts were perfectly shaped with tight, dark nipples. Well-defined ab muscles led down to a dark curly patch of neatly trimmed pubic hair.

Nic waited patiently while Dana studied her, holding herself in check. She wanted to give Dana time to be sure, and to allow Dana to set the pace, to keep her promise. "Ready for that shower now?"

"In a minute. I want to feel you against me first." Dana stepped into Nic's embrace letting her hands travel over Nic's body. She started with her hands on Nic's breasts then slid them down around her back coming to rest on her firm buttocks. She tugged, Nic to her, "My God! You feel incredible." Dana stepped away taking Nic by the hand and leading her toward the bathroom. "Now I'm ready," she said, a smile playing on her lips.

They started out slowly, taking turns soaping each other. Nic turned Dana away from her and soaped her back before pulling the shorter woman against her. She reached around the front of Dana's body sliding her own body against Dana's back and buttocks, each woman enjoying the slippery sensations.

Nic was trying hard not to come. She concentrated her attention on pleasing Dana. Encouraged by Dana's responsiveness and soft moans, Nic was unable to wait any longer. She reached her arms around Dana and slid her soapy fingers of one hand down between the slick wet folds as she stimulated Dana's breasts with her other hand. As Nic kissed the back of Dana's neck, Dana pressed her hands against the shower wall, opened her legs, and pushed her bottom back against Nic as she slipped her fingers into Dana's wet and warm opening. It only took a few strokes for them to groan in mutual release, Dana pulling Nic over the edge with her. The warm water played over their bodies rinsing off the soap as they stood trying to steady their legs.

"Come on." Nic pulled a towel from the rack, using it to dry Dana before she led her to the bedroom. They fell together on the bed. Nic began to kiss Dana and their passion built again. She positioned herself between Dana's thighs after kissing her way to her destination. Dana's hands were clenching the sheets and she was raising herself from the bed.

"I want your mouth on me," she whispered, her breath ragged.

In one quick, fluid motion, Nic raised Dana's legs over her shoulders and pulled Dana toward her burying her tongue deep inside. "Oh Nic, don't stop." Dana's breathing was loud and ragged as she clutched the sheets. Finally, unable to withstand any more sweet torture, she stiffened, cried out in release, and slumped like a rag doll onto the bed, arms splayed out to her sides. It took a few minutes for her breathing to slow to a point where she could speak.

"My God! I'm nearly forty years old and I had no idea sex could be like this. How could I not have known?" She rolled over and fit her body on top of Nic's. "Honestly, that was a rhetorical question. I didn't necessarily mean you have to answer it. I can probably answer that question better than you can. It's because it took me this long to meet you."

Nic smiled. "So you are having a good time?"

"Yes, I am, but I'm about to have more fun. Now, it's my turn."

"You just had a turn. Actually, if I counted correctly, I think you had a turn."

"You need to go back to school—actually I had two turns," Dana boasted with a wicked grin. "However, what I mean is that I want a turn to make you feel good."

"You're certainly welcome to try, but I can rarely do more than one orgasm and I already came in the shower when you did."

"Well, no matter what you think, you can't fault me for trying, can you?"

Nic shook her head and smiled. "I just don't want to disappoint you. Also, I want you to know it's me, not you."

Dana sat up and straddled Nic slowly grinding against her as she played with her breasts, succeeding in getting them to pucker to attention. Dana licked one, then the other, blowing on each in turn to stiffen them, before rolling the now erect nipples against her palms.

"You feel so good." She kissed her way up over Nic's breasts on her way to her destination of Nic's lips. She lingered there kissing her softly on the mouth before she tongued her ear. As Nic started to respond and move beneath her, she pushed Nic's hands above her head before she kissed her way down Nic's arm stopping to tease her armpit with her tongue.

"Umm, that's an interesting sensation. I've never had that done before."

"Do you like it?"

"Yes, I think I do." Nic wiggled her brows. "Interestingly, certain parts farther south on my body, like it too!" They both laughed.

"I don't think I'm accomplishing my mission if we're laughing."

"Why would you think that? Don't you think sex should be fun?"

Dana shrugged. "I don't know, it never really seemed fun for me before. It's always been more like...like work, an obligatory part of a relationship, I guess." While they were talking, Dana's hand explored Nic's southern region with her fingers, stroking softly along the shaft of Nic's clitoris, which she could feel getting firmer. "Can I come inside you, Nic? I won't hurt you will I?"

"Yes, you may, and no, you won't hurt me. Umm...where did that come from?" Surprised at her own responsiveness, Nic began to move her hips in time with Dana's thrusts.

"I'm not sure exactly what I'm doing, but I want to taste you."

Nic's breath was coming faster now. She was already close. "It won't take much. Keep stroking and use your mouth on my clit." Nic groaned when Dana's mouth closed on her. "Oh God! Stroke faster."

Dana picked up her pace.

"Yeah, that's it," Nic hissed as she tightened in response to the motion of Dana's fingers.

Dana switched from using her tongue to sucking a little harder. She knew she was on the right track when Nic moaned and pushed against her. Nic tensed, arching up, before going limp against the bed. Dana kissed her way up Nic's body snuggling against her, resting one palm on Nic's breast. Nic looked at her with half closed eyes. Dana smiled at her smugly.

"Pretty pleased with yourself, aren't you?"

"In more ways than you'll ever know," Dana admitted.

They lay entwined, arms and legs tangled together until their breathing was normal and they were both completely relaxed. Dana laid her head on Nic's shoulder. "Sleepy?" Nic asked.

"No, you?"

"No. I'm just relaxed. Are you okay?"

"What do you mean?"

"No regrets?"

Dana kissed Nic's nipple, worked her way up Nic's neck, along the jaw to kiss her lips. "No, how could I regret what we just did? It was wonderful. I never knew what truly being loved and feeling such pleasure could be like."

There was a relaxed silence between them for several minutes. Nic reached down and covered them with the sheet. "Comfortable?" she asked.

"Yes, very. Am I making your arm go to sleep?"

"No, you feel good."

"Nic, can I ask you something?"

"Anything. Now and forever."

Dana grew serious. "How do I know if I'm a lesbian? I mean I know that I'm here, naked with another woman, wrapped in your arms, and we just had sex. Does that make me a lesbian or is it just that for some inexplicable reason I'm attracted to you?" She paused. "I mean since the day I first met you it was as if I was a moth being attracted to a flame. I couldn't get enough of you. I missed you the moment you left me and couldn't wait for the next day when I'd see you again. I love the way you smell, couldn't keep my eyes off of your mouth when you spoke, had to force myself not to touch you unnecessarily. I have never felt that before for anyone else, either male or female."

"I don't know what to tell you, love. For me, I've known all my life that I loved women. I've never been attracted to a man, ever. Honestly, the thought of having sex with a man makes my skin crawl. It's just creepy."

"I know what you mean. I've only had intercourse once in my life. I decided at that moment that it was nothing that I ever wanted to do with him again. At the time, I hoped it was that he just wasn't the right guy. It wasn't normal to not want to be with someone. So I dated. I dated a lot. Unfortunately, I never felt anything sexual for any of them. The last guy I dated wouldn't take no for an answer. I told him I wasn't interested in having sex with him. I told him repeatedly. He...he tried to force himself on me. I hit him with a heavy fruit bowl I kept on my coffee table—knocked him out cold. I told him if he ever came near me again I'd file attempted rape charges."

"Good for you. He deserved it."

"I'm amazed at how easily I'm sharing all my secrets. I'm telling you things I haven't even told Amanda. Anyway, I haven't dated a man since. Funny, my best friend is gay, as are most of my other close friends, like Tony and Bruno and a couple of others...is it remotely possible that I've been a lesbian all along and didn't know it? How could that be?"

"Well, I don't think even heterosexual women are attracted to all men, so it would follow that lesbians are not attracted to every other female out there. I know I'm certainly not. I haven't been in any kind of serious relationship for over two years. Not that I haven't had sex, but it was just casual. Don't panic, it wasn't that often. It wasn't anything like what we shared tonight. Truth is, I've never had anything as good as what happened between us tonight."

Nic adjusted her position, rolling on her side and propping her head on her hand. "Does the label really matter? I mean if you would continue to be with me, to spend time with me, and continue to make love with me like we did tonight, both getting pleasure from each other...would it matter if you were a lesbian or a bisexual or a straight girl who just happens to have a thing for me and only me? It certainly doesn't matter to me how you identify as long as you continue to want me."

After a few minutes in which they were both quiet, Nic had an afterthought. "You know Dana, you seem to think that identifying as a lesbian has only one criteria on which to base the label and that is a woman who has sex with other women. Many lesbians are married to men and have chosen to remain with their partner for any number of reasons. I've also read that many women who self-identify as lesbians don't have sex with other women, choosing instead to remain celibate. Just as there are heterosexual couples that don't have sex. I know one woman who is in her seventies. She happens to still be a virgin, yet she maintains a lesbian identity. So, I wouldn't let it bother you. Eventually, you'll figure it out."

"Okay, I guess so." Dana was quiet for a moment. "I appreciate you trying to answer the question. I guess, I alone, am the only person who can answer that question. I know I've always been female oriented, preferring the company of women to that of men. I have had mostly gay friends, but just never had the pleasure of meeting you until now. Maybe I was just waiting for you."

Nic wrapped her arms around her lover. She wondered how much sleep Dana would get and if she would have regrets in the morning. Nic pulled her tighter, afraid if she did have regrets, she'd want to pull away in a few brief hours when the light of day brought reality.

Three short hours later, Nic awoke to find Dana staring at her. "Good morning," she said sleepily with a concerned look.

Dana reached out her hand and ran the back of her fingers down Nic's cheek then smoothed the furrow between her brows. "Yes, everything is fine, and no, I still don't have any regrets."

Nic rolled onto her back pulling the smaller woman on top of her, settling the hills and valleys of their bodies into place and fitting them together like perfectly matching pieces of a puzzle. "I love this position. I could hold you like this all day." She ran her hands down Dana's back.

"I think you need to stop that so we can get up. We have to go downstairs and be sociable with our hosts before we catch the train at one o'clock."

"I guess I'll have to explain the finer points of a quickie to you," Nic said with a chuckle.

"No, you won't. Here are my plans...tell me what you think of them." She tilted her hips moving against her lover's. She inhaled then murmured, "Umm." With a sigh, she said, "Okay, when we get back to our hotel, I don't know about you, but there is definitely a nap on my agenda...more specifically, a naked nap with you. Then, after we're refreshed, I plan to tire you out again by making mad passionate love to you...with you. Following that, we're going to have class. I want you to give me lessons on techniques that I can use to better please you in bed."

Dana's serious expression made Nic laugh. "You don't need any ideas and I couldn't have been any more pleased. You are very inventive and have pleased me more than any of my previous lovers ever have. I told you that last night. It was the truth. But we can still do that if you want. It could be fun. Anything else?"

"Well, I expect you to take me out and feed me, of course, because by then we'll have worked up a voracious appetite." She smiled sweetly.

"Well, you have some very good ideas there, my love. I think I'll let you plan my schedule every day. No more of this work stuff. I'd much rather stay in bed and invent ways we can please each other. I think we should probably get cracking though, get up and dressed. I think you're right about that."

Dana gave Nic a long slow kiss, tweaking her right nipple as she got out of bed. "There, that'll give you something to think about until we get back to the city!"

Nic groaned and reluctantly rolled out of bed. "Well, that's for sure."

They washed, dressed, and packed their suitcases before they went downstairs to join everyone for breakfast. It wasn't long after breakfast that the guests started to leave for home. Bruno pulled Dana aside and announced that he wanted to touch up her hair before she left for the train.

"So," he said, once they were out of hearing range, "it is good to see that you are looking very tired this morning. I think you have a flush to your cheeks. I think you made a good decision, no?"

"I made a good decision, yes." She hugged her friend. "Thank you for being so supportive."

"I wish you both much happiness," he told her and squeezed her tightly.

Bruno stayed to tend to the remaining guests, while Tony drove Nic and Dana to the train. When they arrived back in Rome, they followed Dana's agenda to the letter with one exception. They ordered room service instead of going out to eat.

## Chapter 7

It had been a few days since Mallory and Amanda had their video call with Dana. Mallory settled in a comfortable chair in Amanda's living room and propped her feet on the footstool. "I've been wondering if you've made any progress on your book?"

"Not much, although I did finally finish that chapter I've been having so much trouble with. I think I'm back on track, thankfully. I've been working too hard on my real job." Amanda rolled her eyes. "I've fleshed out some of the story in my mind though, and am ready to start putting it on paper when I have a chance to concentrate on it."

"I didn't see the flower delivery truck this morning. Tell me Miss, how does your garden grow today?" A smile played on Mallory's lips as she awaited a response.

Mallory was referring to the fact that since Amanda had given Bernie her location, like clockwork, a new arrangement of flowers with a card arrived each day. The card simply said, 'I'm sorry...come home...'

Amanda shook her head. "You know what annoys me most about the whole flower thing?" She didn't wait for Mallory to respond, assured that she had her attention when she made eye contact. "I'll bet that she's not even in the country. She's simply placed an order with the florist shop to keep the flowers coming. She keeps sending emails like, hush...'Have you forgiven me yet?' or, 'I'll never give up.' Well, you get the idea." She shrugged. "Flowers were always her apology of choice."

"What are you going to do about her? Could you ever forgive her?" Mallory's heart beat a little faster as she waited for Amanda to consider her response to the personal question. She knew, generally, what had happened between Amanda and her partner, but still wondered if they were completely finished with the relationship.

Although the time could only be measured in weeks since their first conversation about it in the hot tub, it seemed much longer somehow. Amanda's response of, 'I don't like to share' when they spoke before about her reason for being at Dana's seemed so long ago now.

As if reading Mallory's mind Amanda said, "I've never really told you what happened between us, have I?"

Mallory shook her head.

*** 

"Bernie and I had been together since we were kids really, me just out of college a couple of years, Bernie a few years older. From the first moment of my initial introduction to Bernie at the party where we met, I thought my heart would pound its way right out of my chest when she shook my hand and looked at me so directly. I don't think I'd ever seen eyes such a deep blue color before and I remember standing there, transfixed, just staring into them. I was so busy watching as her lips curled into a smile, I didn't realize I was still clutching her hand." Amanda's eyes drifted as she recalled the experience. "When I finally released the death grip I had on her hand, I fully expected the connection between us to be broken. I remember feeling pleasantly surprised that, although we were no longer physically linked, I still felt attached to her. There was something magnetic about her. I was drawn to her in a way I'd never connected to anyone before."

Amanda adjusted her position, leaning her head back in her chair. "Bernie's first words to me were, 'Have dinner with me.' There was no 'Hello,' or 'I'm pleased to meet you.' It wasn't even a question but, rather, sounded almost a command. We had a whirlwind first date, ending up that first night in Bernie's bed where we made love. It was magic. Bernie was certainly more sexually experienced than I was and our first few months together were like a tour of the lesbian Kama Sutra. Very few of the conversations we had occurred anywhere other than in bed and those that did usually involved some reference to what would happen when we did get there. As I'm telling you this, I realize how our entire relationship was based on that one particular element. It feels shallow now as I look back."

"Don't be so hard on yourself. It's easier to see those things in hindsight. What do they say...hindsight is always twenty-twenty?"

Amanda shifted in her seat, her mental discomfort seeming to radiate into a physical manifestation. "Anyway, as you could probably predict, it didn't take long for us to begin living together. Bernie's career in hotel management required long, sometimes odd hours, with travel that included extended periods away from home. Initially, Bernie's schedule worked for me. As a freelance writer with a only a part-time job writing monthly and annual reports for a couple of mid-sized companies, every spare minute I had I devoted to locating work, then grinding out stories and articles. Eventually all that hard work paid dividends for me. I landed my current job working for a large direct mailing firm, where I negotiated a mailing fee per ad package sent out by the company, in exchange for a slightly lower flat fee for writing copy. Their massive mailings provided me with a steady and reasonably acceptable income. The company treats me well, I like the people I work with, and the ability to work from home gives me control of my schedule, so I can take on additional projects. More recently, in the past couple of years I think I've mentioned that, in addition to my ad work, I researched and wrote a number of freelance articles and ghosted a novel. In my spare time I started writing short stories, and the novel

I've been working on, as much for my own enjoyment as for any profit I would earn."

Amanda again shifted position so she could better face Mallory who had patiently listened to Amanda's story without interruption.

"A few years ago, a little over two really, I found out quite by accident that Bernie was cheating on me. It broke my heart. I recognize now that there were huge deficits in our relationship, but at the time I was devastated. I'd idolized her. I'd never before responded to anyone like I did to her. For want of a better analogy, she was my Svengali. I fell quickly under her spell, literally seconds after I met her, and it just never stopped. She's tall and I guess I'd describe her as handsome rather than pretty. She has a beautiful smile and those blue eyes the color of the sky on a crisp September morning. Her eyes just get to me somehow. They undo me."

"Obviously you still have feelings for her."

Amanda tossed her head as though she were tossing the idea aside. "We were together for twelve years. No doubt there are feelings, but they've changed," she said ruefully. "When she cheated on me," she paused searching for the right words, "that spell I'd been under was broken somehow. I started to pull away from her and things between us were never the same. She complained that I wasn't as responsive to her sexually and the way she touched me, made love to me altered, too. She was..." Amanda paused again, the correct way to phrase her thought elusive. "I guess less loving, more demanding with me...I don't know exactly how to express it. Don't get me wrong...she never hurt me. There was an edge to her that I'd never felt between us before. She became more aggressive and dominant in bed. Maybe it was her way of trying to get back what we'd lost. I don't know."

"Were you frightened by her?"

"No, I don't believe she would ever hurt me." Amanda thought back to the night she had left. "She tried to bully me into not leaving. Oddly enough, in my heart, I know that in her own way she does love me, even though I admit that sounds strange. It's just that, for some reason, I'm not enough for her. I can't give her everything she needs. I don't know if I fall short in offering her what she desires or if her need is just too great. I just know that whatever I can give her, it's not always enough and that hurts."

Amanda paused, reflecting on her feelings. "In fairness to her, I know I changed then...that I pulled back emotionally when I first found out that she wasn't faithful to me. Anyway, I told her that if I ever caught her cheating again that would be it...that I'd be done."

"So, that's what happened, she cheated again?"

"Yes."

"The woman is obviously a fool," Mallory replied, not missing a beat. "But you still love her?"

"Yes, I still love her...probably always will. If you met her, you'd find her smart, witty, and entertaining. You'd probably love her too." Amanda shrugged. "It seems that everyone does. However, I'm reasonably certain that I'm no longer in love with her," she said with an emphasis on the words 'in love.'

"Reasonably certain, not positive? I mean, could you ever return to a relationship with Bernie?'

It was at that moment that Amanda recognized that Mallory was feeling the same attraction for her as she was feeling for Mallory. It became obvious to Amanda that Mallory was afraid...afraid that she might go back to Bernie.

"Look, I'd love to say with one hundred percent certainty that I'm not going back. Right now that's what I feel and I'm probably ninety-nine and ninety-nine one hundredths percent sure. I'll probably have to talk to her one last time to close that door forever." She knew that was not what Mallory needed to hear, but she would not be less than honest with her. She already cared too much for Mallory to give her any less than the truth. A silence held between them.

Mallory sighed deeply. "I understand."

"No, I'm not sure you do, Mallory, not fully anyway. Hell, I don't even understand fully." Amanda shook her head to gain clarity and courage. "Let me be the first to acknowledge that there's something happening between us. There's no question there's an attraction between you and me." She looked to Mallory for confirmation of the statement.

Mallory nodded and smiled at her. "Yes."

"In a surprisingly short stretch of time I've developed feelings for you and I think you care for me as well." Amanda's expression showed her concern. "We're practically living together...living our lives like an old married couple."

"Except for one thing..."

"Yes, except for one thing." Amanda smiled, knowing she had to respond to the longing she heard in Mallory's tone. In a voice barely above a whisper, she said, "I want you too."

Mallory shrugged and raised her eyebrows. "I know there's a but in here somewhere." She quickly grinned back when Amanda chuckled.

"Yes, I'm afraid there is and it's for your protection as well as mine."

"Do you think we should see less of each other? Is that what you're saying?"

"No. Still I don't want to end up hurting you, ever. So, I need to completely finish up everything with Bernie before I can feel free to become involved on any deeper level than what we have now. She and I have the house to settle, which should be easy. She can definitely afford to buy me out. The house was always more her taste than mine. Still, it could take additional time if she decides she doesn't want to keep it since we'd have to put it up for sale. I need to see or at least talk to her one last time to finalize things. I took the coward's way out by leaving Dodge the way I did." She smoothed back her hair using both hands.

With silence hanging between them, to reconnect Amanda reached for Mallory's hand, drew it to her lips and kissed it. "I want you, but I want more with you than just sex. I think we have a chance to build something very special, something that could be good for both of us. I need to feel that I'm ready for a new relationship being one hundred percent positive that the door to my past is firmly closed. Don't you think that's best?"

Mallory squeezed Amanda's hand then released it. "I admire your honesty and your loyalty. I'm glad we've acknowledged that there's something happening between us besides friendship. However, I agree with you. If we move forward, I want all of you and I'll be happy with no less than that. Running the risk that you'll suspect I'm campaigning, I do want to say that once I commit, I'm a faithful partner and I expect no less in return."

"If we get to that place, you'd never get less." Amanda stood and pulled Mallory into a quick hug. "I'm glad we talked," she whispered. Releasing her, and needing to change the topic of conversation, Amanda said. "Now, that we're clear I feel better."

"Me too."

"So, let's talk about what to do today? I'm thinking I'd like to go back to try to photograph that chipmunk we saw before. Interested? It's a beautiful day for a walk, don't you agree?"

A new level of comfort enveloped them. Some of the sexual tension that had been humming between them had been reduced, although not completely extinguished. It was apparent that knowing that they were not going to take that path any time soon, lessened the intensity of those feelings and made things between them lighter. They enjoyed the walk and had a wonderful day together although Amanda did not get the picture she wanted.

## Chapter 8

Mallory returned to work the next day. Each day for the following week, just as Amanda had promised, dinner was in the oven when Mallory arrived at Dana's house after work. Both women looked forward to Mallory returning each night for dinner.

"Honey, I'm home," Mallory called as she stuck her head in the door.

Amanda rewarded Mallory's effort to make her smile with a hearty laugh, although a part of her wished the endearment could be sincere.

"What's for dinner?" Mallory asked.

"I repurposed last night's leftover chicken into a casserole."

"Hmm, repurposed chicken...sounds yummy."

*Her nickname should be Ms. Sarcastic,* Amanda thought, but kept her opinion to herself. She watched as Mallory investigated the smell emanating from the oven.

Mallory went to the stove and opened the oven door to peek in. After inhaling deeply, she grinned. "Yum! That really smells good."

Amanda smiled because, this time, she knew the compliment was sincere.

"It's a pity though, because I planned to take you out to dinner. I'm sorry, but you just cooked yourself out of a dinner offer. This smells too good to pass up."

"There's always another day, like tomorrow for example."

"How about Italian? The cafeteria at the hospital was cooking something Italian today and the aroma put me in the mood."

"That would be perfect."

Together they served the chicken Amanda had prepared. Amanda and Mallory had established a comfortable routine. They had adopted a tradition Mallory's family practiced where, as they ate, they told of the best and worst moment or event of their individual days. Amanda washed down a bite of her biscuit with a sip of wine. "Okay, you start. What was the best part of your day, today."

"Hmm. Best part was that by the time I left work today I knew that everything was ready for this weekend."

For Mallory, it had been a difficult few days at work. She'd handled more than the usual number of problems and complaints in addition to having to prepare for an open house at the hospital to introduce the upgraded rehab center. It was finally her last day at the hospital for the week. She looked forward to her time off because, usually, the time off meant relaxing, taking her turn cooking, and doing something fun with Amanda.

"Good for you. You've invested a lot of time and effort into making the open house successful. I'm glad you won't have to be worrying about things last minute. I hate that."

"It's one of the character traits we have in common, along with our organizational skills, and our unforgiving standard of punctuality." Mallory patted Amanda's hand.

"So true. Neither of us tolerates tardiness well. So if finishing up your preparation was the best, what was the worst?"

"Well, the worst is that I realized our off time this weekend will be shortened by the fact that I need to be at the hospital for the open house on Sunday. In addition, my new staff members are coming on board on Monday, with one starting on the eight a.m. shift and the other starting at four p.m. I've arranged to work a split shift. I'll be going in around noon and if I take the comp hour each day I'll earn this weekend I can finish by seven p.m. That means I'll be able to be home in time to eat a late dinner with you each night. I know that each of the nurses would be supervised within their departments, but I like to review policy and procedure with each new employee myself.

"I wish you'd be around this weekend, but I'm glad you'll be home for dinner all week. That'll be nice."

"How about your best and worst, Amanda?"

"My best thing is that I finished another chapter."

"That's wonderful. I'm proud of you. Now you're back on track after struggling with that chapter that had you stuck for so long. And the worst?"

Amanda gestured at the two new bouquets that arrived earlier in the day. "The flowers from Bernie are still coming daily.

Mallory glanced around. "It's like a mortuary in here."

Amanda added her laughter to Mallory's. "Isn't that the truth?"

Although some of the floral arrangements were composed mostly of roses, the last few had contained their fair share of carnations. Anger and frustration evident in her tone, Amanda admitted, "I know I've got to figure out some way to make Bernie stop sending them. It's really starting to piss me off now. I've repeatedly asked her to knock it off in my emails to her and even tried calling her. She must be out of the country."

"I think it's the smell of the carnations." Mallory said, almost to herself. "They always make me think of death."

"Wow! Now there's a pleasant thought. Where'd that come from?"

"I don't know...I guess from Piper's viewing."

"I'll get rid of them tomorrow." Amanda promised.

"Don't make that sacrifice on my account."

When Amanda stuck her tongue out at Mallory, the two laughed heartily.

"Come on, there are fewer bouquets in the living room." Once settled in the comfortable room, Amanda asked, "Would you be interested in reading my newest chapter tonight? I'm anxious to hear what you think of it."

"Absolutely. I've been looking forward to reading what you've been working on all week."

Amanda went into her office and brought out a printed copy of her next chapter.

"Here it is, I hope you like it."

"I'm sure I will. I liked the first parts you gave me to read very much. I think you're a very talented writer. I can't wait to read the rest of this chapter. I figure your main characters should be getting together soon. I hope the love scene is as hot as the first one."

"I guess you'll just have to wait and see, won't you."

"I think I'll take it home and read it in bed before I fall asleep. I'm tuckered out after this week. Maybe, if I go to bed now, I'll have energy to do something fun with you tomorrow. Don't forget that I have to go in on Sunday for a few hours, but I won't be home that late."

"I'm looking forward to spending tomorrow together, and preparing to miss you on Sunday."

"Yeah, me too. By the way, I have a question for you."

Amanda tilted her head waiting to hear what Mallory had on her mind.

"Do you know how to two-step?"

"I can two-step so well you'd think I was raised in Texas." Amanda stood, slapped her knee, and hitched up her jeans, before she hooked her thumbs in her belt loops. "Why, would you like a demonstration?"

Mallory giggled. Her giggle was a sound that never failed to lift Amanda's spirits and, truth be told, it made her want to wrap Mallory in her arms and keep her close."You betcha. Show me."

"Nope, my sweet thang, you will have to wait until tomorrow for me to show you my stuff."

Mallory arched one eyebrow, while the rest of her face remained impassive except for a hint of a smile. "Promise?"

Realization of what she had just said dawned on Amanda causing her face to turn red and her ears to burn with the heat of her embarrassment.

"Oh stop. You've already seen my stuff. Besides, I was referring to my dancing and you know it."

Mallory was still chuckling as she stood and pulled Amanda into a quick hug. "You know, I always enjoy seeing your stuff, no matter what."

Amanda pushed her toward the door. "Get out of here before I do you bodily harm. Don't forget the chapter. I expect a full report tomorrow."

***

Amanda and Mallory drove into the city and dined at a cute little Italian restaurant that a coworker had recommended to Mallory. Neither could decide between the lasagna and the stuffed shells, so they agreed that each would order one entrée and they would split them. The waiter who overheard their plan kindly offered to take care of that for them in the kitchen. They were so pleased with the food and the restaurant that they decided to return for dinner again one night later in the week.

At the bar, Mallory ordered each of them a drink, after which they found a table as far from the band as possible so they could talk. When the musicians started to play some slow songs, Mallory stood and held out her hand to Amanda. "Shall we dance?"

Amanda nodded, placed her hand into Mallory's, and followed behind as Mallory led them onto the dance floor. They were closely matched in height, so they fit together well. Mallory was a skilled dancer and Amanda soon relaxed and tucked in close as they moved around the floor. After two slow dances, the band changed the tempo and began to play their version of Mary Chapin Carpenter's *Down At The Twist & Shout*, a song that would be easy for them to two-step to. After a couple more dances, the band played *A Little Less Talk And A Lot More Action*, a song made famous by Toby Keith. The band was good and they had the crowd on their feet. The women joined in on a line dance that seemed to form of its own volition. It was well past midnight when they headed for home.

"That was really fun, Mallory. Thank you very much for bringing me. It was a welcomed change of pace."

"Yes, I agree." Mallory inserted the key into the car's ignition. "We'll have to do it again soon. I had a lot of fun with you tonight. I enjoyed kicking up our heels a little."

The sharp ring of Amanda's phone surprised both of them. It was unusual that she would get a call at this late hour. She checked caller ID and saw Bernie's name in the window on the front of the phone. Normally, she would have ignored the call, since she was with another person. The lateness of the hour made her suspect something might be wrong. Concerned, she pushed the talk button. "Hello?"

"Hey baby. I miss you so much."

"What are you doing calling me at this hour, Bernie? I thought something was wrong."

"I just wanted to talk to you."

"Well, I'm not talking to you now. I'll call you tomorrow, at a more decent time." Amanda pushed the end call button on her phone. She turned to Malory and said, "I'm very sorry."

Mallory reached over and squeezed Amanda's hand. "It's not your fault and it's no big deal. I understand."

"I really need to talk to her sooner rather than later. This can't go on. I've sent her emails, I've left her messages on the phone, followed by text messages, and no matter what I say or do she ignores the fact that I've told her I'm done with our relationship. How many ways do I need to tell her it's over?"

Mallory nodded. "Sometimes it's hard to hear 'no' if you don't want to."

"I think it's particularly hard for Bernie to hear it. It's not a word she's accustomed to hearing, especially from me."

"I know Bernie seems like an insurmountable problem right now, because she's not hearing what you're saying, but I think she will eventually. So don't give up hope and stick to your guns."

"I'm calling her tomorrow and we're having this out. I'm sick to death of my home being filled with flowers that I don't want and phone calls and messages at all hours that I don't need. I've had it. Tomorrow, after I call her, I'm going to block her from my email program and get a new phone number. She has plucked my last nerve. I plan to tell her tomorrow that I want her to get the house appraised and either buy me out or sell it. If she needs to contact me, she can contact me by mail or through my lawyer if that becomes necessary."

"You sound serious, like you've really made up your mind."

"Yes, I have. It's been made up for a while now, but I can't figure out how to get her to understand that." At that exact moment, the phone rang again. Amanda didn't have to check, to know that it was Bernie calling her back. She flipped the switch turning the phone off. "That's enough of her for tonight. We were having such a good time and now she's gone and put a damper on the evening."

"I'm not going to let her dampen my evening and you shouldn't either." It was a few minutes later that Mallory turned into her driveway. "Do you want to come in for a nightcap or some coffee?"

Amanda shook her head. "No, thanks. I think I'll turn in for tonight. I need to give some thought to what I'm going to say to Bernie tomorrow and figure out how I can convince her that I'm completely serious. Because of the time difference, I won't be able to call her until the afternoon. I know it's our day off, but I really need to take care of this. We can still get together later. Is that okay?"

"That works out perfectly because, don't forget, I have to work tomorrow."

"Oh right, I did forget that. I have trouble remembering things I'd rather forget."

Mallory reached for Amanda's hand and gave it a squeeze, releasing it slowly, as if reticent to break contact with her. "I hope your conversation ends the way you want it to. Call me if you need to talk."

"Thanks for a wonderful time this evening. It was a pleasant break from the routine. I'll see you tomorrow when you get home, after I finish talking with Bernie."

"I'll call you if I get a break tomorrow," Mallory said resting her hand on the handle in preparation for opening the car door.

"Okay. I'm sure I can figure out something to make for dinner with the supplies we have left, if I'm creative."

"I have a better idea. Why don't I stop and pick us up a pizza on the way home? Maybe you can make us a salad to go with it?"

Amanda reached over to touch Mallory's arm, reluctant to let their evening end. "Great. I like how you think."

After they decided which toppings they both liked Mallory told Amanda, "I shouldn't be late. I'll give you a call when I'm ready to leave the hospital so you'll know when to start the salad."

"Perfect."

They bid each other good night with a long hug. " Good luck with your call tomorrow." Mallory said, as she released Amanda.

"Thanks. I'll get it over with in the morning when I get up. Keep your fingers crossed that all goes well."

Later, tucked into her bed, Amanda tossed and turned, thinking about the video call she had promised to make to Bernie. She vacillated between a mixture of dread and anticipation. The call would be difficult, and she wondered how Bernie would react to what she planned to tell her.

## Chapter 9

The crisp September morning dawned bright and refreshing with the sun reflecting off the beautifully colored foliage that stood in contrast against the vivid blue of the sky. The first thought that Amanda had, as she looked out the window at the fabulous weather, was disappointment that she and Mallory were missing out on a wonderful day for a bike ride. Maybe, she thought, if she was able to get in touch with Bernie early enough, she could fit a ride in before Mallory got home. She spoiled herself and slept later than planned. Although she wanted to call Mallory to see if she wanted to visit before work, she refrained, hoping that Mallory was able to sleep in, too.

Amanda got up, made tea, and ate some cereal. Following her shower, she took extra time on her hair because she wanted to look her best for her video chat with Bernie. Not that the light makeup she applied would impress Bernie, but if she felt good about her appearance, it might help bolster her shaky confidence. Amanda went into the office, booted up her computer, selected Bernie's name from her favorites list, and pushed the call button. It didn't take long for Bernie's face to appear on her screen.

"There you are. What the hell took you so long?" Bernie's brow furrowed, conveying her displeasure. "I called you four times on your cell already, but got no answer. I've been waiting for nearly an hour."

*If she's trying to win me back, she's certainly off on the wrong foot.* In fact, just their initial encounter this morning was enough to solidify her already strong resolve to inform Bernie that she did not intend to change her mind about ending their relationship for good.

"I slept in this morning." Amanda explained, no regret discernable.

"You know I like to play early when I'm home." Bernie was of course referring to golf. In general, golf was a game Amanda didn't particularly enjoy playing with Bernie. If Bernie had a bad shot, or God forbid a bad round, she could become extremely cranky and impatient. All the past fights about the game, and her eventual refusal to play it with Bernie remained fresh in Amanda's mind.

"I know, Bernie. I'm here now, so let's get on with it. I don't intend to sit here and have you pick a fight with me."

"So, from your attitude today, your emails, and phone messages it would appear I wasted my money sending the flowers."

"Yes, I'm afraid so. They were all beautiful, although it's not flowers I needed or wanted from you." Amanda adjusted the screen a bit to center the picture better. She thought Bernie looked tired or maybe just stressed.

"I've apologized many times over for my little indiscretion. I really don't know what else to say or do to make you happy. We have a lovely home and money is certainly no issue. We can buy anything we need or want, can do anything or go anywhere we want. What exactly is it that you expect from me?"

"I needed and wanted the important things from you, Bernie. Let's start with respect, fidelity, loyalty...I can add a few more if you need me to."

"Sure, this is your show, isn't it?"

Amanda thought about the past few weeks she'd spent with Mallory. She recalled the fun they'd had riding their bikes and the horses, strolling the trails before sunset after which they'd come in and cook dinner together, laughing, especially in the hot tub, and sharing secrets, thoughts, and stories. "You know Bernie, if I have to lay this out for you I will, but it really isn't worth it...trust me."

"I want to hear it."

"Okay, the first two are critical. You lack respect for me or you would hold our relationship sacred and not cheat on me every chance you get. You'd remain faithful to me...to us, and it wouldn't always be about you."

Amanda could list any number of additional elements missing from their relationship, like having fun and laughing with each other, sharing activities they could both enjoy, and even something so small as being able to sit quietly together enjoying a bit of nature. Amanda was certain that all of those things would be lost on Bernie. "Truth is, Bernie, you treated me like a housekeeper that you found it convenient to have sex with whenever you were in town." Amanda watched the smooth, slick facade that she was used to slip into place, the one Bernie so effectively used to get her own way.

"Isn't it amazing how two people can have such a different perspective on the functioning of a relationship?" Bernie smiled sweetly into the camera. "So where does that leave us now. I'll change, Amanda. I know you don't think it's possible, but I can. The other women don't mean anything to me. I've never given them my heart, only my body."

"Be honest for once, how many have there been? Two I know of...how many others were there Bernie?"

Bernie's eyes filled for the briefest of moments and just for an instant Amanda saw the real woman beneath the mask. Amanda, in that moment, believed that Bernie was truly sorry and did genuinely care for her, but it was too late.

"I'm sorry Amanda." One tear escaped and tracked slowly down Bernie's cheek. "There must be something wrong with me. I just can't seem to stop myself."

"Well, it's sad Bernie. I'm sorry. I can't help you with that. If you're honest with yourself, you'll admit that our relationship ended quite some time ago. Let's agree to part now while we still have some kind feelings for each other. Before you enter a relationship with anyone else though, do yourself and her a favor and get some help with whatever it is that drives you."

"Okay, Amanda, although I don't like it. You're probably right. I have a problem. If I get help, will you wait for me?"

Amanda was not expecting that question. She knew that Bernie thought that the primary thing wrong with their relationship was her infidelity. She obviously had not yet internalized the other issues that Amanda addressed. In the end, it really didn't matter. In her heart, she knew with certainty that she was done with this relationship. She didn't want to go back and start over.

It was not until she had been away from Bernie and shared time with Mallory that she realized how unhappy she really was in her previous relationship. More confident in her decision to end it with Bernie, she knew now that she wouldn't go back to that. She wanted a life that made her happy...a life with Mallory. She also knew that if there were no Mallory to turn to, she still wouldn't want to return to her life with Bernie. It took being away to clarify how miserable she had been for the past several years and she felt she was leaving with a clear conscience...leaving for no one other than herself and her own peace of mind. Mallory was a bonus to run to—not a factor in her decision.

"No, Bernie. I can't. I'm sorry. I won't be back."

"Okay, I finally hear you." Bernie smiled. "I know you don't believe it, Amanda. I really do love you. I guess I have to admit that I took you for granted."

"Thank you for that."

"So, what now?" Bernie wondered.

"I think I'm going to make a life here. I like this area...it's close to the city and that provides me with options for work. I'm happy here Bernie, something I haven't been there for way too long."

"What about the house, Amanda? What should I do about that?"

"You decide. You can either keep it or sell it. Buy me out or cash it out for both of us."

"Can I have a little time to decide?" Bernie put her hand to her forehead then brushed her hair back.

"Sure. I don't need any money right now."

"I'll let you know my decision as quickly as I can. Give me a couple of weeks, okay?"

"Yes, that's fine. I can do that."

Bernie sighed deeply. "So, that's it, I guess?"

"Yes, I guess so. I'm sorry too, Bernie. I'll always care for you. It's time for us to call it quits now, and time for me to find someone who will value the same things I hold dear."

"Believe it or not, I do understand, Amanda. Thanks for the good times. I'm sorry for the bad ones. Can I call you sometimes? Just as a friend. You really are the best friend I have."

*I feel sorry for Bernie. I just have no more to give her.* "Not right away, Bernie. Maybe someday—just not right now. We need time before we can be friends. Call me when you've made your decision about the house. Okay?"

"All right. Two weeks, no longer. I'll be here in the States until then. Take care of yourself, sweetheart. Call me if you need anything." One final smile and Bernie was gone.

Amanda exhaled completely for what felt like the first time since the conversation with Bernie started. She shut down the computer and reached for some tissues. She was sad. It was the end of twelve years of her life, although she didn't intend to cry in her beer over a relationship that had made her so unhappy. Amanda blew her nose and changed into shorts and a T-shirt. She knew that Mallory was at work and probably busy, so she'd wait until she saw her later that evening to tell her about her conversation with Bernie. Hoping to regain some of the good spirits she woke up with earlier in the morning, she decided to take that bike ride she wished she could take with Mallory. She was relieved that things with Bernie, except for the house, were finally sorted out.

Amanda strode into the garage, got out Dana's mountain bike, and placed her camera in the seat bag. Maybe, she'd get an opportunity to take that photo of the chipmunk today she'd not been successful in capturing before. It would make a great gift for Mallory.

## Chapter 10

On Sunday, Nic and Dana returned to Rome after leaving Tony and Bruno's party. They made love and talked all afternoon and most of the night, finally falling asleep wrapped in each other's arms. Cuddling together, the conversations centered on the attraction between them and how amazed Dana was that she could feel such a strong physical pull for another woman.

"Being with you is amazing. I can't get enough of you."

"You seemed so sure of yourself and are such a good lover that, if you hadn't told me otherwise, I'd never have guessed this was your first relationship with a woman," Nic said.

"What about you? Have you always been attracted to women or did you start out with doubts?"

"Doubts? I'm not sure I would call what I felt doubts." Nic trailed her fingers across Dana's torso leaving goose bumps in their wake. "I come from a strong Italian Catholic family. Both my father and mother came over from the 'old country' bringing their traditions and values with them." She couldn't use her hands to make quotation marks with her fingers because her arms were wrapped around Dana, but the inflection in her voice made her meaning clear. "It was probably more of an issue of options. I never considered loving another woman an option open to me."

After a brief pause, Nic sighed, exhaling a long breath. "Initially, I didn't think I was attracted to women as much as that I just wasn't attracted to men. I had nobody to talk to about it, so I just maintained, so to speak. I dated...men, but never got serious with anyone. I went to a local college, lived at home, and was...I guess what you could call, naive about the world. It's hard to believe that by the time I graduated college I still didn't have a clue."

"Oh, sweetie, think about it. I'm nearly forty and was clueless until you. Don't be so hard on yourself."

"My first job didn't require much travel. I worked for an agency and most of my jobs involved translating quarterly or annual reports for various large companies. I continued to live at home. Then I met Alex. Alexandra just to be clear." Nic grinned. "I was already twenty-five. She was two years younger."

"So, you realized right away that you were a lesbian."

"No, it took awhile. I wasn't sure until she kissed me and my world went from black and white to Technicolor. Oddly enough, for the first time in my life I felt normal. It was as if I finally understood what all the hoopla surrounding sex was about."

Dana adjusted her position, turning on her side so she could see Nic's face. She slid a leg over Nic's and pulled close against her. Her hand traced lazy patterns across her lover's body.

"So what happened? Did you tell your parents?"

"No, I was afraid and don't forget, I was Alex's first too. So, we were sort of figuring things out together. She was from as strict a family as I was...only hers was Hispanic. It took us a few weeks before we decided we wanted to be more intimate. We made plans to go away for the weekend to New York, ostensibly to see a show." Nick sighed at the memory.

"So what happened next?"

Nic laughed. "Patience, my sweet. I'm getting there," She touched Dana's cheek with her fingertips. "Well, together we figured out what we'd been missing for all those years. We couldn't get enough of each other. Alex was concerned that her parents would become suspicious of us spending so much time together. She told me she'd continue seeing a 'friend' of hers, Mateo, as what I would now call a beard. Alex and I were together for a little over a year. I loved her with all I was until she broke my heart. She came to me one day and said we needed to talk."

"Oh no." Dana whispered. "Was she pregnant?"

"No. She told me that she was getting a considerable amount of pressure from her family to get married, as well as from Mateo. Everything was against me...the church, the family, and tradition. I couldn't compete and she left me."

Dana's heart ached. "You must have been devastated. What did you do then?"

"I ran. Ten years or so ago, I started accepting travel assignments. It didn't make my family happy, but I figured they'd be a lot unhappier knowing why I started traveling. In some ways, it was easier being away from home. I didn't have to deal with the fear of being found out as much."

"So, your family doesn't know yet?"

"My dad died several years ago. My mom..." Nic smiled thinking of her mother. "Well, it just didn't seem worth upsetting her. I'm not home enough for it to matter. If I ever settle back in the States and set up housekeeping, maybe I'll tell her, maybe not. My older sister knows and she still loves me, so I have her to talk with when I get too lonely for family who is supportive."

"So have there been many others since Alex?"

"No, not really...nobody serious anyway. You know yourself it's hard to maintain any kind of stable relationship in a job like ours that requires being away so often. This assignment is unusual because of the length of time we've been in one place. It's unique because you and I had time to get acquainted and come to know each other. It doesn't seem I have that luxury often. Do you, Dana?"

"No, you're right. I think I mentioned before that I haven't been in a relationship for a long time." She shook her head. "It's sad to think about what I've been missing for all that time. It's been years, in fact, for some of the reasons you mentioned, as well as the fact that I just didn't meet anyone with whom I wanted to have more than a casual relationship until you."

"What made me special?"

"I don't know for sure. I think it started when you said 'hello' to me." Dana leaned in and kissed Nic. It was late into the early morning hours when they finally drifted off to sleep.

*\*\*\**

The next morning Nic awoke to find Dana watching her sleep. "Good morning, Dr. Nicolina F. Bianchi. What does the 'F' stand for?" Dana's hand was tracing lazy circles around Nic's navel.

Nic rolled on her side then leaned in and kissed Dana on the nose. "Fabiana."

"Fabiana as in fabulous?" Dana teased.

"No," she smiled knowing that Dana knew it didn't mean that. "Ha! No, its literal translation is bean grower."

Dana giggled. "If it's all the same to you, I'll stick with my definition. It suits you better."

Nic laughed then began to pull away to get out of bed. Dana held on tightly, delaying her departure. "I hate to mention this, but we have to get up and face the harsh reality of work. Although I'd much rather spend the day here with you."

"Ugh! Work." Dana gave Nic a lingering kiss. "Maybe that'll keep me fresh in your mind today."

They got up and showered together. Due to time constraints, they limited their activities there to washing as opposed to what they would have preferred to be doing. Nic pulled Dana close. "Why is it I can't get enough of you?"

"I don't know. Whatever it is, it must be contagious, because I feel exactly the same way."

They headed downstairs and grabbed a quick bite for breakfast before leaving for their meeting. Neither woman wanted to be at work but once there they became engaged in their duties. The day seemed interminable to them, until at long last, their responsibilities for the day ended. Nic pulled Dana aside as they left work, away from the foot traffic on the busy street.

"Where to?"

"It doesn't really matter as long as it's with you."

Nic had a soft look in her eyes as she smiled at Dana. "Let's take a walk. The hotel is not too far from here. We can stop in there until we decide where we want to have dinner."

They opted for an espresso and biscotti along their way. They sat at a small table to enjoy their snacks and make small talk.

"I hope you don't get tired of me." Nic touched Dana's hand.

"How could I?" Dana looked deeply into Nic's eyes. "Oh, I get it. You're afraid I'm just toying with you and soon I'll revert back to my evil heterosexual ways, aren't you?"

Nic glanced down then looked away, taking time to organize her thoughts. She didn't want to leave any room for Dana to misinterpret her. The last thing she wanted was to hurt her or say the wrong thing and make her angry.

"Toying with me isn't exactly the phrase I had in mind. However, I do admit that I have fears that eventually you may have trouble being involved in a lesbian relationship with me. It happened to me before. I have to confess that even in this short time, I've developed strong feelings for you Dana. I don't know where what I'm feeling can go."

"So, where do you want it to go?"

Hoping to lighten the intensity of their conversation, Nic replied. "Immediately or in the future? Immediately is easy to answer. I've been lusting for you all day." She chuckled, as did Dana. "As for the future, my goals include my desire to stop traveling—it's getting old. I want to be settled and have a more normal job, a lover I come home to every day, and maybe a family, although I'm fast becoming too old to hold onto that dream for too much longer. What about you?"

"Hey, you stole my dream!"

They both laughed.

"Think about it, though, Dana. In your wildest imagination, did you ever picture a woman as the person you settled down with in your dreams?"

"I have to admit that I didn't... does it make a difference that I couldn't imagine someone like you?"

"From my experience, obviously, sometimes it does."

"I understand that you're feeling tentative and afraid I'll hurt you. You certainly have good reason to feel that way based on your history. If it helps any, I can unequivocally state that I don't ever want a relationship with a man again. I think that we have to start with the premise that I'm telling you the truth. If I wanted a man, do you really think I'd have waited to get involved with one as long as I have, regardless of the fact that I travel for a living?" She watched Nic mull her question. "So, do you?"

With a twinkle in her eye, hoping for the outcome she wanted, Nic raised an eyebrow. "Maybe you're haven't gotten involved for so long because you're frigid."

Dana feigned shock. "I know one way to prove that theory wrong." She stood, linking her arm through Nic's, thankful that it was commonplace for women to walk that way on the streets of Rome. "Why don't you show me your hotel room?"

*** 

Much later, the lovers lay cuddled in Nic's bed after an exhausting love making session. Dana spoke first. "Well, I hope that proves your theory about my being frigid was totally off base. What else have you got?"

Nic laughed. "I don't know. I just can't help thinking about what if. What if people you know or members of your extended family don't approve—or your friends? If things get tough, will you leave me because you don't want to face the prejudice of those you care for and those who care for you?"

"I know, honey, that you need me to reassure you that this is not a mistake. I think you're seeking an ironclad guarantee."

Nic nodded. She needed to believe that if they moved forward with a relationship, Dana would not change her mind about being comfortable in a partnership with a woman.

Dana propped herself up on one elbow and looked into Nic's eyes. "I'd love to be able to give you a money back guarantee. I know it's what you want. All I can say is that I hope what we have happening between us continues to grow and develop into something long-term. It's what I'd like to see happen between us and I hope you feel the same."

"Yes, I especially like the sound of that long-term part."

"Okay, progress." Dana squeezed Nic's hand. "So, as far as family approval...my parents and grandparents have all passed and I have no siblings, nor is there any other family to be concerned about. Even so, my family was very liberal. They had friends from all backgrounds and occupations, rich and not so rich, gay, straight, and of many different nationalities. I can't imagine that my parents would have been disapproving as long as they knew that I was happy with my decision. As for friends, I only have two friends who would matter. All the rest are mere acquaintances or work friends. You, yourself, admitted that it was difficult to form lasting relationships while on the road. I think that's true of friends as well as lovers, don't you? I have many acquaintances, but few true friends."

"Yes, I can count my real friends on one hand and have a couple of fingers left over," Nic admitted.

"As for the friends I do have, my closest friend, Amanda, is a lesbian, and my other friend is my neighbor. I don't know how she feels, although I suspect it wouldn't matter to her either. She and Amanda have already become good friends, just in the short time I've been here. So, I think all of those concerns are moot. What it boils down to is what happens between us. I don't take commitment lightly and if I make a commitment to you, I promise you I won't change my mind. If we become more emotionally involved than we are now, I can assure you that if ever I were to end our relationship it would be for reasons directly related to just that—our relationship.

It would never be because of what other people think or feel about us. Is that enough?"

Nic paused for hardly a fraction of a second before she pulled Dana close and breathed in her scent. "Yes, that's enough, more than enough. Dana, get ready. I'm coming for you with all that I've got, with all that I am. I want that dream and I want it with you. Think we have a chance?"

"I think we're off to a darned good start. Oh, by the way, I'm going to let you chase me until I catch you!"

## Chapter 11

Amanda was already enjoying her bike ride by the time she turned off the road onto the trail. She hated wearing a helmet because they were hot and made her sweat. She debated about leaving it behind, although in her heart, she knew she had to wear it, despite expecting the ride to be an easy one. *I should have left Mallory a note. Oh well, I guess it really doesn't matter. I'll be home long before she gets there.*

Amanda pedaled steadily up the path. She made consistent progress, stopping twice before she reached the clearing for water and a bite of the energy bar she had stashed in her pack. She was about on track with her timeline. Unpacking the telephoto lens she brought with her on the trip, she decided that she might set up out of sight, hoping she would not scare the animals off this time. Scanning the clearing by peering through the lens, she was disappointed that she was the only one there. She not only missed the animals, but realized that she wished that Mallory were with her as well. Deciding to take shelter near one of the large boulders she hoped that the shielding of the rocks would protect her from the animals seeing her. According to her watch, she had about another thirty minutes before she had to leave to make it back in time to meet Mallory.

Reflecting on her earlier conversation with Bernie, Amanda realized that it was a relief to have that behind her.

Although Amanda was sorry for Bernie, she felt just a little sorry for herself as well, for the years she now felt she'd wasted. Starting over is never easy. Now back in New York State, she was genuinely looking forward to beginning a new life. She had never much cared for California, always feeling threatened that an earthquake, fire, or some other natural disaster would strike. On the plus side, the weather was gorgeous and the coast was beautiful. Sadly, she never seemed to feel comfortable there...just didn't seem to feel at home. How much that feeling had to do with her unfulfilling relationship with Bernie, she wasn't sure. Regardless, she was excited to be back east and was even looking forward to the cold winter.

The scuffling sound in the leaves alerted her to the appearance of the chipmunk. She readied the camera, focusing in on the cute, furry little creature that seemed more at ease than the first time she and Mallory had spotted him. Perhaps the fact that she'd been sitting so quietly in her hiding spot made him unaware of her presence. It came as no surprise to her that she wished at least the tenth time that Mallory were here to share this with her. Even the sound of Mallory's name and the feel of it on her lips gave her a secret sense of pleasure. *Maybe now that things have been resolved with Bernie, there will be a right time for us to move forward and explore the possibilities of a relationship together.* Obviously, they were certainly compatible. After all, they'd practically been living together for the past several weeks—except for the fact that they were still sleeping separately. In reality, they hadn't even kissed yet.

She'd been attracted to Mallory right from the beginning. Having allowed a friendship to develop with Mallory made her desire for her all the sweeter and that much more intense. What she felt for Mallory had developed in layers, and was more than the simple lust that drove her relationship with Bernie. The only word she could think of to describe the multidimensional feelings she had for the warm, honest, and considerate woman she was growing to care for was full. Mallory made her feel emotionally complete. She was anxious to tie up the remaining loose ends with Bernie and feel free to explore a deeper relationship with Mallory, one that included physical intimacy.

Although Mallory and I have yet to share any sexual contact, our relationship is, in reality, more intense and...what? The only word I can come up with is intimate. Yes, I'm more personally intimate with Mallory than I've ever been with Bernie, even after all the years the two of us had together. Because of the depth of the emotional intimacy I share with Mallory, I'd bet a sexual relationship with her will feel like a more complete, more fulfilling experience than all the hot sex I've had with Bernie.

Amanda felt the smile form on her lips as she recalled how she and Mallory could talk together for hours about nothing and everything. Mallory cared about what she thought and felt. Bernie, not so much...not that she and Bernie had not at one time shared secrets, but sex had always been Bernie's communication mode of choice. *When had Bernie ever sat and read or commented about what I had written? Never. I doubt that Bernie would even be able to recall any details about the book I'm writing. Why? Was I guilty of closing her out? Was I less than open about my hopes and dreams with Bernie, and if so why? When had that started?*

I know that I stepped back and withdrew emotionally. It became my method of self-protection after the first time I caught Bernie cheating. I wonder how many others there were before and after. Did it matter? She pondered the cause of the rift between them. She knew that for the past two years she'd maintained more of an emotional distance from her lover, if for no other reason than self-preservation. Wasn't that a byproduct of Bernie's cheating? Or, did I force Bernie to seek shelter in other women's arms because I withheld something Bernie needed from me?

Amanda needed to understand what had gone wrong in her relationship with Bernie so she would be confident that history would never repeat itself. Bernie had been quick to accept the blame for their relationship falling apart, but she'd never said anything other than, 'I don't know why I cheated, I just couldn't stop myself.' *There had to be a reason, didn't there, or could it just be one's nature to be unable to be monogamous?*

Amanda drew her attention back to the chipmunk. He was nearing the spot where she had the camera focused. She'd set the focus and strung a remote release cable back to the position where she hid out of sight behind the rock. When he entered the general area where the camera would capture him in the shot, she depressed the plunger. The click startled the little guy and he raced for the hole. He was so fast that she barely managed to squeeze off another shot, one that would end up becoming one of her favorite pictures of the day. She captured a picture of him as he dove into his home with just his fat little backside and his tail visible as he disappeared into the hole in the ground. She couldn't wait to get back home to share her photos with Mallory.

Amanda glanced at her watch and couldn't believe that it was already time to leave. Carefully, Amanda headed back down the path on her bike. She slowed to a stop just before the steepest part of the trail that Mallory had warned her about and decided that today, because she was alone, she'd walk that section instead of riding it. After she navigated the steepest part of the trail, Amanda quickly covered the ground she needed to make her way back home. A quick shower and she felt wonderful. She made the salad and waited for Mallory to show up with the pizza, while she acknowledged to herself for probably the fiftieth time that day how much she'd missed Mallory.

*** 

Mallory called to let Amanda know that she was on her way. Amanda stood waiting at the door and greeted Mallory with a warm hug before taking the pizza box from her. They headed for the kitchen. The plates, salads, and table settings were in place, the wine was chilling, and two mugs were in the freezer awaiting Mallory's choice.

"Wine, beer, or water?"

"Beer, I think. That would taste good with the pizza." Mallory offered an expression of appreciation for the special treat as Amanda poured the beer into the icy mugs.

Once settled in their seats, Amanda asked, "So how was your day? Start with the good thing."

"Just an average day." Mallory grinned a shy smile, and averted her eyes.

"What happened that you aren't telling me?"

Mallory looked up. "Well, as part of the rehab department opening ceremony, the Hospital Chief honored people instrumental in making the whole thing come together. I was one of the people they honored."

"Oh, Mallory, that's wonderful."

"The bad thing is that it doesn't put any more money in my paycheck." Mallory teased. "Despite that pesky little detail, it was really rewarding just the same."

"I'm so proud of you. It must be gratifying to work for an organization that recognizes and appreciates excellence."

Mallory considered Amanda's observation. "I'd think it would be a difficult aspect of your profession, the lack of recognition, I mean. It'll be satisfying when you sell your novel. Its success will be recognition for all the hard work you put in every day."

"Careful, you'll turn this girl's head."

"So, Amanda, do you feel ready to tell me about your day? I want to hear it all, not only the good and the bad, but all the parts in between."

It was obvious from the directness of the question and the request for details that Mallory was curious about Amanda's conversation with Bernie earlier in the day. "Let's wait until we finish cleaning up, then I'll describe it start to finish."

It took a matter of minutes for them to clean up their dinner plates and move to the living room taking their second beer in with them. Once they were settled comfortably, Mallory said, "Okay, give."

"Well, my conversation with Bernie began with her being a bit on the testy side. She was upset that she had to wait for my call. I'd forgotten to turn my phone on this morning and I slept in a little later than normal, so by the time I connected with her, she was already a little annoyed. However, things got better after that. I think she's finally accepted that I won't come back." Amanda saw Mallory exhale a long breath she'd been holding and a flicker of relief pass across her face.

"No more flowers?"

Amanda shook her head and smiled. "No. No more flowers, at least not from her."

"Is that a hint?" Mallory hoped to make Amanda smile.

"No, at least not in the near term. I think I'm flowered out. But...candy is always an option." Amanda rested her chin on her hand, and rewarded Mallory with the smile she'd been seeking.

"I'll take that under advisement." Mallory leaned forward, placing her weight on her elbows she rested on her knees. "So, what happened after that?"

"Surprisingly, Bernie apologized again, and this time I do believe she's sincere. I'm not sure if it's because of the fact that her cheating and dishonesty cost her something this time or if she's even really internalized that yet. But I think I've finally convinced her that I'm not coming back to her."

Amanda noticed Mallory dip her head in acknowledgement of the information. She heard the conviction in her own voice conveying the truthfulness of her statement and was relieved that she still felt good about it.

"You know what else she said? It amazed me. She told me she just couldn't control herself."

"Maybe she really is sick. Maybe she's a sexual addict."

"Isn't that just an excuse for not controlling your libido? It seems to me that it's just a cop out for all the movie stars and politicians who get caught doing whatever or whomever they shouldn't be doing—then it's off to rehab for sexual addiction."

"Well, I'm not convinced that's completely accurate. I'm sure that may be true in some instances. From the studies I've read, there are definitely some people who have a credible problem. They've lost jobs, homes, marriages, children, and more. There seems to be two camps. I know there are some people like you who are dubious and it's purely narcissistic behavior, while many in the medical field believe it's a mental disorder. Do you think Bernie's an addict?"

"How can I know? She was away from home three weeks of the month. I saw no evidence of it when she was home other than a change in her sexual conduct and preferences after I learned she was cheating the first time. Then again, I have to admit that my feelings about her changed, too, so I can't really blame her. In fact, I still wonder if I didn't drive her to cheat because I never totally forgave her and admit that I pulled back."

"Don't be ridiculous. Don't accept blame for her behavior. If she had a problem with your relationship, it was her obligation to tell you what it was and the responsibility of both of you to try to work it through. Then, if you couldn't, agree to separate. Cheating is never a solution."

Amanda nodded. "Thank you, that helps."

"I do have one concern for your health. Do you know how many others there were or who these women were?"

"No. Not really. Why?" Amanda's expression conveyed her concern.

"I don't want to alarm you... have you given any thought to being tested for STDs?"

"Do you really think that's necessary? I don't seem to have any symptoms."

"Well, there are many sexually transmitted diseases that are asymptomatic for many women—like gonorrhea, chlamydia, HSV, HPV, HIV, hepatitis B and HCV to some extent. A large percentage of them go undetected in women, at least initially. Lesbian women are at lower risk than the heterosexual population statistically, yet it's not something to just take for granted. It's of more concern if a woman is bisexual or is involved with drugs. From what you've told me, bisexuality isn't an issue for her." Mallory paused. "Do you know if Bernie does drugs?"

"I don't think so, at least not at home. When she travels, I can't really say for sure. I doubt it." There was a short lull while Amanda contemplated the information Mallory had provided. "I had no idea about STD's having no symptoms." Concern evident in Amanda's voice, she asked, "What about kissing? Can all this stuff be spread by kissing?"

"There are varying opinions about that, but the consensus is that kissing is considered safe, for the most part. Obviously herpes can be spread, but usually an active case...that's an obvious infection. I'm sure you've seen people with those angry looking sores on their lips."

Amanda nodded.

"Even HIV isn't considered generally transmittable by kissing. So of all sexually oriented activities, that's probably the safest."

"Good thing. If not, people would never get paired up."

Mallory laughed. "I'm impressed by your unfailing ability to find humor in almost every situation.

"It makes life easier to deal with if one keeps a sense of humor, don't you think?" Amanda shifted her position and grew serious. "So you really think I should be tested?"

"Although you probably have nothing to worry about, you know that Bernie's been sexually active with more than one other sexual partner. So I'd definitely recommend it, for your own peace of mind as well as the safety of any future partner you may choose."

"Well, you've got me frightened now." Amanda grimaced. "I'll attend to it this week. I'm sure you have a gynecologist that you can recommend. I'm due for my annual check up anyway."

"I do." Mallory pulled out her cell phone and sent a text with the number of her gynecologist to Amanda. "Don't worry. I doubt that you have a problem. I think it's wise for you to get tested. Besides, before you enter into any kind of monogamous sexual relationship with a new partner where you'll engage in unprotected sex, it's always best practice if you're both tested. Then neither of you has to worry. Many people practice 'safe sex.' To me, that's really a misnomer. I think 'safer sex,' is a more accurate term, because although using some sort of barrier is safer, none of those techniques is one hundred percent *safe*."

"Okay, now that I'm totally depressed, let's change the subject. Oh, just one more thing, Bernie told me that she'd let me know about the house in two week's time. She's not sure if she wants to keep it. Honestly, it doesn't make sense for her to keep the house. She's simply not home often enough to justify the expense. Thankfully, it's not my decision any more. If she decides to sell it, I'll probably have to go back and help close things up. It's not fair to leave all of that to her."

"I know I have no right to interfere. I can't stop myself from hoping you won't have to go back to California. I'll miss you if you do. Let's talk of happier subjects. Tell me about the rest of your day. Did you work on the novel?"

"No, I went for a bike ride."

"Really? Wish I could have been with you. The Open House was successful, but it pales in comparison." She chuckled.

"That makes two of us who wished you could have come with me. I missed you." Amanda reached out to touch Mallory's' hand. "I went back and got some pictures of the chipmunk. Wait, I'll show you!"

Amanda retrieved the camera and showed Mallory the photos she took that afternoon. When she got to the picture of the chipmunk diving into its hole, Mallory laughed out loud. "This is by far my favorite."

"Yes, mine too. I'm going to crop, enlarge it, and hang it in my room upstairs. It just makes me smile. You want a copy?"

Mallory enthusiastically nodded. "Yes, definitely. It'll remind me of the happy time we had shared on our first trip to the clearing."

***

The rest of the week sped by. The two women spent time together at dinner, and in their free time they played cards, word games, or just talked, each enjoying the other's presence. Sometimes Amanda would work on her novel and Mallory would catch up on her professional reading. Amanda was able to take advantage of a cancellation and made an appointment with Mallory's gynecologist for the following week. After her visit, Amanda reported the results of her conversation with the doctor to Mallory.

"The test was no big deal. I was surprised when they told me that I'll have to wait two or three weeks for my results."

Mallory smiled. "That's not unusual. I'm sure everything will be fine. At least you'll have a clear mind and no worries a few weeks from now."

"I know you're right. It's just plain scary. I did like the doctor though. Thanks for recommending her."

"No problem. She's very nice and well respected in the hospital, too." Mallory hesitated a bit before she decided that she'd never know an answer to the question she'd been pondering for a while until she asked it. "I won't be available this weekend. I decided to work and get a jump on my year end reports."

"Oh." Amanda's shoulders dropped and her facial expression clearly indicated her disappointment.

"Don't look like you just lost your best friend. There is a decided upside to me being missing in action this weekend, that I'm hopeful you'll be happy about."

"Really? What could that possibly be?"

"Well, at the end of this month, I'll combine my comp time, my days off, and a couple of days of vacation and get seven days off. I hope it's not too early to ask you this, but I was wondering if you'd want to go on my vacation with me?'

Amanda's body language had gone from dejection to elation with those few simple words. Amanda didn't even ask where Mallory planned to go before she announced her decision about the trip. "The thought of being away from you for seven whole days gives me agita. Yes, without a doubt I want to go. I don't really care where it is, but tell me anyway."

"Agita? I haven't heard that word since I left Philly." Mallory laughed. "Well we certainly don't want you suffering angst and feeling ill. I've been thinking of taking a cruise. There are a few different choices. One leaves out of New Jersey the end of the month bound for Canada with two days at sea, and stops in Halifax and St. John. I'm kind of thinking I like that one. As an alternative, if you prefer warm weather, we could go to the islands or fly down to the Keys."

"I like the first option. I like the idea of several days of pampering. Have you ever cruised before?"

"Yes, once. I like it. What about you?"

"Once on a big ship. I liked that. Then Bernie and I went out with a friend of hers who owned a yacht. Very fancy and very upscale. Not really my taste."

"With your permission, I'll call and book us. They're running some very attractive last minute special prices."

"Just let me know what I owe you."

"No, Amanda, this is my treat. You've been taking care of me for a couple of months, ever since we met. I appreciate it. It's the least I can do."

After unsuccessfully arguing against Mallory paying for her cruise, Amanda gave in. "Well, then I'll pay for the onboard expenses and tours and transportation to and from the ship." Excited by the prospect of their vacation, Amanda suggested that they look up the tours. "We can decide what we want to see in the ports."

They checked the information online. Together they opted for more of the historical overview tours offered in each of the ports they stopped at, with the option for some shopping in the downtown areas afterwards.

***

Planning the trip was great fun for Mallory and Amanda. After they checked the weather forecasts for the areas they'd be traveling to, they began to organize their clothes. Unsure of exactly how warm or cool it would be based upon the fluctuation in temperature in the forecast, both decided to bring clothing they could layer.

Several days before their scheduled departure, Bernie called Amanda to reveal her decision. Having decided to sell the house, she asked Amanda to come to California to go through things and help her divest of their possessions. Despite Amanda's protests that she didn't have anything there that she wanted, Bernie insisted, saying that there were quite a few items she didn't know what to do with.

"Bernie, when I tell you I don't want any of it, I mean it. Can't you just box up everything you're not sure about and ship it to me?"

"No. After twelve years together, don't you think you owe it to me to help?"

"Bernie, you know that I'm not coming back to you, right?"

"Yes, you've told me that repeatedly. How could I not know? Still, I think you owe it to me to look me in the eyes and tell me that."

"Okay, I'm busy the remainder of this week and all of next week, so I can't come now, but I'll come out the following week. Will you be there?"

"I'll have to be, won't I?" There was a pause then, Bernie said, "Let me know your flight arrangements so I can pick you up at the airport."

Amanda completed her travel arrangements, planning the trip to California for the end of the week after she returned from the cruise. She sent Bernie a quick email with her flight number and arrival time. Dread was not an exact descriptor she would use to regarding her trip back to the house she owned with Bernie, but it was darned close. She hated the thought of going through all the stuff remaining in the house and stirring up memories. Spending the extended amount of time with Bernie that the chores would require was definitely not something she looked forward to with any enthusiasm either. She would gladly welcome a root canal over having to deal with Bernie this final time.

Amanda and Mallory checked all their paperwork the week before the cruise was set to depart to be sure that everything was in order. Mallory suggested that they get a document signed naming each other as their medical power of attorney.

"That's a great suggestion, and not only for the cruise. What if something happened to me? I really have no one to speak for me." Amanda admitted.

"I'm in the exact same position. My family is too far away from me, too. There's an attorney at the hospital able to prepare the paperwork for us. It is common place for people to want to do that last minute at the hospital."

Amanda liked that Mallory was someone who attended to all the details without being forceful, obtrusive, or overbearing. With Bernie, it felt as though it were an issue of control. With Mallory, Amanda didn't feel controlled like she sometimes had with Bernie. Instead, she felt like an equal participant in the decision making process. Mallory often had the ideas, although they most often negotiated and decided the details together. They took turns carrying out the decisions based upon which of them had more free time or could do the task with the least hassle.

The day of the cruise, the limo Amanda hired to take them to the dock showed up a few minutes early. They already had their bags organized and waiting on Dana's front porch. Upon their arrival at the dock, their first view of the ship was breathtaking.

Amanda scanned the ship from the bow to the stern, leaning back to take in the height. "That thing is huge, like a floating city."

The porters accepted their bags, along with a generous tip, before they made their way inside the building to get their boarding passes. Signing in was extremely well organized and the processing was quick. In less than fifteen minutes they had their identification checked and completed the necessary paperwork. Amanda gave them her credit card for the onboard charges. They were issued their boarding passes after they stood in the designated place to have their picture taken. As they moved along in line for the next step in the boarding process, they compared photos and teased each other about whose picture was the least flattering—Amanda won.

Next, they were ushered into a large waiting area where they were called, by color code and number, to board. Large buses shuttled the passengers from the registration building to the ship. Once off the bus, up the gangplank they went. Each deck had displays posted with the words, 'You Are Here' clearly marked on the diagram. It took them a few minutes to get oriented to the layout of the ship. By studying the diagram posted on the wall next to the elevators, they found their stateroom with relative ease. Mallory had reserved a balcony room, which contained a queen-sized bed made of two individual beds joined together, a small sofa, one chair, and a dressing table. Mallory looked at Amanda.

"I requested the room to be arranged with twin beds. I'll get the steward to change it."

Amanda smiled and with a twinkle in her eye she quickly replied, "It really doesn't matter. There won't be anything happening there but sleeping. My test results haven't arrived yet, remember."

"That's okay, but don't forget, cuddling isn't contagious in any way. Just in case anyone is interested."

"You know I'm interested, but as we've already discussed, I'm on my best behavior until my test results show me to be healthy. I'll definitely keep in mind the fact that cuddling is acceptable behavior." Amanda gave Mallory a quick hug. "Come on, let's check out the head." The bath was small but functional with the tiniest shower Amanda had ever seen. "Don't drop the soap," she jested, "you'll have to step out of the shower to pick it up."

"I hope you like hirsute women," Mallory quipped, her tone matching Amanda's. "Tell me how anyone could possibly shave their legs in there?"

They were still laughing together when the room steward stopped in to introduce himself and to inform them that lunch was being served in the main dining room. "Your luggage will be delivered shortly, probably by the time you return."

Finding the dining room wasn't difficult, thanks to the signs in the corridors. Following lunch, they spent the next two hours walking the impressive ship from bow to stern, admiring the artwork and displays in the corridors and marveling at the sheer size of the vessel. It was fun walking the corridors, peering into the different cabins to see size and layout of each different type offered. "Next time, I want a small suite, I think," Mallory announced. "There's a bit more room than what we have and a larger bathroom with a tub."

"You really are into that leg shaving thing, aren't you?"

Mallory grinned. "Who knows? Someday you may come to appreciate that aspect of my personality as well as some of my many skills I don't share with just anyone."

"Yes, you never know what could happen." Amanda replied. Sexual tension had been building over the past couple of weeks ever since she had made her decision final regarding ending her previous relationship with Bernie. The only thing that was preventing Amanda and Mallory from moving their relationship to a more intimate level had been the wait for the blood test results. Each of them expected the trip to be an opportunity for them to spend time together unencumbered by any limitations on them growing physically closer. The fact that the doctor hadn't called before their departure was a huge disappointment.

## Chapter 12

Awareness slowly returned to Dana as she came fully awake. Their bodies were entwined, a tangle of arms and legs, as they always were when she and Nic slept. In sleep, as in the private hours when they were awake, rarely was there time when they were not touching each other.

Dana slid her hand down Nic's torso and was rewarded with an appreciative sigh. *How did this happen to me? I've always thought of myself as heterosexual, but there is not even one lingering doubt in my head or in my heart, that I'm in love with the wonderful woman next to me in bed.*

Dana thought back over the past couple of months they had worked and played together. They'd toured the city, spent time together with and without the company of friends they'd made while on assignment in Rome. What could happen next, and where would they go from this point forward? Neither she nor Nic had revealed anything about their feelings regarding their future other than that they enjoyed the time they spent with each other. As Dana cuddled closer to her lover, she realized how euphorically happy she felt and how contented she was since she and Nic became involved. She wondered though, *what would happen in two short weeks when their assignment in Rome ended?* Obviously, they would each most likely return to their homes. Nic didn't really have a home of her own. She tried to book her assignments back to back whenever possible and if she was off assignment for any substantial amount of time, she would most likely return home to her mother's house in Philadelphia to visit with mom and the rest of her family.

How could they possibly remain together as a couple? They each had a life apart from the other that involved traveling. Oh, maybe it would be doable to meet between assignments, but how long would that last? It had taken Dana half a lifetime to find the person she loved. Loved? Yes, I am definitely in love with her and it's going to hurt like hell when we have to say good-bye. It's best, I think, that I not tell Nic the depth of my feelings for her. I'll just keep it light...no confessions about how I can't imagine my life without her now that I've finally found her.

At that exact moment, as the tears came from Dana's eyes sparked by the thought of having to leave the luscious woman next to her, Nic opened her eyes. She was immediately fully awake and alert. Pulling Dana to her, cradling her against her breasts, Nic whispered, "Qual è il mio amore che ti rende così triste?"

"I'm sad because I love you," Dana whimpered, tears flowing freely now. *So much for keeping it light, and not confessing my feelings!*

"I love you, too."

"You do?" A smile of happiness and relief spread across Dana's face.

Nic returned Dana's smile then kissed her lightly on the lips before she used her palm to wipe away the tears from Dana's face. "I absolutely, positively, without a doubt do. I don't understand your tears. Isn't being in love something to celebrate about instead of something to cry over? Why the tears?"

"Normally, it would be something to celebrate. For us, it makes me sad."

"Why?" Nic said simply. "I don't understand."

"Because it will break my heart to say good-bye to you. I can't even imagine what my life will be like without you beside me every day and every night."

"I know," Nic's furrowed brow and serious expression showed that she was equally concerned. "I've had the same thoughts lately." After releasing Dana, she sat up, propping herself up against the headboard, the sheet loosely gathered around her waist.

Dana slid into position next to her and glanced over at her lover. She tugged the sheet. "If you expect to have a serious conversation with me, you had better cover those up." She gestured with her eyes at Nic's breasts. "You know I can't keep my hands to myself where you're concerned. What I can see, I have to touch."

"Yes," Nic admitted, "I know. That's one of my favorite things about you—your inability to resist temptation."

With the mood lightened somewhat by their gentle teasing, they sat together each absorbed in her own thoughts.

"What do you think we should do?" Dana asked.

"I don't know. I hadn't come to any conclusions yet. I wanted to wait to see how you were feeling...I thought you'd think I was crazy if I told you I loved you after such a short time."

"No, how could I, when I feel exactly the same way? Nic, I can't imagine my life without you in it, and I'm not talking about a few short snatches of time between assignments. I mean every day. I want to wake up with you every morning and come home to you every night. Still, I don't know how that can be possible for us to achieve, with the work we do."

"Well, the solution is simple, really. We'll need to get different jobs. Work that doesn't involve travel."

"But, Nic, are you really sure? I mean you have to admit that those are momentous changes in both our lives. How can you be sure it's the right decision? Are we rushing things?"

"Neither of us is a kid any more. We've both been around and met many other people. Now that I've found who I want, why should I wait any longer?"

"What about your fears that I'll go back to the dark side?"

"You mean to dating men?" Nic laughed.

"Yes."

"Will you? Have you changed your mind about that?"

"No."

"That's good enough for me. If you were to leave me, at this point, it doesn't matter who it is you leave me for...I'd be equally devastated if you left me for a man, another woman, or any other reason. You'd still be just as gone from my life. Besides, I think what we have is special. It's something I've been seeking for a long time. Now that I've found it, I can't see how I can let it pass me by or slip through my fingers." She reached over and took Dana's hand into her own. "We'll work things out. We've been saying that we were both a little sick of traveling so much and having many acquaintances and few close friends or any kind of a committed relationship."

"I know. It's true. Even if there were no you in my life, I'm not sure how much longer I could do this job...maybe for another year, two at the most. Where are you after this assignment? I'm off for two weeks after this, what about you?" Dana said optimistically. "I planned to spend it at home, but if you're traveling, I could go with you. I can't bear to be without you yet."

Nic thought. "I can take some time off to be with you at your home. We can see how we feel about things then. If we still feel as we do today, we'll make plans to change our jobs, if that's what it'll take, for us to start a life together. If our company has no home based assignments for me, with my experience and doctorate, I should be able to get a university position again. I started out teaching and I enjoy it. It doesn't matter to me where we live, as long as I'm with you. What about you?"

"I've been with the company a long time. I'm sure there will be something else I can do for them. Maybe not right away, but within a couple of months, something should open up. If not...I live an hour from New York City and ours isn't the only company who needs translators."

Nic slowly slid the sheet away from first one breast then playfully uncovered the other. "Now what was it you were saying about not being able to keep your hands to yourself?"

Dana rolled over and slid on top of Nic relishing the feel of her skin sliding over her lover's. *I'll never get enough of the feel of her and the scent of her.* She slid up to straddle Nic, tilting her hips, and inciting a flash of desire in Nic's dark eyes. "Let me show you what I mean," she replied softly as she began to move against her lover.

## Chapter 13

After consuming a delicious lunch in the ship's lavishly decorated grand dining room, Amanda and Mallory returned to their cabin. They were pleased to find their bags waiting outside their cabin door and made quick work of unpacking their clothes, neatly storing them in the drawers and closet.

"Look, there's a safe. Want to lock up our passports and other ID? I think the only thing we need onboard is our ship card."

Together they decided on a combination and Mallory keyed it in. With their valuables locked away, they slid open the doorway to the balcony. Two chairs sat facing each other, separated by a small table. Amanda picked up the papers the steward had left on the bed detailing the itinerary for the next day and explaining all the activities for their first day at sea.

"I don't think it's too cold to sit out here. Let's look over the itinerary and decide what we want to do tomorrow."

"Sounds like a plan," Mallory responded.

"So, what are you interested in doing? Tomorrow is a day at sea."

"Wow! There are so many different things to choose from, I don't know what to pick. I think I'd like to try the rock-climbing wall. Does that interest you at all?"

"I've never tried rock climbing before. Have you ever done it, Mal?"

"No, it would be a new experience for both of us."

"What else?" Amanda asked excitedly. She had already decided that she liked cruising despite the fact they hadn't yet left the dock.

"Well, I picked one, why don't you select an activity next?"

Amanda pursed her lips in thought. "Maybe we should book a massage after that? Think we'll be sore?"

"That's not a bad idea, even if we're not. I like that idea, something active followed by something soothing."

"Sounds good to me." Amanda read further down the list. "We can also sit up on the deck and read for a while, if the weather is warm enough. Dinner is all set and after that, there's a show. Tonight is a comedian. I'm looking forward to that. Tomorrow is a review put on by the ship's own group of singers and dancers...show tunes, it says."

"Oh look," Mallory exclaimed. "There's an ice skating show tomorrow afternoon while we're at sea. It says we need to get our tickets today at four-thirty."

"Really? This ship is amazing. I can't imagine an ice skating rink on a moving boat."

"Or a rock climbing wall, for that matter." Mallory continued to read. "It also says that skates are available for rental if we want to ice skate. Want to try it on our last day at sea? I haven't skated for years."

"That sounds like fun. Let's go up top to that lounge that has the panoramic view, have a drink, and watch as we set sail." Amanda paused to think for a moment. "Does one still set sail on a boat powered by an engine?"

Mallory smiled in return. "Don't know, but a bon voyage drink sounds good whether we set sail or steam away. Let me use the bathroom before we go."

Amanda was waiting on the sofa when Mallory emerged from the bathroom. She stood up ready to take her turn in the small room. As she and Mallory squeezed by each other, one coming out and one entering the cramped space, Amanda felt her nipples tense as she brushed by Mallory. She took advantage of the moment to inhale Mallory's fresh, clean smell. There was a pregnant moment where they both paused, hands joined, while an internal debate raged inside each of their heads. Amanda had insisted on the celibacy pending her test results. The overabundance of caution contributed to the building desire each harbored and to the questioning the wisdom of committing to it.

Amanda broke the spell first. "Sorry," she said stepping away. "It's just that you smell so good. I'm having a hard time keeping my distance."

"I know. But at least we're together."

"My senses could use a little numbing. If I remember correctly, you promised me a drink."

Mallory laughed. "That I did...let's go."

The elevators were a madhouse with a steadily increasing number of people boarding the ship and making their way to their cabins. After standing for several minutes waiting with a group of other passengers also in line for the cars to stop on their deck, they agreed to take the stairs. They climbed several flights to the lounge, which was beginning to fill with excited passengers, and found a seat on one of the vacant sofas. Each of them ordered a drink from the cheerful waiter. A couple introduced themselves and asked if they could sit on the sofa opposite them.

It wasn't long before Mallory and Amanda were engaged in animated conversation and soon felt at ease with the outgoing and friendly couple—the husband, a retired police officer and his wife, a retired secretary from a shore community in southern New Jersey. They were humorous people, and it wasn't long before the four were laughing like old friends.

Jack and Hannah said in unison, "Look, the ship is moving." The din of conversation reduced dramatically as almost everybody in the lounge focused in unison on the ship getting underway. They passed under the Verrazano Bridge on their way out to sea. Their new friends excused themselves to head to their cabin before dinner. Amanda and Mallory had the early seating. They knew they didn't have to dress for dinner as the cruise ship's newsletter listed casual as the required attire for the first day's evening meal, so they started down to the dining room for dinner.

The maître d' led them to their assigned table where, once seated, the waiter greeted them and asked them for their drink order. All four people were amazed when Jack and Hannah were led over to join them at their table.

"What are the odds that we'd be seated with you two?" Jack's voice carried the amazement that each member of the group felt.

With the preliminaries already out of the way, the two couples picked up their conversation where they'd left off earlier, in the lounge.

"If you're planning on going to the show tonight, would you like to join us?" Hannah asked them.

Mallory and Amanda looked at each other and signaled wordlessly that they felt it would be fine to accompany them. Amanda answered for both of them. "Sure, why not?"

Hannah suggested, "Let's leave after dinner and get there early. I understand the seating is not reserved. It's first come, first served. Maybe we can stroll along the promenade and see what's there on our way to the theater."

***

The two couples strolled along the ship's main thoroughfare, which was lined with shops and stores, a cafe, an ice cream shop, several bars and lounges. A fabulous two-story stairway located toward the stern of the boat provided entryway into the two-tiered showroom.

Everyone enjoyed the performance which was a song and dance review put on by the ship's own dance company, followed by a juggler who was a comedian. He was very entertaining and there was something in the show to appeal to any age. All the humor was 'G' rated even though there were very few children on the cruise, and none present at the evening performances. Afterward Mallory and Amanda, accompanied by their new friends, stopped in at the cafe in the promenade for some coffee, tea, and snacks.

"It's already clear to me that I'm going to expand my waistline on this trip," said Jack as he patted his stomach. "The food is certainly impressive so far." He had one of each of the three cookies being offered that day on a small plate in front of him. He broke each large cookie into quarters. "Come on, everyone help me eat these so I'm not the only one to gain weight on this trip."

They all agreed that splitting the treats was a perfect way to share the enjoyment and the calories.

"So, are you two going to the disco later?" Hannah wondered.

Mallory and Amanda loved dancing with each other. As their eyes met it was evident to them that neither was sure about dancing together in such an overwhelmingly heterosexual environment. Mallory looked to Amanda, who shrugged, so Mallory replied. "Sure, why not? We'll check it out with you."

The crowd in the cafe had thinned to just their table and two other couples at separate tables in the back of the room. Hanna leaned in and spoke. "Do you mind if I ask you two girls a question? It's a little personal."

Again, a glance between them conveyed a message. This time Amanda nodded and responded with a smile. "Sure. What's on your mind?"

"Well, I hope we're not overstepping. We don't want to insult you, but Jack and I wondered if you two are a couple."

Amanda turned to Mallory and smiled. "You want to take this one?"

"You don't have to tell us if you don't want to. It's just that because our daughter is a lesbian, we have developed what she calls gaydar and we sort of thought you two made a cute couple. We weren't sure though. I hope you don't mind our asking."

"No, Hannah, we don't mind your asking. We're working on the couple thing."

Amanda turned to look at Mallory as she bumped her in the ribs with her elbow and finished the thought. "Right now we're just friends, but a girl can hope."

A bright flash of a smile and a wink were directed at Amanda, quickly followed by a squeeze of Amanda's knee. "This girl hopes so, too."

"Good," said Hannah. "You seem so good together."

Despite their fears, they had a great time with Jack and Hannah in the disco. They fast danced together and did several line dances. Jack danced with each woman in turn. He was a fantastic dancer and they all had a wonderful time. The couples bid each other good night at the elevator. Jack and Hannah were in a suite on the deck above them.

"See you at breakfast," Jack and Hanna called as the elevator doors closed.

It was after one o'clock when they slid the key card into the slot in their cabin door. The cabin was made up for them, with the sheets turned down and their tickets for their first land tour laid out for them on the bed. Mallory took Amanda's hand and pulled her close in a traditional slow dance hold.

Amanda snuggled close. "I had a lot of fun with you tonight, but I missed being able to dance with you."

"Yes, I agree. Still, it was a fun night."

"There's not much room in here, is there?" Mallory winced as her knee knocked against the coffee table. They stopped dancing, but remained holding each other.

"So you're hopeful?"

"More than hopeful. Don't you think of us as a couple already? I certainly do. I wasn't sure how to answer them. We're at an awkward stage in our relationship. Emotionally, I feel like we're a couple, but we don't yet have a physical relationship. I know I was jealous when you told me you were going back to close up the house in California and that you'd be spending time with Bernie. You once told me she was your Svengali. I'm ashamed to admit that I'm jealous. I'm afraid I'll lose you before we really get a chance."

"You have nothing to worry about. You know, I've been thinking about intimacy over these past couple of months. When I met Bernie, I fell immediately in lust and couldn't wait to get my hands on her. Yet, our relationship wasn't intimate. We didn't share what we were thinking and feeling like you and I do. I think that's why I always felt so lonely in my relationship with her. It's hard to explain. Does what I'm saying make any sense to you at all?"

"I know precisely what you mean. I had intimacy with Piper and the sexual component of our relationship developed from that emotional attachment. Our relationship seems to be following that same course. I never thought I'd be lucky enough to find that kind of relationship again. To me, it's the total package."

"I'm not denying that I checked you out and found you attractive from the moment we met. Still, I like the way this feels. As you've described it before, it's like getting a total package. I feel passion, but it's different somehow than what I felt before. It feels deeper and richer." Amanda took Mallory's hand and held it to her cheek. "I'm in love with you Mallory, and I can't wait to get you naked. I want to kiss you and touch you everywhere and make you call out my name in need, and then again in satisfaction."

"God, Amanda, you're going to make me come just listening to you." Mallory turned her hand over to cup Amanda's face in her palm, her touch soft and loving. She drew Amanda toward her to place a gentle kiss on her cheek.

Amanda closed her eyes as Mallory kissed her, enjoying the closeness they were sharing. She pulled back to meet Mallory's eyes. "And to answer your question, I've felt like you and I were a couple from not too long after we met. However, until Bernie accepted that the relationship she and I had was over, I didn't feel free to move forward with you. That impediment no longer stands in our way, nor does my visit to California. I've told you that part of my life is over and it's definitely a closed issue in my mind. You have no reason to worry. Still, it's sort of cute that you're jealous."

Mallory moved her hands to Amanda's face, one palm on each of Amanda's cheeks. As she leaned forward to kiss her, she whispered, "I love you, Amanda."

Amanda turned her cheek and slid into a close embrace. "I love you, too," she murmured against Mallory's neck as she inhaled the scent of the woman she so desired.

"What's the matter? Why won't you kiss me?"

"I've told you before and I'm very serious about it. I'm afraid that I may be carrying some kind of disease."

Mallory sought Amanda's eyes, and found tears there. "Oh sweetie, I told you that kissing is considered safe."

"I don't care. Just because we're onboard a ship doesn't change the situation. We have to follow the same rules we've been following…no physically intimate contact until I get my results. It would kill me if I passed something on to you."

Mallory sighed. "Obviously I did my job too well and have scared you half to death. That was certainly not my intention."

"That may be true, but now you're going to pay the price, right along with me, because I'm going to do everything in my power to drive you just as crazy as you've made me." Amanda slipped her hands beneath Mallory's shirt and slid them up her back, lightly using her nails.

"Umm, that feels so good, even if it's not playing fair." Despite her verbal protest, Mallory settled in, enjoying the embrace.

"I know. Nobody ever said I had to play fair. So, you love me, huh? When did you know?"

"I don't know, one day I was driving home to you and it just came to me that for the first time since Piper died, I realized that I was happy. I think it was at that moment, that I knew your presence in my life was responsible for much of my happiness. I realized that I'd fallen in love with you—plain and simple. What about you, when did you know?"

"I guess my feelings started to change the night I fixed us that leftover chicken casserole for dinner. That night, I realized that you were more loving and caring to me, after knowing me only a few short weeks, than Bernie had been in twelve years. Much like you, I just gradually realized that I never wanted what we have together to end."

Resigned to her fate, Mallory smiled. After she kissed Amanda on each cheek she pulled away, taking Amanda's hands into her own. "Well, if you're not going to kiss me, I've no hope for anything else. We might as well get in bed and get a good night's rest." They prepared for bed, each dressing in new pajamas before sliding between the sheets to cuddle together.

"We must be in some kind of relationship hell." Mallory said kissing the top of Amanda's head.

"I hate to bring this up, but you made me get tested and you told me that before entering any sexual relationship both partners should be tested."

Stopping her before Amanda had to ask her, Mallory responded so quickly, she almost interrupted. "I haven't been with anyone since Piper. Still, I told you both people should be tested and I meant it, so I went for my tests the same day that you went for yours. You see, I was hoping for a romantic cruise, but the damned results didn't come back in time. Undoubtedly, it was poor planning on my part. Really Amanda, there are safe things we can do."

"I know. I want my mind to be clear, and I don't want to have to worry about anything even remotely related to disease or illness when we finally make love for the first time. We can still be romantic, but no kissing and no touching each other below the waist."

"Oh God!" Mallory exhaled. "No kissing and no sex. This is going to be a long week."

Amanda rolled to her side and kissed Mallory's neck before working her way up to her ear, which she tongued, eliciting a moan from Mallory. Her hand slid under Mallory's pajama top stopping to tease her already erect nipple. "Who said no sex? I said no kissing and no touching below the waist."

"Oh God, you're killing me here. You're toying with a woman who hasn't had sex in over two years."

Amanda rolled Mallory's nipple between her thumb and forefinger then used her palm. The sensation of Mallory's flesh against her palm was exciting for both of them. She stopped long enough to replace her hand with her mouth. Sucking and tonguing the aroused nipple elicited a moan as she rolled on top of Mallory. She slid her thigh between Mallory's legs and shifted so that Mallory's thigh was between hers. Amanda looked at Mallory as she pressed her thigh more firmly between Mallory's legs. "So, what were you saying about no sex?" Amanda asked with a chuckle?"

"Now, I'm not complaining, mind you, but this isn't exactly what I had in mind for our first time."

"Oh, really? I can make you come like this, don't you think?" Amanda pulled back to analyze the look on Mallory's face. "Is that a look of disappointment I see on your face?"

Mallory laughed. "Isn't that one of those questions like, 'Do I look fat in this dress?' There's no good answer to it. There's no doubt that it wouldn't take much for you to make me come, obviously. Still, it's not the way I imagined our first time together would be."

Amanda sighed. "Well, I admit that it's less romantic than we might want, but I don't want you to forever accuse me of being a tease. Tell me how you would want it to be different."

"Well, for one thing I want us naked. Also, there needs to be kissing, lots of kissing...and exploring...finding all the places you like to be kissed and touched. I'd spend a substantial amount of time on your breasts."

"Hmm. You certainly have my attention. What else?" Amanda adjusted her position so she was farther away from Mallory. She looked Mallory directly in the eyes and deliberately ran her hand over her own breast stopping to flick her finger back and forth across her nipple repeatedly. "I know you want us to wait to touch each other, but there's nothing stopping us from touching ourselves, is there? Show me how you want me to make love to you," Amanda said as she opened her pajama top and kneaded her own breast, looking Mallory directly in the eyes."

Mallory blushed bright crimson. "I uh...uh..."

Amanda quickly stopped what she was doing and pulled her top closed. "Oh sweetheart, I'm sorry. I didn't mean to embarrass you. Are you shy about sex?"

"You have to remember I've only ever been intimate with one other woman all my life, and she only had me for a partner as well. Not that our sex life lacked variety. It's just that I'm sure that judging from what you've told me about Bernie's experiences you've probably had a lot more variations in your sex life than I've had. It's just that I've never done anything like this before. I'm not sure shy is the right word. I'm not normally modest. I will admit however that I'm feeling a little embarrassed. You seem so confident about all this and I feel like such a novice."

"Experience comes from doing, don't you think? I've already seen you naked before, so there's no need for modesty. Come on. Are you willing to try again? We can have fun." Amanda unbuttoned Mallory's top and kissed her way from one breast to another. She slid off Mallory's pajama bottoms and trailed her hands over Mallory's torso. "Now, show me what you like," Amanda requested playfully as she slid out of her pajamas and moved far enough away to have a view of Mallory's body. She noticed that Mallory had her eyes closed this time as she played with her breasts, stroking her own body.

"I love you Mallory," she whispered.

"I know you do. I love you more and I'm about to prove it." Mallory opened her eyes and looked directly into Amanda's. It was obvious that she was aroused already. "Okay, here we go. I like to be kissed on my neck and of course here," she said pointing to her lips. "There have to be soft, long kisses with tongue. Just a little tongue," she smiled. "No tonsil tickling."

"Got it. No arguments there. What would be next?"

Mallory slid her hand from her breast down her side and across her thigh and traced the route back up to her breast.

Amanda saw Mallory's eyes darken as Amanda slid her own hand between her thighs. Mallory swallowed hard, but continued to hold Amanda's gaze.

"I like to be touched and kissed anywhere in these areas." Warming to the experiment, Mallory gave a shy grin. "Feet are off limits, too ticklish."

As Mallory picked up her pace, Amanda matched her stroke for stroke. Mallory continued, breathing more heavily now. "There's no wrong way to touch me here. Oh God, I want you so much."

"Then, come with me, baby." Amanda encouraged.

They masturbated together until they each moaned in release. Only then did Mallory release Amanda's gaze. She closed her eyes, a smile on her face. It took a few moments for their breathing to return to normal. Not forgetting for a minute why they weren't touching each other intimately, Amanda rolled off the bed and went into the bathroom to wash. Mallory waited for her to exit the bathroom before taking her turn in the tiny room, putting on pajamas, and joining Amanda in bed.

"Umm," murmured Amanda, "that was fun." She pulled Mallory to her and softly stroked her back. "How was that for you?"

"Well, without a doubt, I'm sure it won't compare to the real experience of you touching me. It was hard at first, but once I got over my initial reservations and started to get excited, it was definitely sexy looking you in the eyes as we came together."

Amanda touched her lover's face. "Thank you for trusting me enough to risk doing something new with me."

Mallory grinned. "Now, when do I get my lesson on how to make love to you?"

"Later. For now, I just want to feel you next to me. Hold me and tell me again how much you love me."

They slept holding each other and awoke the next morning in time to meet Jack and Hannah for breakfast. After they finished eating and they bid their friends good-bye, Mallory said, "I'm going to stop by the Internet cafe. I need to check in to see if I got any messages from work and send out a couple of emails. I'll meet you at the rock climbing wall in about half an hour."

## Chapter 14

Amanda was still breathing hard. "Well, that was fun, but I think I'm really out of shape."

Mallory laughed. "Yeah, me too. I think maybe we shouldn't have tried to beat each other to the top of the rock wall the second time we climbed."

Amanda checked her watch. "We're short on time. Want to just grab a quick bite in the cafeteria instead of eating a full meal in the dining room? I don't want to be too full for our massage."

"Good idea. A salad would be great. We can eat in the dining room tonight, but I need a shower before we go anywhere in public."

They returned to their cabin. "You want to go first?" Mallory offered.

"Sure. Thanks."

Amanda stripped to her underwear before going to the dresser to select a new set for after her shower. Looking in the mirror, she watched Mallory's reaction as she reached behind her and unhooked her bra and slid it off then slipped her pants down and stepped out of them. A flash of desire in Mallory's greenish blue eyes rewarded her.

"Wow! You're so easy to torture." Amanda placed a quick kiss on Mallory's cheek. When Mallory reached for her, she quickly slipped into the bathroom giving a playful wave as she pulled the door shut. Sticking her head out she asked, "Think it'll be safe if I leave this door cracked?"

"You'll never know, till you try," Mallory replied tossing a wink in Amanda's direction.

Amanda adjusted the height of the showerhead and fiddled with the water temperature until she had it perfect. She reached for the soap and began to lather her torso when she became aware of Mallory standing behind her. "Need someone to wash your back?" Mallory asked in a husky voice as she stepped into the shower with Amanda.

"That's not my back," Amanda giggled as Mallory's hands slid up her body to caress her breasts.

"Amanda, I don't think we'll both fit in here," Mallory whispered, rolling Amanda's erect nipples in the palm of her hand.

As Amanda turned around hoping to make room for Mallory, she hit her funny bone on the soap dish. "Ouch!"

"This isn't quite what I had in mind," Mallory said with regret.

"I know, but it doesn't matter. You're still very cute and I love you to bits." She held Mallory's face in both of her hands and kissed her on the nose.

Mallory grabbed a towel and wrapped herself in it before she retreated to the cabin.

Amanda emerged from the bath wrapped in a robe. "It's all yours. Let me know when you're done and I'll mop up in there."

"No, I made the mess, I'll clean up."

Amanda went over to Mallory taking her hands to pull her tight. She snuggled into her neck. "You're very cute when you're disappointed, you know."

"It's just that I wanted everything to be perfect for us on this trip. I wanted so much for us to have time to enjoy a new aspect of our relationship."

"Well, this is certainly a new aspect, all right, frustration. Still, it doesn't matter. We're together and we have the rest of our lives to make love and be raunchy in the shower together." Amanda laughed. "However I do agree with you, next time a larger cabin with a tub will be a great idea."

Mallory groaned. "I do love you."

"Yes, I know you do. You show me every minute of the day."

"That's the problem. I want to show you every minute of the night, too."

Enjoying that even disappointment could be relieved through their mutual laughter they finished getting ready and headed for the cafeteria for a light lunch. The massage was relaxing. They strolled back to their room to have a quick nap. They awoke with less than an hour before their dinner seating.

Amanda stretched. "Think we should get dressed?"

"Yes, let's."

"We promised to meet Jack and Hannah for dinner and the show tonight. Hope it's good."

A preoccupied Mallory responded, "Yeah, me too. Can we stop at the Internet Cafe? I want to check mail."

"Are you expecting something important? You don't even check mail this often at home."

"Yes, I hope so. Let's go see."

Mallory became impatient when she had trouble logging onto the computer. Finally successful she typed in the address and after a slight delay she pulled up her list of emails. There it was—a response to the email she had sent earlier in the day. Amanda was on the other side of the room watching the people strolling down the promenade. Mallory clicked to open the message.

*Hello Mallory:*

*In response to your request, I contacted the lab. The report wasn't finished yet, but I was able to get your results from the lab early, via oral report. You owe me. Congratulations! You had no positives on your tests. Have fun.*

Mallory hit print and retrieved the copy from the printer. She logged off her email program and called Amanda over. "Do me a favor and check your email, please."

"Why? I'm not expecting anything important through email."

"I think you might be surprised. Please, just trust me and do it. Pleeeeease," she begged.

Amanda sighed, but complied. "You're so cute when you beg."

"I hope you'll think I'm even cuter after you read your email."

Mallory stood impatiently as Amanda logged in and pulled up her email. Leaning over Amanda's shoulder, Mallory said, "Here, click that one," She pointed to the email from the doctor.

Amanda glanced back over her shoulder at Mallory. "Did you get your results just now?"

"Yes and I'm okay, no positives."

"Mal, I'm so nervous. What if something is wrong?"

"Don't worry. I'm sure nothing is wrong, Even if by some remote possibility it is, I want you to know that it won't change a thing. We'll just deal with it together. I love you, no matter what."

Amanda exhaled a nervous breath and clicked. She quickly scanned the document. "Look! All tests results are negative. 'You're good to go,' she says."

It was a good thing they were alone in the room because Amanda reached over and kissed Mallory firmly on the mouth. "Do we really have to go to dinner and the show?"

"We did promise. What do you think?"

"As much as I want to say we don't have to, we've waited this long. Another couple of hours won't kill us. Let's not disappoint them."

"You're obviously a nicer person than I am," Mallory said adding a chuckle. "I agree with you, though, so let's go. The sooner we get there, the sooner I'll be able to ravish you in our cabin."

"I can't wait."

Dinner with Jack and Hannah was enjoyable, although Mallory and Amanda kept willing the waiter to serve more expeditiously. They managed to sit through the first half of the show. It started with the kids who had performed the previous evening, singing and dancing their hearts out again. Amanda and Mallory took small pleasure from pressing their legs against each other during the show. Mallory's free leg bounced up and down constantly, indicating her energy level. She kept glancing over at Amanda, eager to get her alone. Amanda's drumming fingers on the arm of her seat indicated she was equally anxious for the show to be over. They couldn't believe their good fortune as the lights came up for intermission, when Jack said that he hoped they wouldn't mind if they left before the second half of the show began. By way of explanation, Hannah told them that they had an early morning tour the next day and they wanted to get a good night's rest.

"Certainly, we understand. Trust me when I say that we are just as happy to turn in early as you are."

"That's probably the biggest understatement you'll ever hear," Amanda deadpanned. "We've had a busy day too. We're definitely eager to get into bed too," she said with a smile, never meaning anything more sincerely in her life.

They walked the older couple to the elevator and bid them good night when they exited on their level. Mallory pushed the button for their deck and they stood quietly next to the eight other people in the lift with them. They leaned close to each other, eagerly anticipating what would happen when they got to their cabin.

As they stepped off the elevator Amanda whispered, "Hurry up."

They quickly navigated the hallway, nearly speed walking their way to their cabin. They stopped in front of their door as Mallory searched her pockets for the door key. "Oh, I left mine on the desk, I think. Where's your key?"

Amanda moaned. "Oh no, I didn't bring it...I thought you had yours. I can't believe this. It's some sort of cruel joke. What do we do?"

"Let me see if I can find someone." Mallory sped off down the hallway in search of someone who could help. She finally found their cabin steward folding towels in the service area down the corridor from their room. It took only a few minutes for Mallory to return with the cabin steward in tow. He slipped his master key in the slot and the light on the lock turned green.

"There you go madam," he said, a broad grin lighting up his handsome young face.

"Believe me when I say I can't tell you how much I appreciate your help," Mallory said sincerely as she slipped a tip into the steward's hand.

As the steward stepped away, Mallory placed the, 'DO NOT DISTURB' tab into the slot in the door and turned to face Amanda who was waiting for her on the edge of the bed.

Their eyes met across the room and they smiled at each other shyly. Mallory approached slowly, coming to a stop a few feet away from Amanda. "It seems like forever that I've been looking forward to this minute when I can finally show you how much I care about you, how much I love you. Now that it's here, I have to admit that, especially after our shower fiasco, I'm nervous."

"I know exactly how you feel." Amanda stood and pulled Mallory to her. "I'm sure we'll be fine. It seems like I've been waiting to kiss you all my life." She closed her eyes and leaned in to bury her nose in the tender skin in the hollow of Mallory's neck, lingering there, taking pleasure from inhaling the now familiar scent of the woman she loved. Using her tongue, she circled Mallory's ear placing little kisses along her jaw line, and then did the same to the other ear and the other side of Mallory's face. She saved the treasure of Mallory's lips for last, almost as one would savor the last morsel of a favorite sweet treat. She nibbled her way around Mallory's lips tasting small bits before firmly taking her mouth with her own.

The kiss was like a puff of air added to a long smoldering fire. Their tongues met in a dance designed to stoke the flames. Nervousness forgotten, as their passion took over, it required barely seconds for them to strip their clothes off. Amanda allowed herself the pleasure of feasting on Mallory's body with her eyes for at least a heartbeat before Mallory reached for her. When their bodies pressed against each other, a mutual groan escaped their lips, which were soon again pressed together. Later, neither would remember which of them had instigated the move to the bed. Once there, they began their long awaited dance. They explored all the places they'd waited to touch for much longer than they'd wanted.

"You're so smooth." Mallory said as she traced her hand down Amanda's body.

"You taste so sweet," Amanda whispered as she sucked Mallory's nipple into her mouth and teased it with her tongue. Unable to wait any longer they entered each other and stroked until they had a quick but mutual orgasm. Mallory succumbed first to the exquisite pleasure and Amanda's moan in release quickly followed.

The lovers lay wrapped together savoring the final afterglow of their lovemaking. Mallory surfaced first and now that their urgency was somewhat sated, began a slow, gentle, and long awaited exploration. She stroked and kissed the soft skin the length of Amanda's body taking her own pleasure from the sounds her partner made when she discovered a particularly sensitive spot. Each location was committed to memory for future exploration. Amanda exhaled a long soft moan as Mallory's mouth first explored the slick folds at the apex of her thighs, before she plunged her tongue into her. Amanda gasped as Mallory's tongue slid up, swirling and teasing the sensitive areas already on fire with sensation. Mallory drew her into her mouth and used her tongue to apply the pressure Amanda needed to rocket to another orgasm.

"My God," Amanda sighed as she lay limply on the bed. "I think I'm paralyzed."

Mallory's infectious snicker was music to Amanda's ears. "I don't think paralyzed was exactly the effect I was going for. I was kind of hoping for mind blowing or phenomenal or maybe..."

Finally able to move, Amanda rolled over to lie on top of her lover, her weight melding their bodies together, fitting them to each other like perfectly matched pieces of a puzzle. Amanda's lips covered Mallory's, extinguishing the rest of the sentence. "That was all those words and whatever you were going to say next as well." Amanda pulled back, looking down at her lover. "Have I told you yet today that I love you?"

"I'm sure you have. I'm curious though. Am I rationed to only hearing it so many times a day?"

"No, Mal. Never rationed. From this minute on, you will hear it at least one more time every day than you need to hear it to be satisfied, but one less time than it takes for you to not need to hear it again. Now," after a series of gentle biting kisses on Mallory's neck, "anything special I can do to please you?" She slid to her side, leaving her leg still draped possessively across Mallory's thighs, while her hand idly explored the contours of Mallory's tight body.

Circling Amanda's back with her arm and pulling her close, she responded, "Nothing. Anything. I'm happy. I just need you to be close to me. Being with you like this is the realization of a dream well beyond my imagination. I never expected to fall in love or to find this kind of joy again. It scares me a little to care so much so soon."

"Don't be afraid. Let's just savor every minute we have together and treasure whatever time we have till forever. Forever is a long way away."

"Promise?"

"Absolutely. Now, relax and let me show you how much I love you."

A few minutes later, nearly breathless after a moan of pleasure escaped her, "Hmm, how am I supposed to relax when you're doing that?"

Amanda chuckled, but didn't stop.

## Chapter 15

Mallory was awake and simply appreciating the fact that she and Amanda were naked. Still asleep, Amanda had one leg flung over her own, in an unconscious gesture of possession, her hand resting comfortably on Mallory's forearm. During the night, between their lovemaking sessions, they had both shared that they wanted to be with each other forever. There existed a joy within her from having heard Amanda express her deepest hopes, dreams, and fears for their future together. After last night, each knew that they would be facing whatever life dished out to them, no longer alone. She loved that they talked about all the good things in their lives and were able to share their fears and concerns as well. She thought about Piper, too. *Was it wrong to be wrapped in her new lover's arms while thinking of her former partner?* Wrong or not, thinking about her was what she was doing. She still missed Piper every day. However as feelings for Amanda grew, the missing changed from pain and loneliness from her loss to more of a recollection of fond memories of their happy times together.

Piper would have liked Amanda. She would have enjoyed her devilishness, intelligence, quick wit, good humor, and ready smile. After careful rumination, she decided that she had no guilt associated with falling in love again. Piper would have wanted her to be happy. Lovemaking obviously involved familiar moves although, she thought with pleasure, that last bit Amanda did was new to her. Yes, familiar, but not quite the same...different enough for it to be a completely unique experience, similar enough to feel like coming home.

"Happy?" Mallory asked when Amanda's eyes fluttered open for the first time that morning. After making love, they'd cuddled and talked until the first rays of the sun were only a few hours away from appearing on the horizon. The ship had docked a few minutes earlier and sounds of workers on the pier, as they went about the business of tying up the ship and readying the gangplank for the passengers, drifted through the open sliding door of their cabin.

"Umm hmm," Amanda replied sleepily. "You?" A momentary frown flitted across her face as she glanced quickly at Mallory, assessing. She forced herself to come awake and pull Mallory to her. More awake now, she stroked up and down Mallory's back enjoying the feel of her firm body and smooth skin as her palm moved over her.

"Been awake long?"

"A little while."

"Been thinking?"

"Um, hmm...just a bit."

Amanda took a deep breath and exhaled slowly. "Is everything all right?"

"Everything is perfect," Mallory said with a smile.

"It's okay you know, to be thinking about her. When I first woke up, after thinking how nice it is to be with you, my first realization was what an odd feeling it is for me to have a lover my own size. Now, holding you, how it's unusual for me to be the one doing the holding. I like it that we take turns. It's different, but seems comfortable and natural with you. I do love you, you know," she said her own hazel eyes meeting Mallory's greenish ones. She noticed that Mallory's eyes had darker flecks of green in them and that the clear greenish blue of the center somehow seemed brighter this morning.

"At the risk of being redundant, I love you too. And to answer your unasked question, yes, I did think of Piper this morning. Don't worry...I'm okay. I think she'd have approved. Let's talk about us. We're lucky. Statistically speaking, what do you think the odds of us finding each other were?"

Amanda smiled. "Oh, I don't know, Doctor Barnes. You're the one with the advanced degree, so you tell me."

"Okay, I can see you either aren't awake enough or aren't in the mood for a serious discussion. Let's see what I can do about waking you up!"

Amanda was expecting a kiss, instead Mallory started to tickle her till she begged her to stop. "I'm sorry, I'm sorry," she gasped between bouts of uncontrollable shrieks.

"Okay, are you awake enough now to enjoy what I plan to do to you next?"

The question proved to be moot as they melded together in mutual passion.

Much later pushing Amanda's roaming hands away gently, Mallory said "Come on. One of us needs to be responsible. We need to get up or we'll miss our tour." Mallory pushed herself upright to sit on the edge of the bed. "I'll shower first, okay?"

"Mmm, good idea," mumbled Amanda.

"Don't go back to sleep or you'll pay the price again," Mallory teased as she reached for Amanda's ribs.

"No, no. I'll get up, I promise," Amanda replied sincerely as she restrained Mallory's hand from its target.

Mallory put a little extra wiggle into her walk as she sashayed into the bathroom. She could feel her lover's eyes following her as she retreated into the shower and was thankful for the many hours she spent riding her bike.

***

They grabbed a quick bite to eat before making their way down the gangplank to join the crowd that was headed for the bus they were directed to board by the tour guide. They saw Jack and Hannah getting on one of the other buses and waved. Their friends had opted to take two tours that day.

"I'm glad we only booked an afternoon tour today," Amanda whispered.

"Well, I admit preplanning when we booked, selecting later tours when they were available, with great hope that we'd need our rest in the morning. I think it was a great strategy."

"Yeah, right." Amanda raised an eyebrow doubting she was hearing the truth.

"It's true," Mallory swore as she crossed her heart with her index finger.

They boarded their bus, taking a seat not far from the guide. The tour of Saint John was excellent, with a tour guide who was extremely humorous and very informative. They received an historical overview of Canada's oldest incorporated city, Saint John. During their stop at the Carleton Martello Tower, Amanda took some great photos of the harbor from the old stone fort and of the famous reversing falls rapids at Fallsview Park. There, twice each day, the strong tides pushed the river water upstream. The bus drove past Fort Howe, which offered another fine view of the harbor. Their last stop was at the Old City Market where they bought some candy for themselves and a shirt to take back for Dana.

They returned to the ship and sat around the pool where a marimba band was entertaining the crowd. Afterwards Mallory and Amanda went back to their cabin for a quick shower before dinner. Their brief kiss when Mallory finished her shower had exploded into a quick but passionate session of lovemaking. Running late, they hurriedly dressed and tried to compose themselves before they met their dining companions. During dinner, they compared notes with Jack and Hannah who had taken the brewery and pub-crawl tour. Mallory and Amanda laughed when they said their tour was known for having the happiest tourists on their return to the ship and the fewest complaints. Begging off from attending the show that night, they opted instead to return to their room to enjoy some time alone to read, talk, and make love.

The next day the new couple toured Halifax. The kilt-wearing guide on the bus was a retired history teacher. The bus took them first to Peggy's Cove, touted as the world's most photographed fishing village. One of the passengers willingly used Mallory's digital camera to take their picture with the scenic lighthouse behind them. They were pleased that he managed to frame it so that it didn't appear that either of them had a lighthouse growing out of the top of her head.

On their way to Peggy's Cove, the bus drove them through the harbor area where they learned about the Halifax Explosion of 1917. The explosion occurred when a French munitions ship, the Mont Blanc, collided with the Imo, a Belgian relief ship. Because of the collision, fires began on the ships. The enormous explosion, in addition to killing and injuring thousands of people, left a large portion of the population homeless. To make matters even worse, the next day one of Halifax's worst blizzards arrived and didn't end for six days.

Mallory and Amanda glanced at each other, each with tears in her eyes. They were not the only ones crying and many others could be heard sniffing because of the guide's description of the terrible tragedy. On their return from Peggy's Cove, the tour made several other stops including a maple sugar farm and the gorgeous Public Gardens.

At the final stop, the tourists were set free on their own to explore the shops along the waterfront. Amanda bought a lobster roll for them to share as they strolled through the marketplace. Each bought a Halifax T-shirt as a souvenir of their memorable tour. After passing through customs, they climbed the several story high series of ramps to get back on the ship. A bagpiper was playing on the dock as they boarded. They slowly made their way to their room and sat out on their balcony to watch and listen.

As the ship pulled away, too tired to go to the dining room, they opted for room service. A couple of hours after dinner, they felt refreshed enough to venture out for a cup of tea and a couple of cookies at the cafe on the promenade.

It was an early night as they cuddled on the bed in their cabin and talked about the horrible story of the fire that their tour guide had related. Mallory said, "I thought the saddest part was when he told us that when the ships caught fire, many people gathered on the shore to watch. Then, when the explosion happened, many of them were drowned by the huge waves washing ashore."

Amanda agreed. "That and the fact that so many children were killed. Such a terrible tragedy."

***

The next morning they met Jack and Hannah for breakfast and each couple described what they had seen the day before. Already anchored off Bar Harbor for over an hour, the captain announced that tenders were now available to take anyone interested ashore. After she'd booked their cruise, Mallory had arranged for a visit with an old college friend, Ren and her partner Lindy, who ran an Inn situated on an island off the coast of Bar Harbor. Ren and her brother Jack owned The Inn, which was built by Ren's grandfather many years ago when the orphaned siblings came to live with their grandparents.

Waiting in line to board the tender, Mallory said, "I think you'll enjoy this couple. Although we speak on the phone all the time, I only got to see Lindy and Ren a couple of times a year when I lived in Philly. Maybe that'll change now that I'm living closer. Lindy is very warm and has a devilish personality. She's an author too, so you should have something in common with her. Along with, or in addition to, running the Inn, Ren is an artist. They met a couple of years ago when they collaborated on a book about fairy tales from different countries."

"I'm excited to meet them. So are we going to have lunch at a restaurant or their Inn?"

"At the Inn. They're closed for the season now, Ren said we'll have the place all to ourselves."

Amanda looked puzzled. "Ren is an unusual name. I don't think I've ever heard it before."

"Well, her given name is Lauren, but when she was little she could only say Ren, and the nickname stuck."

"Have she and Lindy been together a long time?"

"Only about a year and a half, I think. Brooke, Ren's first partner, died in a plane crash shortly after nine eleven. It was a crash of a private plane, not related to the terrorist attack. Ren had a hard time of it until she met Lindy. The two of them seem to be happily settled now."

"So, you've known Ren since college?"

"Yup!"

"It's wonderful that you have a long time friendship with her...it's like Dana and me."

They boarded the tender for the trip to the port. As they pulled in to the dock, Mallory waved. "There they are," she exclaimed excited to see her old friend and her partner.

Ren and Lindy waved back. They greeted Mallory and Amanda with hugs. With introductions and greetings completed Ren said, "Our boat is just down the way a bit. Do you still want to go to the island or do you want to wander through town?"

"Well, it's only nine-thirty now and we don't have to be back here until five. Let's head over to your place and come back here this afternoon to stroll through the town so Amanda can see it. It's chilly, so maybe it'll warm up by then."

"Great idea. We started a fire at home," Lindy said. "The ride over to the island will be a bit chilly, but it'll be toasty at home by the time we get there."

They boarded Ren's boat and within twenty minutes it was tied up at the dock on Sunset Island and they were climbing the stairs to the Inn. "What a beautiful setting," commented Amanda, admiring the sweeping views of the water and the rugged coastline. "The Inn is lovely."

"Thank you. Would you like a quick tour?"

"Don't forget to show her some of your artwork," Lindy admonished. Then as an aside to Mallory, she confided, "She's so modest, she'd never even mention that she's a gifted artist if I didn't bring it up." Lindy, with a twinkle in her eye, changed the subject. "So, Mallory, it appears you have someone new in your life. How long has this been going on?"

Mallory pointed to her watch. "It would be more appropriate to measure it on a watch than on a calendar." A broad grin beamed from her face. "Although our relationship is very new, I'm gone, hook line, and sinker. I can't imagine my life without her. It's happened so fast, I didn't have time to worry it to death...we met, got on well together, and it just worked." Mallory grinned, then launched into a description of how they'd met and gave a brief run down of their cruise so far. "We've made a commitment to share our future with each other, so I hope you and she will hit it off. She's a writer too."

"Really?"

Before Lindy could ask any more questions, Ren returned with Amanda. "Lindy, Ren said you'd show me your books."

Ren arched an eyebrow in mirth when Lindy looked in her direction. "Turnabout is fair play, dear."

Lindy stood and kissed her lover on the cheek. "Come with me, Amanda, for Bring and Brag, the adult version of Show and Tell!" She led her guest down the hallway to her office to show her their book on fairy tales.

\*\*\*

"These illustrations are gorgeous. Ren is very talented. All she could talk about though, is what a wonderful and interesting writer you are."

"I hope we're not boring you with our accomplishments."

"Not in the least. I'm always interested in meeting other authors and learning about the work they've done." She pointed to a book on the shelf. "This is on my list of books I want to read. Mallory's friend, Jo, loved it and told her she thought we'd enjoy reading it. She must be a new author, since I've never read anything by her before."

"Not really a new author," Lindy corrected with a mysterious smile, "but this genre is different for her. I think she has another book coming out, hopefully, as quickly as possible after I finish editing the last chapter."

"You! You wrote this book?"

"Guilty as charged." Lindy gestured at the manuscript on her computer table.

Lindy and Amanda spent the next twenty minutes talking about their work, concluding that they definitely wanted to stay in touch to share work, proofread, and problem solve for each other.

"I'm glad I had the opportunity to meet you, Amanda. It'll be fun sharing our writing experiences. I think we'd better get back to see what Ren and Mallory are up to...be advised, you never know what those two are cooking up."

They found their partners in the kitchen. Ren was making sandwiches and Mallory was putting the final touches on a salad. The two couples sat down and enjoyed the meal together, discussing a variety of topics. They lingered over coffee, tea, and the cake Lindy made for their dessert.

Time passed all too quickly and before they knew it, it was time for them to head back. In town the group strolled through several of the shops. The visitors bought a couple of T-shirts before stopping in one of the little restaurants to order drinks. The group lingered over the tea until it was time to catch one of the last tenders back to the ship.

"Wish you guys lived closer," Lindy said. "It's beautiful, but relatively quiet and lonely here during the winter. Maybe you could come back and stay with us for a real visit. It's just the two of us rattling around the Inn. We'd love to have you stay for longer."

Ren agreed. "That would be great."

"It's not all that far to drive," Mallory said. "Maybe you'll get down our way too."

Lindy said. "That's a possibility, too. We might go to the city before Christmas to do some shopping. Now that the Inn is closed, we're free to travel. We're so busy during the season, it's nice to have more free time now."

"We'll work something out," Mallory promised, "so we can get together again soon. This has been a great day."

Reluctantly, they all hugged good-bye.

"Don't stand here until we go, it's too cold. Go home to that cozy fire we left. We'll be in touch soon," Amanda promised.

They joined the tender line standing with the others waiting to return to the ship, after waving a final good-bye to Ren and Lindy.

"I like your friends, Mallory."

"I hope we can see them again soon."

"I'll work something out with Lindy for when they come to the city in December. " Amanda promised.

"That would be great."

\*\*\*

The ship was at sea the following day for the last day of their cruise, allowing for a lazy morning. In the afternoon, Mallory and Amanda went to see the ice show. On the walk back to their room, Amanda chattered about how she couldn't get over how those skaters can do all those spins, jumps, and turns on a moving ship. "It must take hours and hours of practice."

"I could practice forever, and still would be unable to do it," Mallory grinned.

Much later, with dinner concluded, they bid farewell to Jack and Hannah after exchanging phone numbers and promising to stay in touch.

"We're taking the longer cruise to this same general area next year," Jack told them. "It stops in several more ports and even goes as far as Quebec. You should come. We've enjoyed sharing our experiences with you girls."

Hannah added, "If you decide to come, we could maybe pick some of the tours to do together."

"That sounds like a great idea," Amanda replied enthusiastically. "We'd love to if our schedules will allow it.

Mallory added, "We'll keep in touch and book when we're sure of the dates and of what's happening for vacations next year. Don't forget, we're still working for a living, so no promises."

Back in their room, they began to sort their clothes, separating the clean from the dirty. They packed one suitcase with clean clothes and put their dirty clothes and their shoes in the other. Mallory set the bags in the hallway while Amanda finished packing the remaining items they needed for the next morning in their carry-on bags.

"Well, I guess that's it," Mallory grumbled.

"I'm sorry our trip is over, too." She circled her arms around Mallory's waist and pulled her close. "Thank you so much for bringing me. This was a great trip and a wonderful, romantic start to our relationship."

"It didn't start out that way. Remember the shower fiasco?"

"Yes and the no test results kinda put a crimp in things too. Thank goodness I have a honey with some clout in the hospital."

*We laugh so easily together,* Amanda thought. She enjoyed that their relationship was one where they could spring from serious to playful in an instant and could talk about any thought or feeling without worrying the other would disapprove. Decisions were generally easy, because they tended to want the same results, but when there were differences of opinion, they were able to compromise with each being rewarded by getting at least some of what she wanted.

"You know that Dana is going to think something is wrong. I haven't written anything more than a few brief notes to her for a couple of weeks."

"Nor has she written much to us," said Mallory.

"True. Well, on our end, we've been extremely busy getting ready for, then taking our cruise. Maybe her relationship with Nic is going hot and heavy and she's been too busy, just like we have."

Mallory moved the carry-on cases to the floor so they could sit opposite each other on the sofa and chair. "Want to go get a drink and continue this conversation?"

"Sure. We're basically finished here until tomorrow morning."

Settled at a table in one of the lounges they placed their drink order and chatted as they waited for their drinks to arrive. When they did, they raised their glasses, clinking them together in a toast.

"To the best little honey any gal could ask for," Mallory said with a wink and the tip of an imaginary cowboy hat.

They both laughed. "You know, for someone with a doctorate, I'd expect a more erudite toast."

"Okay, Miss Author. Why don't you try one if you think it's so damned easy?"

"Okay. Let me think. Uh, how about this, roses are red..."

Mallory groaned, "Are you serious?"

"Oh my. Now, after it's too late, I find out that you have an impatient side. Hear me out, I promise you'll like it."

Mallory grinned. "Well, if you promise."

Amanda smiled and in a sexy manner, complete with breathy voice, she started over. "Roses are red, violets are blue, come upstairs with me now, I want to make love to you."

Mallory squeezed Amanda's hand. "I'm sorry that I cast aspersions upon your poetic abilities. You're quite obviously a true and gifted poet. I concede that your poem is much better than mine."

"Come on, let's go. I want you right now."

Barely making it through the door to their cabin, they stripped quickly and fell on the bed locked in each other's arms. On their backs, side-by-side after their passionate encounter, with hands linked, they waited for their breathing to return to normal. Mallory rolled over and propped on her elbow, smiled down at her lover.

"I have no idea where that came from. Wasn't it fun though?"

"Yes and sexy."

Mallory agreed. "Yes, that too. Definitely sexy."

Amanda buried her nose in the soft skin of Mallory's neck as her lover's arms circled around her. "I don't want to go home. This has been like being in a vacuum or a protective bubble. I don't want to go back to face Bernie in California. I don't want to go back to reality."

"Do you want me to go with you...to California, I mean?"

Amanda considered the offer. "No, but thanks for being willing. You have nothing to worry about, you know."

"I believe you. I just wish you didn't have to face that turmoil on your own."

"On the plus side, soon I'll be able to look forward to coming home to you every day." She playfully touched her pointer finger to Mallory's nose.

\*\*\*

In the morning, they awoke before the alarm, packed up the last few items into their carry-on luggage, washed up and dressed. They ate breakfast and as they were leaving the cafeteria, Amanda noticed Jack and Hannah were just coming in to eat their morning meal. Hugs were shared all around.

Hannah whispered in Amanda's ear, "I still say you two would make a cute couple."

Amanda whispered back, "Done deed."

Hannah pulled back to look Amanda in the eyes. "Good job. I told Jack it would happen for you two this trip."

"What secrets are you two cooking up?" Jack asked.

"Come on, I'll tell you later. It'll make you happy." Hannah gave a quick wave good-bye and led Jack to an empty table for two that she spotted.

"Lovely people," Mallory observed. "Did you tell her?"

"Yes."

"Good. It seemed to make her happy."

Bags in hand, they made their way to one of the lounges to await the announcement for their color to be called for debarkation. As they got close to their color code, Mallory called the limo service to update their pick up time. Less than an hour later, they were in the limo heading for home.

Amanda used her cell phone to send a quick message to Dana saying she and Mallory were just returning from a cruise, explaining that she was set to fly to California in a couple of days. She promised to contact her by video when she got back from California.

Dana's return text said that their job was ending a little sooner than they expected and she would be home in about two weeks. "There's tons of news to share. I'm in love. I can't wait for you to meet Nic."

Amanda showed the text to Mallory. "Sounds serious, don't you think?"

"I certainly hope, for her sake, that he's as serious as she is."

Later that evening, once all their chores were completed, Mallory and Amanda slid into Mallory's bed together. "Mal, doesn't it feel strange to you for me to be sleeping here in your bed?"

"Strange? No, not strange, just different...but it's a good different. Does it feel strange to you?"

Amanda slid over next to Mallory and snuggled in. "There that's better. As long as I'm in your arms, it feels like home to me."

## Chapter 16

Mallory and Amanda woke up the next morning, made the bed together before moving into the kitchen for breakfast.

"Not much to eat here," Mallory commented. "We mostly cleaned out the kitchen before we left. I have to go in to work for a few hours and dig out my inbox. I'm sure you have some catching up to do, too. Would you rather I stop and pick up supplies on my way home or do you want me to bring home some Chinese or a pizza and then the two of us go to the store together after dinner?"

"Truthfully, the latter sounds good. With Dana coming home, I want to restock her food supply. Having to buy food for all of us, it'll be easier with two of us shopping. What time do you expect to be home?"

"I'm not sure. I'd guess four or five, but it depends on what I find when I get there. I'll give you a call a little before four and let you know. Is that okay?"

"Definitely. I'm sure I can keep myself busy." Drawing Mallory to her she admitted, "I will miss you though."

"Yes, me too, Amanda. I love you and I'm glad you're here. When all this is over with Bernie, I'd like to talk about where we go from here. We've already agreed we want a future together. I want us to discuss what that will be. Would that be okay with you...I mean are you ready for that discussion?"

Amanda smiled at her lover pulling her close again. She nodded. "I love you too. And yes, I'm ready now. Still, I think your suggestion of waiting until I get back from California is the best. There is no doubt that you can be certain that I'll be back. It doesn't really matter if we talk before or after, because my hopes and dreams of a life with you won't change."

Mallory gave Amanda a quick kiss. "Thanks for that. It's what I'd hoped to hear." Slowly Mallory pulled away. "Well, the sooner I get going, the sooner I'll get home to you."

Amanda walked Mallory to the car and leaned in the window to kiss her good-bye. "Okay, see you soon. Hurry home to me." She waved till Mallory drove out of sight.

Back in the house, Amanda checked the time—ten o'clock. *Too early to check in with work...it's only seven out there.* She read through her emails, sent a breezy note to Dana saying she and Mallory had taken a cruise and that they had a substantial amount of news, too. Still, she didn't say anything about her new relationship although she assumed that Dana might suspect it based on the fact they had taken the cruise together. She knew that Dana would be happy for the two of them, but might be worried that Amanda had gotten involved with Mallory too quickly after she'd left Bernie. It had not been her intention to keep her relationship with Mallory a secret. It was just that there had never seemed an opportune time to really talk to Dana about it. They'd both been so busy lately. Primarily, she wanted to speak privately with Dana, not wanting to have to address that concern in front of Mallory. She was confident that Dana wouldn't have an issue with their being involved just with the time frame. Amanda wanted to spare Mallory's feeling awkward if Dana questioned the timing of their involvement so soon after separating from Bernie.

Amanda sat at her computer and pulled up her book. Nope—not in the mood. She sighed. *How quickly I got spoiled spending days and nights with Mallory. Yes, let's not forget the nights and the afternoons and the mornings.* She smiled recalling their times together. *It didn't seem to matter time of* day, she wanted Mallory. Plain and simple—she couldn't get enough of her.

Okay, enough of that. Poor thing won't make it in the door tonight without me jumping her. Maybe a bike ride would help take the edge off of my energy. That'll work I'll take a ride, come back, check in with work, do whatever I need to do and then wait for Mal. Maybe I'll write some more of my book in my mind while I'm riding. Sometimes the best solutions to her writing roadblocks came when she wasn't really thinking specifically about her story.

No sense leaving a note since I'll be home well before Mal calls and way before she returns home. She strapped on the helmet and mounted up. Wonder if I can ride the whole trail this time? In the past, she always walked down the steep part. Today, she was feeling more confident of her skills. I'll see how I feel when I get there.

Amanda started up the slow climb to the clearing where she and Mallory always stopped. She dismounted and drank a long swallow of water from her bottle then replaced it into the holder strapped to the body of the bike. *No sign of the chipmunk today, humph.* After a brief rest, feeling refreshed, she mounted up and started for home.

The trail narrowed and started to get steeper. Just below her, there was the portion where not only did the trail drop more quickly, but the drop off to the right was more like a cliff than an embankment. *Maybe I'll get off and walk anyway in another quarter of a mile or so.* She pedaled forward cautiously. Suddenly, without warning, a buck came running from the left across her path. She hit the brakes. *Too hard!* That was her last thought as the bike skidded and she flew over the cliff, just before everything went black.

\*\*\*

Mallory called home a few minutes before four. She was puzzled when there was no answer on the home phone. *Maybe Amanda went back to Dana's house to do something there.* She rang Amanda's cell. No answer there either. *Maybe she caught up with Dana online.* She smiled wondering how Dana would react to the news of their relationship. *Surprise for sure, happiness, I hope.* She also hoped that Dana wouldn't tell Amanda she was rushing into something. Amanda had mentioned this concern several times to Mallory.

At first, Mallory was concerned about the same thing. Despite the fact that she and Amanda had only known each other a few short months, they'd spent the majority of every evening together and every one of her days off in each other's company since Dana's departure. They just seemed to fit together with such an effortless ease. When Amanda assured her that her relationship with Bernie was over, she believed her. Amanda didn't seem to be wavering in that position at all and certainly behaved like someone in love. No matter what, it was too late for her now. She was head over heels, madly and deeply in love with Amanda. Moreover, she was ecstatic about it.

At four-thirty, Mallory ordered the pizza and called home again to tell Amanda she was on the way. She was puzzled when Amanda didn't answer. *Maybe she's taken a ride at the end of the day and jumped in the shower or hot tub.* Still slightly uneasy, she drove to pick up the pizza and hurried home.

Calling Amanda's name as Mallory entered the house produced no response. She placed the box on the counter and made a search. Worried now, Mallory went out the back door, checked the hot tub, then cut across the yard to Dana's house. The same routine at Dana's place yielded similar results. A check of the garage revealed that the bike was missing. With some degree of relief she thought, *well at least I know where she is.*

She went back inside the house to look for a note, but found none. *Well, I can't blame her, she didn't know exactly when I'd be home, although I did tell her I'd call.* A glance at her watch told her that she was home about a half hour earlier than she'd predicted, so she anticipated that Amanda would be home soon.

Pacing in front of the window, peering out with each pass, she waited impatiently watching the driveway for Amanda to appear, checking at each little sound she heard. By six o'clock, it was nearly dark. It was already too dark to see the trail clearly and in another a half-hour or less it would be pitch black. Mallory was becoming distraught, her concern from earlier now well into fear. She didn't know if she should call 911 or if she should call a different agency. She recalled hearing that the police wouldn't do anything about missing persons for at least twenty-four hours. She decided she'd ask her police officer friend. She located and selected Jo's number on her cell phone and was happy when Jo picked up almost immediately.

"Joanna Martin."

"Jo, it's Mallory Barnes. I have a problem and need your advice."

She responded immediately, "How can I help?"

Mallory quickly explained her dilemma ending with, "She should have been home by now. I'm sorry I'm such a wreck, Jo, but...." Mallory paused. "I'm not sure who I should call. I'm a nurse, for God's sake. Don't you think that I should know what to do?"

"Don't worry about that. It's always easier to know the proper procedure when it's someone else's emergency. I'll call 911 when we hang up. They'll probably contact Fire and Rescue Services. That's who we'll need if she's hurt, to locate and haul her out of there."

"I'll gather some blankets and things we might be able to use from here, too."

"I'm off duty but I'll stop off and borrow some radios. Also, I've got a couple of friends here playing cards who I'm sure will help with a search. Are you sure she's on a ride and hasn't gone somewhere else?"

"Well, the car is still here and the bike is gone...seems logical to me. There's nothing disturbed in the house, so I don't suspect anyone took her." A brief thought of Bernie flashed through her mind, but was immediately discounted since she and Amanda seemed to have come to a peaceful resolution to their relationship. "I'm concerned because I don't know what time she left. Last time I saw her was around nine-thirty this morning. Jo, she's very important to me."

"Okay, sport, I understand what you're saying. Don't worry until we have something concrete. When we hang up, I'll call 911 and I'll get there as quickly as I can. Hang tight, we'll find her."

"Thanks, Jo. I really appreciate it."

Although it seemed like forever, it was probably closer to twenty minutes after they hung up when Jo and three of her friends showed up. Jean and Pam worked as police dispatchers and Meg was a physician's assistant for a group of doctors with a large practice in eye care. All the women were into hiking and would help them cover more ground in their search. They could see the rescue vehicle approaching and when it stopped, Jo made introductions. She pointed to the tallest woman in the group.

"This is Meg, a good friend of mine who volunteers for Emergency Services.

"Yes, I've seen her in the ER." The rescue team nodded hello.

"Those last two are Jean and Pam, friends of mine who were at my house playing cards and volunteered to help. The rescue team is Chuck, Pete, and Toni. The four legged, furry one there is Fella."

Fella wagged his tail.

With introductions quickly out of the way, Mallory explained the situation. "Amanda likes the lower trail. Although we've ridden several others, it's the one she's most familiar with and the one she likes the best. We often walk and bike it."

Chuck took charge immediately after Mallory finished bringing everyone up to date. "Mallory, can you get an article of clothing or something that might have her scent on it?"

Mallory nodded and sped to their bedroom to hunt for something. She quickly returned with a pair of socks that Amanda had taken off the night before. She handed them to Toni.

"Perfect," Toni responded as she took the socks.

Chuck continued with his directions. "Mallory, give your radio to Meg." They agreed which channel they would use to contact each other, and Chuck divided them into teams. "Mallory, you go with Toni. Chances are that Fella will be the one to find her first. As a nurse, you'd be the best one to be there. I'll go with you. Grab a couple of blankets and give one to Meg. Bring the other with you. Grab one of the first aid kits, Jo. I have one for our team. Jo, Pete...you and your group can start up from the south end of the trail. Our team will begin where it starts north of here. We'll work from both ends toward the middle. Whoever finds her first can radio the other team."

He raised his radio and did a radio check. Assured that they were all able to communicate, he turned to delineating safety instructions. He gave Jo a hat with a flashlight on the brim similar to those miners wore. He gave one to Mallory also. He gave the other women handheld flashlights.

"Sorry, no more hats, but you can use these to search the sides of the trail better than you can with the head lamps. Now remember, stay together with your group. We don't want to lose anyone."

All arrangements complete, the two teams headed out. Fella found Amanda's scent before they were out of the driveway. By the time they left, it was completely dark and the temperature had dropped to the point that even though they'd be hiking, everyone needed a jacket. Mallory soon learned that traveling in darkness was much more difficult than it was during the daylight hours.

Mallory's group hiked steadily and quickly, following Fella's lead. Chuck, Mallory, Fella, and Toni were already beyond the clearing and had been moving quickly down the trail when the radio beeped. Pete, his tone excited, relayed the news. "We've got her. She's not that far from home, just north of the steep drop in the trail. We found her bike on the path, but she's gone over the side. We'll need help getting her out of there. Rope too. I think I have enough with me to reach her, but not to get her up without help."

"Okay, if we cut across on the east-west trail, I don't think we're too far from you," Chuck radioed back. "We'll be there as soon as we can."

Mallory was grateful they'd found Amanda, but worried that she didn't know her condition. It took them another twenty minutes of fast hiking to reach the other team's location. When the two teams came together, Jo explained that Meg was with Amanda. Pete descended the hill on a rope harness as Chuck and Toni played out line for him. Next, Mallory navigated the hillside down to Amanda's position. Her heart pounded, not so much from exertion, as for fear of what she would find at the bottom of the hill. She was encouraged when she found Amanda conscious and talking.

"I think I broke both arms and did something to my leg. Everything seems to work, thanks to my helmet, I guess. I mean, I don't think I hurt my neck or back. Can I have some water, please? And I'm so cold."

While Pete unloaded supplies and got the blanket, Mallory opened her own water bottle. "Just a sip honey, until we check you out."

Once Amanda had taken a few sips of water, Mallory removed Meg's coat she'd used to warm Amanda when she got there and began to assess Amanda's condition, finally agreeing with Amanda's own evaluation.

"I think you're right—both arms are broken and your leg is swollen. It may be just bruised or it could be a possible fracture."

Pete covered Amanda after Mallory stabilized Amanda's arms with two blow-up splints she found in the first aid kit and immobilized the injured leg as best she could with the remaining supplies. She wrapped Amanda in a blanket and carefully removed her helmet. She wrapped the leg in a couple of layers of ace bandages.

"Pete, I'm not sure if the leg is broken, but it's swollen, so we need to be careful with it when we get her on the stretcher."

With their initial assessment accomplished, everyone waited impatiently for the stretcher to be lowered to them.

Mallory held Amanda's hand, hoping it gave her lover some degree of comfort. Although the team worked as quickly as they possibly could, hauling Amanda up the slope once she was secured to the stretcher was an arduous task. Pete, Meg, and Mallory worked from below as the others pulled from above. It was tedious, but they finally got her up to the trail. They slowly carried her down the narrow path on the stretcher, equally difficult in the dark with only flashlights and helmet lights to show the way.

It was after midnight by the time Amanda was admitted to the emergency room at the hospital. Amanda's right arm required surgery to repair it and she was placed in a cast from her armpit to her knuckles. Her left arm only required a cast from below the elbow to her palm, leaving her thumb and fingers free. She had an air cast on her ankle for the sprain.

Mallory was sitting at Amanda's bedside when she opened her eyes. "You're going to be fine, honey," she told her when Amanda was alert enough to understand. "Still, you've done some damage," she said bending over the rail of the bed to kiss her softly on the lips and gently touch her hand.

Amanda focused on her lover and smiled. "Hi sweetie. I'm sorry. Mal, it really wasn't my fault. It was that damned deer."

Thinking that Amanda was delusional, Mal asked, "What deer?"

Amanda told her story about her encounter with the big buck. "Bambi's daddy was no light weight," she quipped.

"Well, no matter what, you'll be here a couple of days then probably in rehab for a little while, until I can arrange for help at home. You have two broken arms and a severely sprained ankle. So you'll need someone with you all day."

"Bernie—I have to call her and tell her I'm not coming." Amanda hated to drag that out, but there were obviously no other options.

The call to Bernie went much easier than anticipated and Bernie accepted the change in plans surprisingly gracefully. "I understand, Amanda. Do you need me to come there and help you?"

"No, I have a friend here...my neighbor who works at the hospital. She's arranging for me to go to rehab. After that, I hope to be able to go back home."

"Okay, we're going to need to get this stuff out of here so the realtor can show the house, so I'll start to pack it up. Anything I have doubts about I'll put aside and put into storage. When you get here, we can go through the boxes of stuff I'm unsure about. Anything you feel you need specifically, just let me know. Otherwise I'll just use my best judgment."

"Mostly, I think all I'll need from there are my clothes. I already packed up the office, as I'm sure you've seen. Other than that, I don't think there's anything else there I'll want to ship here."

"I'm very sorry you're hurt, Amanda. Call if you need me."

"Thanks Bernie. It was thoughtful of you to offer to come help. I do appreciate that."

"Don't forget that I still love you, sweetie. If you ever change your mind..."

"No, Bernie, that won't happen. I do still care for you, probably always will, but I'm no longer in love with you. Admit it. Neither of us is happy being together any more."

"Well, I won't admit that. I was happy. I'm sorry you weren't. We've been over this all before and it appears nothing has changed from your perspective. Call me when you're feeling well enough to fly out."

"I'll call you in a week or so and let you know when I'll be able to come and what I want to do with my stuff. There won't be that much, other than my clothes. I trust you to be fair."

"Okay, I'll be out of town off and on, and will work on packing up when I'm home, so there's no hurry. I'm hoping to get the house on the market right after Christmas. The realtor tells me nobody will be buying during the holidays anyway, so there's no rush. I'll talk to you soon. Take care and feel better."

"Thanks. I doubt I'll be able to travel until a week or two before Christmas. Then, there's difficulty traveling at the time of year because of the holiday. I'll do the best I can. Sorry to stick you with all the packing."

"It's okay. As I recall, you did most of the work when we moved in here. Fair is fair, after all."

"I'm sorry Bernie...about everything."

"I know...me too. Good-bye Amanda."

"Bye."

## Chapter 17

Mallory spent the night, or what was left of it, in the hospital with Amanda, returning home after Amanda was settled. She fell into bed completely exhausted. After a few hours of deep sleep, she showered, dressed, and wrote a quick email to Dana. The email correspondence provided a short but detailed explanation of Amanda's accident and the injuries she suffered in her fall from her bike. She was quick to reassure Dana that Amanda, given time and medical attention, would fully recover despite the fact that she had several difficult weeks ahead of her. In her note, Mallory added that as soon as Amanda was released she'd be staying at her house, because she knew the injured woman would be most comfortable there. Before that could happen, Mallory needed to arrange for her to have someone to help her with Amanda's care.

Returning to the hospital to report for work by noon, Mallory stopped to check in at her office before going to see Amanda. She was alert but uncomfortable.

"This is going to be a long six weeks," Amanda complained. "I can't even scratch if it itches, nor can I do any of the other necessary things related to my own hygiene."

Amanda's right arm was in a cast, which didn't allow her to bend at the elbow. The left arm was broken, closer to her wrist, so at least she could bend her arm. Eventually, as soon as the swelling went down, she would have better use of it than she had right now. For the time being, she wasn't moving it too much, because it ached if she did.

"This is so humiliating," Amanda whined.

"It's only temporary, honey. Are you in pain?"

"No."

"You'll improve, given time. Be patient."

"Yeah, I know. It just feels good to complain. I'm sorry."

"Complain away. I can take it. I'm a nurse." Mallory winked.

"Humph! By being so damned agreeable, now you've taken all the fun out of it." Amanda stuck out her bottom lip in the best impression of a pout she could muster.

For a moment, Mallory thought Amanda was serious. However, Amanda's wink brought a relieved expression to Mallory's face. "You had me going there for a minute."

"Good. I've got nothing else to do but lie here and rest. Poking a little fun at those around me is all the entertainment I get."

Mallory wiggled her eyebrows and with an evil chuckle, she responded, "You'll have plenty to do once they transfer your butt to rehab."

"I'm looking forward to it...the faster I get there, the faster I can get home."

"Impatience is not your most endearing quality, I see."

When Amanda stuck her tongue out at Mallory, she leaned over and whispered something into Amanda's ear that made both of them laugh.

"Ha! You're bad and don't I like it." Amanda struggled to scratch her nose.

"Okay, I've got to go to work. I'll be back to visit when I get a break. See you soon."

Mallory gave Amanda a quick kiss before going to talk to the nurses at the main desk. She had already provided the hospital with Amanda's medical power of attorney, so the medical staff were free to discuss Amanda's condition with her. Once she was assured that her lover was stable and plans were underway to make the transfer to the other department, she returned to her office.

She called to schedule an appointment to see her supervisor before sitting down at the computer to type up a request for a modified schedule. Finishing that chore, she checked her email to see if Dana had responded. She had and with good news. She'd be home in a week. Luckily, Nic was arriving a few days before her, by the end of the week. She added that between them, they would arrange for at least one of them to be available to help full time for at least two weeks. She told Mallory that Nic had volunteered to help as well. So, between Dana and Nic during the daytime and herself in the evenings, she wouldn't have to worry for three weeks. That information really took the pressure off Mallory and gave her time to plan to provide the remaining coverage for Amanda's care. *Perfect timing,* she thought.

\*\*\*

Amanda worked hard in rehab and was now able to transfer from the bed to a chair and achieved the other goals that were set for her. She was ready to be released. The rehab department didn't feel it was necessary for Amanda to have a hospital bed. Instead they suggested a recliner with a power seat to help her stand more easily, since she was unable to use her arms effectively to help when transitioning into a standing position. Mallory purchased the chair the rehab counselor recommended and planned for the delivery to her home on Friday. Amanda was going to be discharged on Thursday and Nic was due to arrive on Friday. All arrangements now in place, Mallory thought that she was more anxious for her lover to come home than Amanda herself was.

"What's wrong, honey? You don't seem very excited about coming home."

Amanda thought for a moment. "I can't wait to be home with you. It's just that I hate feeling so useless and I'm already sick to death of watching television. What am I going to do for another five plus weeks? I'll be a burden to you. It's not the way I wanted our relationship to begin."

"You'll feel better when we get you settled. I'll get your laptop set up for you. Didn't you say you could voice control it? Once you can get back to work, you'll feel better. You may even finish your novel. Besides, I miss sleeping with you."

"We can't sleep together. If I have a nightmare, I might club you to death with my cast."

"I think I'll just have to risk it. I'm sure we can work something out."

\*\*\*

Thursday, discharge day, finally arrived. They settled her in the living room and with Amanda's guidance, Mallory set up her computer for her while they awaited delivery of her recliner. Mallory was taking a couple of days off from work to help Amanda until Nic could get there. Via email communication, Nic expressed a desire and willingness to be useful.

"It'll only be bad for a couple of weeks," Mallory promised. "As you begin to heal, you'll get more mobile," she told her, hoping to reassure Amanda that her entire six or more weeks of recovery would be less difficult as the time passed.

"What am I going to do about the bathroom while Nic is taking care of me? I don't care how super a guy he is or how much Dana loves him," she complained. "He's just not going to take me into the bathroom or worse still, come collect me and help me off the throne when I'm done in there. I'm sorry, I hate to whine, but really, Mal. It's beyond what I can tolerate."

Mallory worked hard to control her smile, knowing Amanda was feeling better if modesty was her primary concern. Up until this point, Amanda had tolerated her injury reasonably well, except for the bathroom issue. It took a few days, but she'd finally adjusted to the nurses helping her while she was in the hospital although she complained bitterly about having to use a bedpan. Now that the swelling in her less injured arm and fingers had subsided she was able to use the better of her two injured hands more effectively. She insisted on taking care of business herself once she was at home and able to use the toilet. However she still needed Mallory's assistance to help her stand, pull down her pants, then pull up her clothing once she was done using the toilet.

"We'll work something out, Amanda. Maybe I can come home for lunch to help. It'll only be a few days with Nic. Before you know it Dana will be home. Then she can help you. We just have to get through the first three or four days till Dana gets here"

This statement elicited another groan from Amanda. "Just hire a nurse to help me when you can't. Please," Amanda begged.

"Okay, if that's what you want, but..." It was at that moment, before Mallory could finish her thought that the doorbell rang. "That must be the chair."

Mallory opened the door and found a tall, slender, dark haired woman standing there. She was dressed in black slacks and a white shirt, the collar open a few buttons, enough to tease the serious observer with a glimpse of cleavage. *Gee, delivery people sure seem to be better dressed than I recall them to be and a hell of a lot more attractive than I remember.* "Hello. You can put it right over there," she said gesturing to the empty spot she had created in the living room for the new chair.

"Excuse me?"

"The chair. Just put it over there, please."

"I think there's a misunderstanding here. I'm Nicolina Bianchi, but my friends just call me Nic. Dana told me to come here and you'd help me get settled in her house."

Mallory's jaw literally dropped open. "Nicolina?" She said flatly. Then in an incredulous note, "You're Dana's Nic?"

"Yes, is there a problem?"

Mallory's laughter took Nic off guard. Although Nic's expression clearly conveyed her opinion that Mallory had lost her mind, Mallory chose not to explain. Instead, she opened the door to its widest angle. "Look Amanda, Nic is here."

Amanda's face initially displayed absolutely no expression, but that was soon replaced by genuine puzzlement, bewilderment, followed by a slow dawning of comprehension. "Oh my God! I can't believe it. You're a woman."

Mallory thought Nic was considering turning around and leaving what was obviously a group home for the seriously challenged. "Of course I'm a woman. What else would I be?" Then it dawned on her. "Oh, I get it, Nic, from my name. Oh no, you thought I was a man." In a second, she joined Mallory in laughter, followed quickly by Amanda.

At that precise moment, the chair delivery team showed up to find the three women still laughing hysterically.

"What's so amusing?"

"It's a long story. Basically, we thought she came to deliver the chair."

"Hmph, I don't get it," he replied. "Whatever. Where do you want this thing?" All three women pointed to the empty spot in the room as they dissolved again into laughter.

"Here, sign this," he said before he left. "You're a group of nuts," he said with a smile. "Still, at least you're happy. Enjoy the chair. See ya."

With the door closed on the still puzzled delivery man and Amanda comfortably settled in the new recliner, all attention turned to Nic.

"So you thought it was a man that Dana was involved with?"

"Yes, I don't think she ever said 'he' or 'she,' only Nic this and Nic that when she was describing you and the activities the two of you were sharing. Considering her past dating history, we just assumed you were a man."

"I can't wait to tell Dana this story." Nic grinned. "It really is humorous when you think about it."

"I can't wait to hear how you two got together. In all the years I've known Dana, I never would have expected she could be interested in a woman," Amanda said.

"Well, I think it was a bit of a revelation to her as well. When our friendship developed quickly and we found that we had strong feelings for each other, I guess she just decided she'd waited long enough for happiness and that it didn't matter what form it came in. I don't really want to speak for her. I'm sure she'll want to talk to you about her feelings and what happened from her perspective. From my viewpoint, I simply can't imagine my life without her and she says she feels the same. So, we're moving forward. She tells me that you two are her closest friends, so I'm hopeful that we'll be good friends as well."

Amanda and Mallory replied in unison. "We hope so, too."

Mallory took Nic over to Dana's house and got her settled. "I'm sure you'll want to get cleaned up and maybe have a bit of a rest. Dinner is at six at our house. We hope you'll join us."

"Thanks that would be great. Promise, though...no peals of laughter when you open the door next time. It could seriously damage my confidence."

"That's a promise you can count on. See you later." Mallory was still chuckling when she returned to her house and to Amanda, who started talking the minute Mallory opened the door. "

"Can you believe it? A woman. Nic is a woman. All this time I'm figuring some guy is going to be decorating Dana's arm when she shows up and it's a woman...a fabulous woman, I might add." With her best approximation of a lecherous look, Amanda wiggled her eyebrows and pretended she had a cigar. No easy feat considering the cast.

"Yes, I agree, she is fabulous, but what's more important, she's a terrific woman. I really like her. You can see why Dana fell for her."

Amanda's face switched from lecherous to fake concern. "Do I need to be jealous?"

Mallory approached Amanda and gingerly embraced her. "You need not have one moment's doubt, my little plaster laden princess." To soothe, she crooned, "I love no one but you," before planting a kiss on Amanda's forehead. Mallory was rewarded with a giggle.

"Yeah, you think you're funny, but you're not." Amanda laughed, her good humor restored again.

The rest of the day seemed to pass without further incident. Nic showed up at five with an offer to help with dinner prep. She and Mallory had the meal ready in record time. Together they transferred Amanda to the wheelchair and moved her into the dining room to eat.

"A change of scenery will do you good," Mallory ordered when Amanda protested. "You can't grow roots in that chair."

Dinner conversation was light and lively. Nic told them a bit about her background and a few more details of how she and Dana had fallen in love.

"Well, it's rumored that Rome is certainly the place to do it." Amanda loved Rome. "May I ask you a sort of personal question?"

"You may ask me anything you'd like to know." Nic followed her response with a sincere and welcoming smile.

"Did Dana seem to find it difficult when she realized she was attracted to you? I mean, as far as I've ever known, she's always been straight."

"It was a concern for both of us in the beginning. Well no, let me restate that. Initially, I think neither of us recognized what was happening. We were just hanging out with a group of people working on the project together. Then, we just seemed drawn to each other somehow and our friendship seemed deeper than those we developed with the others on the team. At the end of each dinner when everyone separated to go home, she and I would find ourselves lingering over a final espresso or strolling along the street, looking for any excuse not to let the other go back to the hotel. At least that's how I felt."

Nic pulled on her left earlobe, a trait Amanda and Mallory would soon recognize as something she did when she was thinking about what she wanted to say.

"Soon, it seemed we preferred to just spend time alone together instead of, or sometimes in addition to, the time we spent with the group. We spent every moment we could together. When we recognized that there was more than friendship...that we were attracted to each other as more than just friends, we talked about it. I was concerned on more than one level that we shouldn't get involved and shared that with Dana. I promised her that despite how much I was attracted to her, I wouldn't make the first move. If she wanted me, she would have to be the one to take our friendship to the next level. I also shared that I was afraid that if we did get involved, it would be what she called 'a walk on the wild side' for her. You know a fling, something temporary."

Nic stopped the story. Amanda and Mallory waited expectantly. "What?" Nic blushed. "You don't expect details, do you?"

"No, I'll get those from Dana," Amanda assured her. "That can't be the end of the story."

"Okay, let's just say we finally realized that the attraction we felt, and the feelings we were developing for each other, were something we both wanted to pursue further, and I think needed at this point in our lives. We each admitted to having many acquaintances and few friends and agreed that we were tired of that...tired of traveling so much and each of us wanted more out of life. We both want roots and someone that we're in love with to come home to every day."

"I can't believe it. Dana made the first move?" That bit of information surprised Amanda.

"Yes," Nic grinned. "My story is that she chased me, so to speak, until I let her catch me."

They all laughed.

"And the rest is history," Mallory smiled.

"So you'll live here?" Amanda asked.

"We still have some details to work out. This is an extremely new situation for both of us. Because we each travel so much, some adjustments to our lifestyles will need to be made if we hope to live together as we want. We have a couple of weeks now to begin to resolve all the issues associated with how we're going to accomplish being a couple. We don't know if it's possible to arrange to travel together or if one or both of us will have to get a different type of job or go to work for a different company. We do hope to settle here at Dana's eventually. Logistically, how that works out remains to be determined, but those are our plans right now."

"If you can't stay at your current job, what would you do?" Mallory asked.

Nic explained her options, her background, and training.

Reassured that Nic had a variety of choices available to her, Amanda grinned. "Okay, Nic, you're off the hook. We're convinced you and Dana have the bases covered. We hope the two of you will be very happy."

"Thank you. From what I've seen here, I assume that you two have become a couple as well. I don't think Dana knows that. Does she?"

They both shook their heads. "No, we decided we wanted to tell her together either through video conference or in person. When we found out she was coming home we decided to do it in person. It's no big deal…really. We just wanted to see her reaction. She'll be surprised that I got involved so soon." Briefly, Amanda summarized her situation with Bernie. "So, I was booked to go to California and did this instead." She gestured as best she could, considering she had two casts.

The three talked about inconsequential topics, getting to know each other better. Amanda and Mallory soon realized how Dana could have so easily fallen in love with Nic. She was polished, witty, and had a seemingly unending number of entertaining stories about her travels. She was a good listener as well, often interjecting astute observations or humorous comments as Mallory and Amanda shared their background stories with her. The hour grew late.

Nic checked her watch and smiled at her new friends. "Thank you for a wonderful evening. I think its time for me to go back to Dana's house. I've enjoyed spending time with you."

"Including the grilling we gave you?"

"Yes, even including the grilling. I'm glad to see that Dana has friends who care enough about her to be wary of someone new in her life. You two are obviously good, caring friends and Dana is lucky to have you."

"Well, we're glad that she's got someone in her life. It's no fun being alone in this world." Mallory smiled as she squeezed Nic's shoulder.

"I'll stop over tomorrow morning, before you have to leave, for any last minute instructions. Amanda, don't worry...we'll survive the entire experience, including any residual embarrassment." Nic winked at Amanda as she closed the door.

"Cad," grumbled Amanda, although she was secretly happy that Nic was so kind and willing to help her.

## Chapter 18

The next morning, Nic presented herself at the door about fifteen minutes before Mallory had to leave for work. She and Mallory reviewed the transfer procedure they'd practiced the previous evening.

"I'm sure we'll be fine. At the risk of sounding excessively macho, she's such a little bit of a thing." Nic's grin was followed by a chuckle. "If all else fails, I'll just pick her up and carry her where she needs to go."

Mallory left for work. She was relieved that she wouldn't have to take off work again so soon after being away on the cruise for a week. Nic and Dana, being able to help would certainly take a considerable amount of pressure off her. By the time they had to return to work, Amanda's ankle should be much improved, as it was already showing evidence of healing. Once in her office, Mallory put her head down and dug into the pile of work waiting for her on her desk.

\*\*\*

"Hello. Is anyone here?" Amanda called when she awoke.

"I'm here," Nic said, as she appeared at the door to the bedroom. "Good morning, Sleeping Beauty. It's nearly eleven. Did you sleep well?"

Amanda smiled. "Yes, thank you, but I'm afraid we're going to have to face my greatest challenge first thing before we've even gotten a chance to break the ice this morning. I have to pee like a race horse."

"Humph! I've never quite understood that expression. Never mind, let's take care of your issue before we talk about its origins and meanings."

Not waiting for an invitation, Nic flipped the covers back and before Amanda knew what was happening, she leaned down, lifted Amanda into her arms and carried her quickly to the bathroom. She gently stood her on her feet.

"Grab onto the counter there to steady yourself." When Amanda complied Nic said, "Okay, normally I'd have a gentler touch and a great deal more finesse, but this is not a normal situation."

Before Amanda could respond, Nic bent over and stripped Amanda's pajama bottoms to her ankles in one smooth move. Nic popped back to her full height before Amanda even realized she was standing there naked from the waist down. She quickly sat down.

Nic turned away and headed towards the door. "Call me when you're finished and I'll come collect you." She pulled the door to, but not closed, and Amanda could hear her footsteps heading down the hallway to the living room.

Amanda appreciated Nic's consideration and no-nonsense manner. She wasn't nearly as embarrassed as she thought she'd be and was appreciative of Nic's kindness at allowing her some privacy. It was not easy with the cast and the limited finger dexterity she had, but she managed to take care of drying herself. *At least*, she thought, *I don't have to suffer that indignity.*

Nic knocked softly. "Ready to get out of there?"

"Yes, thanks."

Nic opened the door and noticed that Amanda had managed to get her pajamas back to her knees. "Okay, let's get these bad boys up where they belong."

She pulled Amanda to her feet and steadied her. Again, she speedily tugged the pajamas up. "Stay here a minute and I'll get the chair."

Backing the wheelchair into the bathroom, Nic locked down the wheels. "Lock your arms around my neck, and we'll just pivot you clockwise and you should be able to just sit down."

They completed the maneuver and finally Amanda was settled. Nic reached outside the door and retrieved a throw, which she placed carefully over Amanda's legs. She left her patient at the sink to wash up and brush her teeth. Nic waited outside the door and when it sounded like Amanda was finished, she stuck her head around the corner saying cheerfully, "Now, let's go get you some nourishment."

Something about Nic's business-like and matter of fact demeanor combined with her unfailing good humor made an uncomfortable situation reasonably tolerable for Amanda. The day passed quickly. They used the time to talk and get to know each other better. Nic made French toast for brunch, then gave Amanda a snack of fruit and cheese around two o'clock. For the most part, they talked about their childhoods, growing up, and coming out as lesbians.

Amanda asked, "Do you think Dana will have a hard time identifying as a lesbian at this point in her life?"

"I don't know. She seems to be struggling with the label. In practice she seems to be very matter of fact about falling in love with me, at least so far. In some ways, I think it was easier there in Italy. We could stroll arm and arm with no one paying attention, something not acceptable here. I'm not sure how she'll feel once we're back in the real world. Once we went beyond a certain level of caring, it didn't matter any more. I couldn't stop myself from falling in love with her even if I'd wanted to, so it was a moot point for me." Nic tugged her ear. "We seem to be able to talk about things honestly, so I'm hopeful that we'll be okay. Besides, she's got you two to talk to as well. She seems to feel that you fall in love with a person and that gender is not a critical element.. I hope she continues to feel that way."

"I'm sure she will. One thing I will say, for a novice lesbian she has good taste in women."

"Thank you. What a lovely compliment."

The rest of the day was uneventful. Nic was impressed with the dictation software that Amanda used and as she started to work on her next chapter, Nic began reading Amanda's novel. She quickly became immersed in it "

"Oh, Amanda, I found a typo here. Do you want me to make note of it for you?"

"That would be very much appreciated. That one and any others you find, or anything that just doesn't read right."

Nic nodded and went back to the story. Around five o'clock, Nic stopped reading and began dinner. Amanda had fallen asleep around three and was still resting peacefully when Mallory came home.

After checking on Amanda, Mallory entered the kitchen to find Nic peeling potatoes. "Can I help?

"No, I've got it. We had a good day."

"Thanks, Nic, for helping out. I'll be able to get caught up at work with you doing this, so if I need to, when you two go back to work, I'll be in a better position in terms of my work obligations. I talked with my boss today and told him I might need to split my shifts for the next few weeks. Fortunately, I didn't get any negativity. I felt that everyone I spoke with was supportive."

"That's great."

"Nic?" Amanda called from the other room. "I need some help, please."

"I'll go," Mallory said.

Entering the living room, Mallory called, "Will you settle for me? I'm awaiting my assignment."

"Oh honey, you're home." Amanda replied with a large grin. "Of course, your first assignment is to come give this girl a kiss."

Mallory complied with the request. "Okay, what's next?"

"Well, I'd like to go to the bathroom and clean up a bit. Any chance I can wash tonight? I'd kill for a shower."

"After dinner, when Nic goes home, we'll see what we can manage."

Nic excused herself shortly after dinner. "I'm sorry, you two, but for some reason I'm really sleepy, I must be jet lagged. I'll see you in the morning, Miss," the comment directed toward Amanda. "Mallory," she said with a nod before she exited through the back door.

Mallory sat opposite Amanda on one of the recliners. "So how did you and Nic make out today?"

"Fine." Amanda nodded. "Yes, really fine. She's a wonderful person, Mallory. Nic is so calm and measured. She has good values and seems to really cherish Dana. I'm still having trouble wrapping my mind around Dana being involved with a woman. It will be interesting to see how Dana interacts with her. I wonder if she'll be shy or demonstrative in front of us."

Mallory shrugged. "Yes, it is different from what we're used to thinking about her. Coming out is always an interesting process. Remember Dana is in the process of coming out to herself, too. Nic told me that Dana seems to be surprisingly accepting of this new dimension of her life."

Amanda nodded. "She's made a good choice in Nic. They make a wonderful couple. I'm so happy for her."

"Yes, me too."

"Okay, enough about them…let's talk about me."

Mallory laughed. "Okay. What's on your mind?"

"Honey, I can't stand myself. Is there any way to hose me off?"

Mallory was expecting this request and was prepared with cast covers for the big shower event. She wheeled Amanda into the bathroom and stripped Amanda of her clothes before putting on the cast covers. Next, she removed the brace from Amanda's leg.

"We need to be careful of your ankle. Try to keep your weight off of it as much as you can. Also, it's important that we keep these casts on your arms dry."

"Okay, just tell me what to do."

"Let's get you up and we'll then have you sit on the edge of the tub. Once you're stable there, I'll help you get your legs over and into the tub. Then we'll stand you up again inside the tub. I'll turn the water on. Try to keep your arms up, but your hands away from the direct spray of the water throughout the shower. The object is to keep water from running down into the cast. These covers are good, but not perfect. You have to help keep them dry."

Amanda's eyes became large as she watched Mallory strip off her own clothes. "Ooooh! You're showering with me?"

"Yes, but don't get too excited about it…we're showering, nothing else. I need to get you in and out of there, as quickly as we can manage."

Amanda grinned devilishly. "Then you should have left your clothes on. I wonder, Dr. Barnes, do you do this for all your patients?"

A quick smile and a kiss placed lightly on Amanda's cheek was Mallory's response. Amanda faked a pout. "No. They seem to be less demanding than you are and are happy with just a sponge bath. Enough of that…it's chilly. As my mother would say, let's get on with it before we both catch a cold. I know that's not possible, but no sense tempting fate."

They managed to successfully get Amanda into the shower and stabilized in a corner. Mallory scrubbed Amanda's hair. "Oh, that feels so good…clean hair. I'm in ecstasy, nearly orgasmic." Amanda crooned as the water sluiced over her body from the handheld shower and Mallory began to wash her in earnest. They giggled as Mallory made her spread her legs so she could scrub there.

"Sort of takes the romance out of showering together when you're really showering to get clean, doesn't it?" Amanda noted. "Also, it's torture to watch you all naked and soapy and not be able to touch you." She gestured with her plastic covered hands.

Mallory helped Amanda turn around to face her and finished up washing her partner. "Now, it's my turn." Amanda watched with an increasing amount of lust in her eyes, as Mallory soaped her own body and slid her hands between her legs to wash herself.

"Hmm...from ecstasy to torture. It's torture not being able to touch you," Amanda whined.

"Just think how great sex will be when we can have it," Mallory exclaimed as she turned off the shower.

"So, Mallory, are you one-hundred percent sure you don't give all your patients this treatment? You're very good at it."

Mallory grinned, a wicked expression spreading slowly across her face.

"Nope, only the cute ones." Mallory kissed Amanda on the nose. "Okay, you sit." It wasn't long until Mallory had Amanda dried off and in bed.

"I'm horny." It wasn't so much a complaint from Amanda as it was an observation.

Mallory smiled. "Really, how did that happen?"

"From watching you wash yourself."

Mallory sat on the bed next to Amanda and placed a soft kiss on her lips. "Would you like me to do something about that for you?"

Amanda heaved a deep sigh. "No, it wouldn't be fair to you. I can't make love to you in return because of these," she said raising her hands.

"Oh for God's sake, Amanda. How long have you been a lesbian? Rely on all that sexual experience you have under your belt." Her teasing tone removed any possible perceived insult from Mallory's words. "You don't need your hands...that's what you have a mouth for." Mallory helped Amanda slide down in the bed. "Now, stop feeling sorry for yourself, and come over here and see how inventive you can be without using your hands. To keep it fair, I won't use my hands either."

Amanda brightened at the challenge. 'I'm sorry," she said contritely. "It's just that this is so frustrating, and embarrassing, and annoying, and inconvenient, and well..."

"Okay, I get it." Mallory leaned over and kissed Amanda thoroughly and completely. "Now, let's see if I can't improve on that sour mood you're in."

The next morning, Amanda woke up with a smile on her face. It returned many times during the day, every time she thought of their love making session the night before. *Maybe having broken arms won't be as bad as I thought it would be.* Amanda sighed with relief.

Amanda and Nic spent the day together again. They discovered they had a mutual enjoyment of word games. They each had tablets, so they set up a game and found that Amanda could manage to move her letters with her left hand if they propped the tablet on a pillow next to her on the recliner. They played a couple of games and were evenly matched. At four o'clock, they were tied at one game to one and their scores were close on the third game.

"I need a glass of water. Don't cheat while I'm gone," Nic teased. "Want anything?"

"No, the more I drink, the more I have to pee and you know how much I enjoy that."

Nic laughed. "You should be used to that exercise by now. I'll be right back."

Nic stood, preparing to go to the kitchen. There was a quick knock at the door and Dana burst in calling, "Nic, are you here?" She stopped for a heartbeat and launched herself into Nic's arms. The kiss she planted on Nic's lips was anything but tame. "I missed you so much."

"I missed you too, sweetheart." Nic wrapped her arms around Dana and pulled her close.

Their eyes met and Amanda could feel the connection they had. *Well, I guess that answers the question about how demonstrative they'll be.*

Dana kissed Nic, more demurely this time before pulling away to approach her friend. She leaned over and gave

Amanda a hug and kiss. "Look at you. Are you okay?" She gave Amanda a thorough assessment.

"Really, Dana, I'm fine. Truthfully, Nic and I have been having a pleasant time getting to know each other."

"That's exactly what she said. She told me about her initial meeting with you and Mallory. Too funny."

"It was a memorable introduction for sure."

"So, you two didn't know that Nic was a woman. I can't believe that. I wasn't trying to hide anything, honest. I'll have to go back and re-read my emails to you two. I can't believe it wasn't apparent through them."

"Well, not knowing did make for an amusing introduction. I think my mouth actually dropped open."

"Yes, I can imagine it did." Dana reached over and took Nic's hand into her own before she turned to fix her gaze on Amanda. "And what about you two. You kept a big secret from me, didn't you?"

Amanda turned to Nic and exclaimed, "Big mouth."

"Sorry, it sort of just came out when I was talking to her about the misunderstanding when you and Mallory first met me."

"Mallory and I wanted to tell you either in person or at least on video chat, but it seemed that the timing was always off. We had a hard time catching you online because Mallory was working different shifts and you were so busy with Nic. After that, it was the cruise, and then you said you were coming home soon. It wasn't like we were keeping secrets...we just wanted to see your face when we told you. So, we decided to wait. Forgive us?"

"There's nothing to forgive, really. I'm happy for both of you and for me, too. Now I'll have the two friends I treasure most coming in a package deal."

Sensing that Amanda and Dana might like to talk privately, Nic excused herself and went to the kitchen to fix tea.

"So that's it? You're not upset with me or worried that we got involved so soon after Bernie?" Amanda asked.

"No. You're a smart and capable woman. I think you know your own mind and your own heart. It's not for me to judge you. Honestly, I'm happy for both of you and thrilled that you've found each other." Dana moved her chair closer to Amanda. "What about you? Are you shocked?"

"Shocked? You mean about you and Nic?"

Dana nodded.

"Shocked, no…surprised, definitely. Mostly, I'm just exceedingly happy for you. Nic is great, I love her already." Amanda wiggled her eyebrows. "I certainly can see how you fell for her. She's hot, hot, hot. I'm puzzled though because all these years I've known you, you've always been into men."

"Dated men, perhaps…been into men, not so much. Besides, you know that I haven't really dated anyone for a number of years."

"Have you ever been attracted to other women?"

Dana considered her answer carefully. "No, never the way I feel about Nic." Dana smiled and whispered as if she were thinking aloud. "There's just something about her. I can't get enough of her. I love how she smells and how we fit together. I love her walk, her voice, her sense of humor, and her calmness. I can go on, but you get the idea."

Amanda grinned at her friend. "Oh man, have you ever got it bad."

"Yes, I do. I gladly admit it."

"I don't want to be a wet blanket, but you and Nic were living in a vacuum in Rome. Will you hang in when things get tough? Not everyone approves, you know. Remember how my friends and family reacted when I came out?"

"I considered all that, but in the end it just didn't matter. Look, I'm not a kid any more and as you well know, I've always felt that the person one chooses to love is a personal decision. I know there may be people who'll disapprove. It doesn't matter because the important ones, the people closest to me, seem to be happy for me and that's all that matters to me."

Dana smiled as she thought about her lover. "I miss her the minute she's out of my sight. When we're together, just being in her presence makes me feel like I want to burst with the sheer joy of it." She leaned in to whisper a confidence to her friend. "And the sex, my God, Amanda. You should have told me what I've been missing out on all these years. It's incredible. I had no idea it could be like this." She giggled at Amanda's expression at the frank confession before leaning back and seeking Amanda's eyes with her own. "I love her Amanda…the head over heels, jumping on the couch, rooftop shouting kind of love I've only read about in books or seen on television before. That's the bottom line."

"Well, you made an excellent choice, and you two make a wonderful couple. Mallory and I like Nic a lot already. We're very happy for you both."

As if on cue, Nic returned with the tea and the three women chatted together amiably. After taking the last swallow of the soothing liquid, Dana turned to Nic. "Hon. I'm going over to unpack and take a shower. Do you have dinner planned or do you need me to run out and get something?" Without waiting for a response, Dana said, "You know, ladies, I'm really craving a steak sandwich from McMurthy's. Anyone else interested?"

Everyone agreed that would be better than the frozen chicken breasts Nic was planning to prepare for dinner. "Let's call Mallory," Amanda suggested. "She can pick up the order on her way home if we call it in."

*** 

Dinner was delicious and everyone enjoyed it. Animated conversation ensued throughout the meal. It was as if the two couples had been friends forever.

"Thanksgiving is just about four weeks away," Dana said. "Has everyone made plans already? If not, maybe we could do dinner here together?"

Amanda looked at Mallory. "Mal, have you decided if you're going home?"

"No, I think I'll just stay here with you. I'll probably have to work part of the weekend anyway. Time kind of got away from me. I might invite my folks up here for Christmas to spend a few days and let them meet you and our friends." She turned toward Nic and Dana. "What about you two, any plans for the holidays?"

"I'd like for my mom to meet Dana," Nic replied. "We haven't discussed it, but maybe Mom can come here for a couple of days for Christmas, too. I'd like to be more settled than we are now before she comes."

Mallory responded enthusiastically. "That'll be fun. A celebration."

Dana added, "Maybe you can invite your brother and the kids, Amanda?"

"I'll invite him, but you know he won't respond. Still, I never give up trying. I'll give it another shot when I send his Christmas card. The children are hardly kids anymore. His twins, a boy and a girl, will soon be fifteen and the oldest girl, the apple of his eye, is already eighteen."

Mallory said, "Then, it's settled. It'll just be us for Thanksgiving and we'll have family in for Christmas."

"Mal, why don't you ask Jo and her friends who helped find me after my accident to join us?"

"That's a great idea. I'll give her a call. If she and the rest of the rescue team have plans for Thanksgiving, maybe we can do a small dinner party for them after the holiday."

When the conversation reached a comfortable lull and dinner was over, Dana said, "Come on, Nic. Let's clean up while these two relax."

Mallory and Amanda talked privately while their friends washed up the dinner dishes. Amanda repeated, virtually word for word, the conversation that she and Dana had earlier. Dana and Nic returned just as Amanda was finishing the story. Dana sat on the arm of Mallory's chair and put her arm around her shoulder.

"Quick work there, Doc...I'm impressed," Dana said with a smile.

"The same could be said about you, Miss Thing!" Mallory replied, sliding an arm around Dana's waist.

"I'm sorry I let the cat out of the bag," Nic tried her best to look contrite.

Mallory and Amanda both smiled at her. "Not to worry," they said in unison, before they both laughed at their mutual response.

\*\*\*

The next two weeks were tolerable for Amanda. Nic, Dana, and Mallory took turns in providing care for the steadily improving patient.

During the week, Dana and Nic met with their respective bosses to see what the opportunities were for them to reduce or eliminate their travel. Dana's boss said he could probably arrange to reduce her travel by at least seventy-five percent. The work would, of course, be much less varied and therefore less interesting. But it was a sacrifice, in her opinion, worth making.

Nic didn't fare as well and decided to call her educational contacts. She was offered a position as a substitute for a professor who had suddenly taken ill. It would be a temporary position, but would last through the first few months of the coming year. She opted to take it despite the cut in her salary after Dana and she determined they would be able to afford their expenses.

"This job is not my dream position," she explained to Mallory and Amanda, "and it'll involve an ugly commute, but it'll pay the bills while I look for something better. Also, it allows me to stay here with Dana and serves as a foot back in the door of the hallowed halls of education for me. At least I'll have a job while I'm searching for something more permanent and maybe a little closer to here."

"We know it's a less than ideal work situation," Nic said. "But we're deliriously happy that we're able to begin our lives together. It's a start for us, and it enables us to be together more time than not." Nic squeezed Dana's hand. "We'll work to make it better and for now it will be enough."

## Chapter 19

On Thanksgiving Day, Amanda watched as Dana, Nic, and Mallory worked together to prepare a traditional turkey dinner. Once everything was sliced, diced, and in the oven, they formed teams to play table games as the turkey cooked. It was just the four of them. Jo had declined the invitation, having already agreed to join her family's holiday gathering at her parents cabin near Edinborough, New York.

Amanda demonstrated steady improvement, and the day after Thanksgiving, roughly six weeks after her accident, she was relieved to have her casts removed. The itching had driven her crazy. Fortunately, Mallory had a trick or two up her sleeve to help keep her comfortable. Using a hair dryer set on low to cool the cast and reduce the itching had made her more comfortable. Her ankle was nearly better, but she would still have to wear a blow-up brace for a few more weeks. Eager to begin her therapy, Amanda and Mallory made the rehab center their next stop. She began physical therapy the next day. Motivated to be fully functional as quickly as possible, she worked hard to regain her strength and dexterity. A week after their first Thanksgiving dinner party, the four women were sitting around the table playing Scrabble in teams when Amanda's cell phone rang. Mallory answered it for her and after a few seconds, she turned to Amanda and said, "It's for you."

"Who is it?" She asked.

"It's the San Francisco police wanting to speak to you."

"Put the call on speaker, Mallory."

"Amanda James speaking. How can I help you?"

"I'm looking for the Amanda James who lives at the following address." He read out the number and street of her home with Bernie.

"Yes, that's me. What's wrong? Did something happen to the house?"

"No, Ms. James. This is Officer Patrick Murphy with the San Francisco Police Department. I'm sorry to have to tell you, but Bernadette Maxwell was killed in an automobile accident this morning. You were listed on a card in her wallet as the person to contact in case of emergency."

"She died?"

"Yes, ma'am. I'm sorry."

Amanda looked to Mallory. "Officer Murphy? This is Mallory Barnes. I'm a friend of Ms. James. If it's okay with you, I'll take down whatever information you have for her."

Mallory hung up the phone and found Amanda dry-eyed, but dumbstruck by the news. "I can't believe it. She's dead. I'll have to call her family. She had prearranged her funeral. I hope they respect her wishes. She didn't want a big funeral service. It was her wish to just be cremated."

Amanda called Bernie's family and gave them the news. She explained that she was in New York, recovering from a biking accident and would fly out as quickly as she could make the arrangements.

Bernie's mother said that they were aware of their daughter's wishes and would arrange the cremation. They would also take care of planning and arranging for a memorial service at a future date. Bernie's mother revealed that Bernie left instructions that she wanted her ashes spread near her home in Brazil at a private funeral service.

That revelation puzzled Amanda, but Bernie's family made it clear that they would be taking care of all the arrangements.

They left little doubt that they didn't want her involved in the arrangements at all. Legally, she was powerless. Obviously, Bernie had made her parents well aware of her wishes. Maybe she'd already told her parents that they had ended their relationship and they assumed she wouldn't care.

Mallory arranged for the two of them to fly to San Francisco on the earliest flight available. Amanda called and told Bernie's family the flight number and arrival time. They requested that Amanda meet them at their hotel upon her arrival, after informing her that they would send a car to meet her.

\*\*\*

Mallory and Amanda caught the red eye to the coast the next day. By the time they arrived in California, Bernie had already been cremated. Mallory waited in the hotel lobby while, per their request, Amanda met Bernie's parents at their hotel. They were cordial, just not overly welcoming to Amanda. During their brief meeting they introduced Amanda to Bernie's lawyer, Mr. Johnson.

"We'll give you some privacy with Mr. Johnson," Mr. Maxwell said. "Good-bye Amanda." He shook her hand briefly and gave her a quick pat on the shoulder. Bernie's mother already had her hand on the door and merely nodded in Amanda's direction before the couple left her alone with Mr. Johnson.

She didn't have enough time to process the strange encounter with Bernie's parents before the lawyer began speaking. "Here is my card with the address and phone number of my office." He handed her a sealed envelope.

The envelope was thick, but she could feel that there was a key inside it. "Ms. Maxwell instructed me to give you this letter, in the event of her death, and asked me to tell you to not open it until you were alone, inside your home."

"I don't understand, Mr. Johnson. What's all this about?"

"The information in the envelope will make everything clear, I think. I am permitted to tell you that I am available to assist you with any questions you have after you read the contents of the envelope. I can assure you that Ms. Maxwell was extremely thorough in her preparations for her death. You may begin sorting your belongings from hers in the home you shared with her. You are restricted from removing anything from the house other than your own personal property before you have read the enclosures."

"Thank you, Mr. Johnson." Amanda replied mechanically. She was so perplexed by the interview that she felt overwhelmed and so unsure of what was happening that she stuffed the envelope into her purse without further thought.

"I understand there will be a memorial service, but no arrangements have been finalized yet." Mr. Johnson responded with a sympathetic smile. "In keeping with Ms. Maxwell's wishes, the family is thinking they will opt to hold it in Brazil where Bernie's life was centered." He stood, gathered his belongings then nodded in her direction. "Miss James."

Before she could utter another word, Amanda found herself sitting in the room alone pondering the oddly formal and personally distant meeting. She thought that the statement about the memorial service was a strange comment but by now had internalized that, without a doubt, she was obviously being excluded from any further arrangements for Bernie and might possibly not even be included in the memorial service. Feeling bewildered and off center by the dismissal, Amanda left the room and made her way to the lobby to find Mallory. They took a cab to Bernie and Amanda's house. On the way there, Amanda described the strange meeting to Mallory.

"Maybe they just didn't approve of the fact that Bernie was a lesbian." Mallory suggested by way of explanation. "I mean, how many horror stories have we all heard about surviving partners being excluded after their partner passed away."

"Yes, I know. It seems that they're at least allowing me to get my personal belongings out. I have little there, but once I get my things sorted, I'll call the lawyer and find out what will be done about the house. I assume I'll get something from that when they sell it. I know Bernie has a will, so I assume all will be made clear once they get everything settled."

They pulled to a stop in front of the house she had shared with Bernie and went inside. "Geez, Amanda. This is certainly some place. Look at the view."

"Well, it was really mostly Bernie's house. Her taste, not mine." Amanda turned from the window and focused on Mallory. "I'm looking at my favorite view right now."

Mallory took Amanda's hand and kissed it. "It feels a little...what? Odd, I guess. Yes, odd to be here in Bernie's and your house. I know it's not true, but it feels a bit like I've been having an affair with you instead of a relationship."

"No, Mallory, please, don't feel that way. Bernie and I had come to a peace. I was done when I walked out of here, if not before. I wouldn't have done that to her, or to you, and you know that. I've kept no secrets from you about my relationship with Bernie and the fact it was over long ago, although I only left her recently."

"I know. I didn't mean it that way. It's just weird to be here."

Amanda looked around. Bernie had made good progress packing up the contents of their home. Several boxes in each room had Amanda's name on them with the contents of each clearly labeled in a neat, precise hand. As she looked around, tears filled her eyes.

"Poor Bernie."

Mallory walked over to the mantle where there were individual pictures of both Amanda and Bernie.

"She was very attractive."

"Yes, and she knew it, too. And charming, as well, especially when she wanted to be...yes, let's not forget that."

Amanda walked around the room looking at the boxes one more time, then made a tour of the house to check the contents of the rest of the containers that Bernie had set aside for her.

"There really is nothing here that I want. I took everything from my office that I wanted."

"Maybe you should read the letter she gave you."

"I will, but not tonight. I'm exhausted. Let's go upstairs, find a guest room, and get some sleep."

Mallory took one look at the sweeping circular stairway and commented. "That's a long way up for you. Aren't there any bedrooms on this floor?"

"Don't worry," Amanda smiled. "There's an elevator."

"Of course there is." Mallory rolled her eyes and assumed an expression indicating she should have expected no less.

They exited the elevator and entered one of the large guest suites on the second floor. Mallory helped Amanda prepare for bed. As she started to unzip her pants, Amanda said, "I can do that now."

"I know you can, but I've grown to like undressing and dressing you." She kissed Amanda on the nose then finished up by unbuttoning her shirt for her before she slipped a nightgown over her head and placed a kiss on her lips.

"Thank you, Mallory. I know this must not be easy for you. Emotionally I don't think I could have done this alone. I love you. Don't ever doubt that for one nanosecond."

"I know you do...and I love you, too." Mallory looked around. "What are you going to do with all this stuff?"

"I don't know. Maybe it won't be mine to dispose of. The lawyer asked me not to remove anything but my personal property and to just to sort her things from mine. As I told you before, there was very little here that I wanted. This place is her taste, not mine. I much prefer your cozy nest with the two recliners in front of the fireplace where we sit together, read, and talk. Nothing like that ever happened here. Especially for the past two years, Bernie and I lived separate lives here, together. I'm not the least bit sad to say good-bye to this house and these possessions. I was never completely happy here. Despite what Bernie told me, I honestly find it difficult to believe that she was happy here either."

They climbed into bed and Mallory pulled Amanda to her. "At least tonight, I don't have to worry about you clunking me on the head with one of your casts," Mallory teased, hoping to lighten Amanda's mood.

## Chapter 20

Amanda arose early and showered. She dressed in tan slacks and a dark brown sweater before taking the elevator downstairs to the kitchen where she prepared coffee for them. Mallory was following close behind having gotten in the shower when Amanda finished. The coffee was ready by the time Mallory came downstairs with her bag in her hand.

"I'm so sorry that I have to leave you to face this alone." Mallory lamented. "With all the time I've taken off lately, I can't get any more leave or I'll run the risk of losing my job."

"I know baby. I'm glad you came with me even if it was just for a short time." Amanda looked around gesturing at all the boxes. "As you can see, Bernie made a sincere effort to get things in order here. There's little left to do. I don't want anything from here but my clothes. There's nothing personal in any of these boxes. I just don't know what to do with all this stuff. I checked the bedroom this morning and there are boxes full of my clothes. I'll have to go through them, donate the ones I don't want to charity and ship the rest home. That should keep me busy. I'm assuming I'll have to go for the reading of the will to know whose responsibility it will be to get rid of the rest of all this. If I'm lucky, she'll have left everything to her parents and I won't have to deal with it."

Mallory pulled Amanda close to her and held her for as long as she could. "I've got to go. Are you sure you'll be okay here alone?"

"Yes, I'm sure. You, Dana, and Nic all used your vacation time to take care of me with my broken wings. I know you'd have been here with me if you could. I'll be fine, really." Mallory seemed to be suffering from threshold paralysis, unable to leave. Amanda reassured her. "Really...now go. Your cab is waiting for you."

"It's hard to leave you here with all this to deal with on your own." The cab driver, obviously growing impatient, announced his annoyance with a toot of his car horn. "I have to go. I love you."

"I know you do. I love you, and I can't wait for a time when everything is past us. My injury..." she glanced around, "all this."

"I know, but you can be sure of one thing, our home and I will both be waiting for you whenever it is you can come back to us."

"I won't be long." They kissed. It was a kiss filled with longing and sadness over having to part, but with promise of better times to come. Amanda stood in the door and watched until Mallory's cab disappeared. The house felt so empty without Mallory and so sad with all the boxes stacked around her. She went back to the kitchen for another cup of coffee. Her head was beginning to pound. She reached for her purse to get a couple of aspirin and found the ignored letter the lawyer had given her the day before.

Speaking aloud to no one but the boxes, she said, "I guess there's no putting it off any longer. I've got to see what the note says." She pulled the letter from her purse and ripped open the flap. A key fell onto the counter as she slid the letter from its envelope. She slipped her glasses into place and read:

*My Dearest Amanda:*

*In our bedroom, you will find a metal box in the top of the closet. It is hidden in a shoebox I kept there. Inside you will find another letter from me with an explanation and some instructions. I hope you will follow them...and I hope you will understand and forgive me.*

*Bernie*

**What the heck is this all about?** Amanda went to the bedroom and located the box Bernie mentioned in the letter, exactly where she had described. She took it down and placed it on the bed. After discovering that it was locked, she remembered the key that had fallen out of the envelope when she opened the letter. She quickly retrieved it from the kitchen table and opened the box. Inside, she found two envelopes. She opened the thinner one labeled 'READ THIS FIRST.' *Bernie was nothing, if not organized.* She looked at the letter and noticed that it was dated just two months ago.

*Dear Amanda,*

*This is the third time I have written this letter to you. I update it every couple of years or so. Hopefully, it will be reasonably current when you get it. I try to update it if a major event in our lives occurs. Obviously, our lives are changing now since we have separated. I still harbor a desire for us to work things out. If we are unable to do that, I want you to know that I accept full responsibility for the ending of our relationship. I have been under considerable stress lately. Both here and well, as you read on, I'm sure you'll understand better.*

*If you are reading this, you already know that I'm dead. I hope it is a long time from now that I will die. One never knows though, so like a good girl scout, my motto has been 'be prepared!'*

*I travel so much that there is always a risk I'll die in an accident instead of from old age. Oh well, let me get on with it...it doesn't matter the how, only the reality. If you predecease me, you will be spared all these details and your sense of what I'm sure you will view as betrayal. If I die before you, I'm sorry, but I'll have to end up hurting you one more time in order not to hurt someone very important to me who should not be involved, two others really. Just like you, both of them are completely innocent in all of this. I have chosen to make an effort to protect the one most vulnerable, my daughter. Hate me if you must, but please hear me out.*

"Daughter, what daughter?" Amanda continued to read, this time with more urgency.

*I have several things that I need to get off my chest and a few apologies to make. Then I have one final favor to ask of you...and it's a big one I'm afraid. I hope, after you learn everything, you'll understand and not think so unkindly of me that you'll deny this last request of mine. I trust you enough to have hope that you will do as I ask even though I know you'll be hurt and probably a little more than pissed at me.*

*First, let me tell you that I did and still do, love you. I loved you from the minute I laid eyes on you. I will always love you. Now, you have left me and I do understand why. I tried to give you my best, at least the best I could, which you are about to discover, was not all that it should have been. I never meant to hurt you, although it's already obvious that I have and will continue to do so, even though I'm now on my way out of your life permanently. Again, I ask that you pardon my shortcomings and hope you will find it in your heart to forgive me. Our attraction was so strong and the rush I got from you so great that I couldn't deny myself loving you. It was true, I found myself unable to resist pursuing a life with you.*

*If you will recall, during that time, I was working almost exclusively in Brazil. I had just started servicing this area and was only here maybe one week a month. When we met, things were so magical and new for us, and the sex was incredible. We quickly moved in together and we were happy. We'd probably still have been happy if you hadn't called me at my home in Brazil that day two years or so ago.*

"Wait a minute. Called your home? Weren't you in a hotel? When did you get a home in Brazil? What the hell are you talking about?" mumbled Amanda.

*I've told you in the past, when you accused me of being a cheat and a liar...that 'I couldn't help myself.' That much was true. I really couldn't help falling in love with you although, honestly, I was not exactly free to do so.*

Amanda's brow furrowed as she tried to understand what Bernie was saying. "Not free? What's that supposed to mean?"

*By now, I'm sure you are asking yourself, 'What the hell is she talking about?' Well, Amanda, you see, you were not the first woman I fell in love with, which I'm sure will not be a surprise to you. When you and I became involved, I led you believe that I was available when, in fact, there was another woman, my partner, living in Brazil. We have a family, a little girl, and a life together. I really thought we'd be happy forever. And then I met you and was not strong enough to resist you.*

"Oh my God! I'm the other woman." Amanda closed her eyes in an effort to give herself a chance to absorb this new and stunning information. "How can this be?" After a few seconds, the pulse pounding in her head slowed. She shook her head in denial. "Bernie, what have you done?"

*My job and my constant travel made keeping you separate from each other easy at first. Her name is Aline, by the way. The day you called, I was in the shower, and she answered my phone. When she wanted to know who you were, I did the only thing I could think of on the spur of the moment, I told her a bold faced lie. It was not to be the first or, unfortunately, the last lie I told either of you. I'm sorry for every one of them. Anyway, that day you called I told her you were my cousin that I lived with when I was in the States. She believed me or at least I think she did. After that, things got easier for me with her. Since she believed you were my cousin, I didn't have to be as careful there...I could even tell her about some of the things we did, you know, things I did with 'my cousin, Amanda'.*

*Our relationship (meaning your and my relationship) changed after that day. You suspected me of being promiscuous, something I could never convince you was not true. Your suspicion made our relationship different, your suspicion. You began to pull away from me. I was frustrated that I couldn't win you back. I even considered confessing to you about Aline, so you wouldn't think I was a womanizer. I hated that you thought that I wasn't true to you when, for the most part, I really was, at least in my mind. I loved both of you, you and Aline, and would never have cheated on either of you.*

*Other than a few occasional one night stands, totally meaningless sex with no emotional commitment, there were never any other women for me, other than Aline, of course. You never understood that I considered cheating as sex with emotional commitment. Sex for pure sexual release was just that for me and had no impact on my committed relationships to you and Aline. Seriously, although I won't deny there were a few, there were far fewer of those others than you accused me of, because for the most part I was with Aline when I was not with you. I never strayed when at home with either of you. My only transgressions were committed when I traveled away from my homes.*

*As I am writing all this down, I realize how bizarre this all must sound to you but, for me, it makes sense. Financially, I could comfortably provide for both of you, could certainly keep up my end of the relationship sexually and, from my perspective, emotionally (although you've told me you disagree about this.) So, from my perspective, I didn't see why I couldn't have both of you.*

*My two lives were separate. My parents knew about both of you and, of course, although they disapproved of my behavior, for the sake of my daughter, they kept my secret for me. I'm afraid I've now come to another apology I owe you. Initially, they didn't know that you were unaware of Aline's existence in my life. Eventually, I had to tell them so they'd keep my secret. They didn't like it, having to keep a secret like that, but for their granddaughter's sake, they did it. You always thought they didn't approve of you when, in reality, they remained reserved because they didn't want to have to tell you direct lies. It made it easy that they didn't live near us and we saw them so rarely that it wasn't that onerous. I didn't really want to hurt anyone, and I'm sorry that I have to hurt you this way by asking you a favor.*

"Bernie, you egocentric bastard...if you weren't already dead, I'd kill you. Oh my, what your parents must have thought of me. No wonder they always acted like they never liked me."

*So, now we come to your part in this tale. I'm sure that after my recent revelation above, you're feeling disinclined to honor it. I'm begging you to reconsider that position and hear me out, not for my sake, but for the sake of my daughter, Anna.*

*Aline will probably have to come here for the reading of the will and to settle my affairs, so the chances are good that you may run into her. I am begging you to keep my secret and for appearance sake, if your paths cross, continue the pretense with her that you are my cousin. I ask this not for me and not even for Aline, but for Anna. For her to learn all of these details would serve no purpose, and I hope you will accept and believe that.*

*You will not need to go to the reading of my will, as you are not named there. I have left you a sizable insurance policy that I'm hopeful you will find sufficient to cover your needs. Please don't view it as a payoff. I took the policy out when we first got together to protect you. It was meant then, as it is now, as a way to assure that you were cared for in the event I was no longer alive to do so. The policy is included in the next envelope, along with the address and phone number of the agent. She will help you submit the proper paperwork. She will need a death certificate to process the claim. I already arranged for my lawyer to have one delivered to her, so everything should be in order. It won't be long now and you will be gone from my life entirely. I'll be able to destroy this letter and you will not need to know any of this. If I have died before that eventuality, I implore you, once again, to please keep my secret.*

*I have placed the insurance policy and a few items you may or may not want to keep in the second envelope. I hope you will find it in your heart, someday, to forgive me for falling in love with you and not being strong enough to resist loving you.*

*Bernie*

## Chapter 21

Stunned...Amanda was just plain stunned. There was no other word for it. She put down the letter from Bernie. She didn't know what to feel other than numb. *For all those years, how could I have been so blind...so stupid?* She wanted to just leave. Leave and go back to Mallory. She lifted her phone to call, but closed it up when she realized that Mallory was probably in the air, on her way home. Home, where she wanted to be. Already in a few short months, Mallory's house was more of a home to her than this house ever was. She felt relieved she would have no more responsibilities for this place and she would be free to go.

Amanda folded Bernie's letter and placed it back into the envelope along with the second envelope labeled READ SECOND.

That's about all of that I can take right now, Bernie.

At that moment, all she wanted to do was to get out of the house before Aline showed up. The last thing she wanted to do was to have to lie to the poor woman who Bernie had deceived more harshly than she had deceived Amanda herself. She got the phone and called the moving company she'd used to move her belongings a few months earlier. Once connected, she explained what she needed.

"I only have about an hour's worth of work, but I'll pay you a two hundred dollar bonus if you can be here within an hour and get this stuff out of here and deal with it for me."

"Hell, for that kind of money, I'll do it myself. Unfortunately I can't be there in an hour but should be able to make it in two hours or so if that works for you. I'll get there as soon as I can, hopefully in a couple of hours, but definitely by lunchtime."

True to his word, the mover showed up more quickly than Amanda imagined possible. By the time he arrived, she had finished sorting the clothing from the boxes in the bedroom. There were only six boxes in all, two of which were full of clothing that she was shipping east, while the remaining four were to be delivered to Goodwill. When the man left, she closed the door and returned to the kitchen where she opened a can of soup.

Finishing her meal, she knew she had to open the other envelope so she could get the address of the insurance agent. Before she opened the flap, she thought about what Bernie's letter said about the insurance money not being a 'payoff,' and the fact that she wasn't named in her will. Since Bernie always made considerably more money than Amanda had, she had bought the house mostly with her money and only a small contribution of cash from Amanda. Still, over the years Amanda had helped support the expenses associated with the residence, helping to pay for the taxes, mortgage, utilities, and maintenance. Since she'd not realize any gain on the value of the home, she did feel that Bernie owed her something for her contributions to their living space. After all, how could she walk away after twelve years with literally only the clothes on her back?

She tore open the envelope and dumped the contents on the table. Enclosed was a release for the lawyer to sell the house, including a waiver for any proceeds from the sale of the property. An insurance policy with a note attached fell out, as did a pile of pictures, some with notes clipped to them but most without. She quickly sifted through the photos, most of which were of her and Bernie. There were two with notes attached. One was of a cute little girl about ten years old. Beautiful dark eyes stared back at her from the page. She was dressed in a fancy white dress and sported a grin from ear to ear. The note read,

> This is my daughter Anna three years ago, at about ten years of age, ready for her Confirmation. I've attached a picture of us as a family. I don't do this maliciously. I just thought that if you are going to keep my secret it would be probable that you would have at least seen pictures of my partner and my daughter. Please keep her in mind as you make your decision about what you'll do.
> B

Amanda studied the photo. The house in the background of the photo was very picturesque, although not as lavish as hers and Bernie's. The woman standing next to Bernie in the photo had one arm linked through Bernie's and the other draped casually over her daughter's shoulder. The family looked happy.

Amanda turned the insurance policy over to get the name of the agent from the attached note. It was then that she noticed the amount of the policy—two million dollars. She reread it to be sure that the amount was what she thought. *My God, Bernie! Next thing you know the police will be after me to see if I bumped you off to get the insurance money.* It took her a few minutes to absorb the amount and realize the impact it could potentially have on her life. She'd never have to write another advertisement again unless it was something she wanted to do. She'd be free to write what she wanted to write, instead of what she had to write to preserve life and limb.

"Thank you, Bernie," she said aloud, hoping that somehow Bernie would hear her.

The insurance agent was very kind. When Amanda called, she told her how sorry she was to hear of Bernie's death and reassured Amanda that she had received the death certificate from Bernie's lawyer. The agent promised her that she would process the claim as quickly as she could. Amanda gave the agent her contact information and hung up. She signed the release for the lawyer, opened the front door, and put the self-addressed return envelope into the mailbox.

While she was waiting for her tea water to heat in the microwave, she called the airlines and arranged for her flight home the next afternoon. The message Amanda left on Mallory's cell phone stated she would be flying home the next day.

"I'm okay, but just feel drained, and plan to go to bed early. I'll call you tomorrow before I leave. You won't believe what I've learned. I wish you were here, I miss you so much."

Amanda fell asleep early, feeling lonely and missing Mallory. The next morning, she packed up her suitcase and carried it downstairs to the kitchen. With a couple of hours left to kill before she left for the airport, she decided to have another cup of coffee. The coffee was brewing as she cleaned out the refrigerator and freezer and placed the bags of trash in the cans outside. Finally, the coffee was ready, but before she could sit down, the doorbell rang.

Amanda stood and walked to the entry hall to answer the door. Her stomach flipped. Somehow, she knew in her heart that she would find Aline at the door when she opened it. She pulled the door open and found Aline standing there. *I hate it when I'm right.* Before she mustered up a welcoming smile, Amanda sighed deeply as she met the eyes of the attractive, dark haired, petite woman standing before her.

"Aline. Hello. Come in."

"Thank you Amanda."

Before Aline entered, she took a few seconds to allow her eyes to travel from Amanda's face to her feet and back up to meet Amanda's eyes. Amanda led Aline into the kitchen.

"Would you like a cup of coffee? I just made myself some."

Obviously, Aline knew who she was. "I'm sorry about Bernie's death. It must be a huge loss for you and your daughter."

Amanda hoped they could change the subject soon, because that was about the extent of the knowledge she possessed about this woman sitting opposite her and her daughter. If they continued talking, Amanda knew she couldn't maintain the ruse much beyond hello. As a cousin, she should have better knowledge about Bernie's family. So, she decided to try to stick to a safer topic.

Grasping for a neutral topic, Amanda asked, "Did you have a hard time getting a flight up?"

"There is no need to make small talk, Amanda. I know who you are." Her English was perfect, but with a strong Brazilian accent. "I can tell from your lack of response that I failed to make myself clear. What I mean is that despite what Bernie told me, I know you are not her cousin."

Amanda felt her face flush. The coffee she'd already consumed mixed with her churning stomach acid and threatened to burn a hole in her stomach. Hoping her voice would not betray her anxiety, she responded in as level a voice as possible, considering the circumstances.

"I see."

"I know you had a relationship with Bernie. I have known for some time now, since the time I answered the phone when you called her. How long were you with her?"

Never having wanted to lie to the woman who was as much a victim, if not more of a victim than she was herself, Amanda told her the truth. "Twelve years."

Aline's pupils dilated, and her eyes opened slightly, her only reaction to the news. "Really? That I did not know."

"Honestly, you have me at quite a disadvantage, Aline. I had no clue that you and your daughter existed until less than twenty-four hours ago. It was indeed a shock for me to discover that I could be considered 'the other woman.' I hope you will believe me that I would never have started a relationship with Bernie had I known she was involved with someone else. You have, of course, no way to know that I am telling you the truth, but I hope that you'll believe me when I tell you that we were both deceived."

"Oh, I believe you. Bernie was a wonderful person, a good parent to our daughter, and a good provider. Still, there was no doubt she had a wandering eye and that she cheated on me, and I guess, on you as well." Aline smiled kindly. "For a smart woman, Bernie seemed to think that I was too naive to know enough to check. She stupidly used our daughter's middle name as her email password. It's certainly not something to be proud of, but I admit that whenever I had the chance, I'd log into her email and find out what she was up to…or should I say who she was up to. Every time I would accuse her, she would be so sorry and would say that they didn't mean anything to her. I think that is true, until you. I don't think she could help herself. She loved women and she was good at making them find her attractive. I chose to turn the other way. She was always well behaved around home and never brought shame to me there."

Amanda nodded to indicate nonverbally that it was the same for her.

Aline shrugged. "I was less careful than I should have been, and in an argument with her, I revealed something I learned from her email. That's when she figured out that I could read her email. All of a sudden, the only emails addressed to her account became notes from friends and family. I lived in ignorant happiness thinking she had stopped cheating. I became suspicious when she would sometimes get phone calls that she would need to take in privacy. I read her emails, but nothing showed up there. Then, that day a couple of years ago, you called and she was so concerned when I answered the phone."

Amanda remembered. "Yes, Bernie always preferred to call me rather than have me call her when she traveled. She said she was so busy when she was away that it was better that she phone me so we would have time to talk without interruptions."

"Well, after she told you she would call you back later, she revealed to me that she was living with a cousin when she was here in the United States. This was information she had never mentioned before. I thought it strange and I became suspicious. It took me awhile until I figured out she had changed accounts and was using a different email for her communications that she didn't want me to know about. It took me some time and a little…I don't know the word to say looking where I was not supposed to…"

"Snooping or detective work?" Amanda offered.

"Yes," she smiled. "That's the word—snooping. I was snooping and eventually I found the other email address she was using. Thankfully, Bernie was a creature of habit and she used the same password." She gave a genuine smile. "That is when I learned of you. I admit that when I found out that she had a relationship here with you that I was hurt, upset, and worried about how you would affect my relationship with her. After reading your emails with her, I guess I resigned myself to the fact that if she was here with you, I knew she was safe and not with anyone else. I felt that one competitor for her attention was better than many others. It seemed for a while that she had stopped cheating. There were no more emails from many different women...only from you and rarely, maybe only once or twice, others. Mostly, they seemed casual and of no importance to her. I came to think of you as a member of my extended family. Someone who helped me keep Bernie mostly for just us."

"We all contend with difficulties in different ways. I ended up leaving, but you had your daughter to consider."

"Yes. I guess so, but what were my options? I had no means of support, so I kept quiet, took care of our house, and took care of our daughter." Aline paused as if reviewing the decisions, the choices she'd been forced to make. "If I left Bernie and took my daughter to be on our own, we could never live the same way as we did with Bernie. So, I swallowed my pride and looked the other way. I don't mean it to sound so calculating, because I did love her and aside from her cheating, she was good to me and our daughter."

"I was always aware that Bernie was capable of cheating on me. I guess you probably already know this if you have been reading our emails. Just a few months ago, we had a terrible fight, and I left her because I found a note from another woman in her jacket pocket thanking her for a wonderful night together."

"Yes, I knew. I'm sorry."

"Aline, Bernie cared for you and your daughter. You and Anna were her first priority. She left a letter for me, telling me about her relationship with you and about her daughter. I swear, I didn't know about you or I would never have gotten involved with her."

"I know that. It should not be your guilt to live with, only Bernie's."

"Thank you for that. But, in the letter she left me, it's important for you to know that its purpose was to inform me about your existence in her life and that you would be coming for the reading of the will, telling me that I was not named in it. The rest of her letter dealt with asking me to protect her secret...to protect you and Anna. She didn't want you to know the true nature of our relationship. She wanted me to continue with the ruse that I was her cousin. Bernie's first priority was that you and your daughter not learn about me and the extent of my relationship with her."

"Thank you for sharing that. You didn't have to."

Amanda checked her watch. "I have to leave now, Aline. I have a flight to catch. I'm going back to New York." She washed and rinsed her cup and placed it on a paper towel to dry. Amanda picked up her bag and turned to face the woman who had shared Bernie's life with her. "I guess this is good-bye. Here are the keys to the house."

"Yes, thank you. Given different circumstances I think we could have been friends. You were good to Bernie, I think. When she spoke of you, as her cousin of course, she had nothing but good things to report about how good you were to her. Take care, Amanda."

It was an extremely strange situation. Oddly, she felt close to this woman who was, in reality, a stranger. "You too, Aline." The two women embraced briefly. *Oh, this is too weird,* Amanda thought. She turned and let herself out.

\*\*\*

Amanda took a cab to the airport. She didn't look back as the cab pulled away from her previous residence. She preferred to look ahead to where she was going. *Home...home to Mallory.* When she arrived at the airport, she called her partner.

"Hi honey." Mallory smiled at hearing Amanda's voice. "I miss you."

"I miss you too. You'll never know just how much."

"When do you think you'll be able to come home?"

"I'm sitting in the airport as we speak."

"Seriously? Oh good. What about the reading of the will and all those boxes?"

"Oh, long story. I've had the most bizarre couple of days you can imagine."

"Well, you can tell me all about everything when you get home. You sound tired."

"Yes...exhausted."

"Okay here's what you do. Go to the airport bar and have a couple of drinks to help you relax. Then, when you get on the plane, take off your shoes and get a blanket and pillow. I want you to sleep all the way home so you'll be rested when you get here. I have plans for you."

"Whatever they are, will be absolutely perfect to me as long as it involves being with you."

"Have you been doing your exercises?" The PT had given Amanda some exercises to help her build strength back up in her injured arms.

"Yes, my little slave driver, I have." It was then that Amanda's flight was called to board. "I've got to go honey. They just called my plane to board."

"I'll pick you up. What time does your flight arrive?"

Amanda provided the flight number and projected arrival time. "I'll see you there. Love you."

"I love you. I can't wait to see you. I have another assignment for you when you get home!" Mallory said seductively.

Amanda knew what Mallory meant. At least she was hoping she knew. "Do I need to be dressed to do it?"

"No, I am reasonably sure clothes would be optional...definitely not required."

"Okay, I'm eagerly awaiting my assignment. I'm sure you can provide any added details once I'm there and ready to comply." They both chuckled, happy to know they would be together in a few short hours.

## Chapter 22

Her flight landed and Amanda exhaled a deep breath of air. *I'm home at last, and am coming home to the woman I love with a free heart and a clear mind.* Amanda hurried down the ramp, her eyes scanning the waiting crowd for Mallory. Their eyes met across the room. *I am totally and absolutely, completely in love with her. Not a doubt in my mind. We've been through so much in the few months we've been together. Even when I was cranky or frustrated while I was recovering, she was the epitome of patience. I never once doubted that she loved me, even when I was at my worst. What can I do to make her life easier? She works so hard. I don't know what it'll be, but I'll do something.*

Amanda had not yet told Mallory about the life insurance policy. She wanted to wait to let Mallory read the letter Bernie left for her. First, she wanted them to talk about their relationship. Once that was settled, she would share the news and show Mallory the policy. That way the money would not become an issue between them and whatever decision they made about their future together.

Mallory asked. "So, I'm surprised you could come home so soon. Glad, but still surprised." She winked. "Tell me what happened. How come you didn't have to stay for the reading of the will? What changed?"

"Remember the envelope the lawyer gave me at the meeting with Bernie's parents?"

Mallory nodded, her attention focused on pulling into traffic.

"Well, it was very interesting. There was a letter in there from Bernie and some pictures and a few other surprises." Downplaying the importance of the contents of the envelope, Amanda said, "I'll show you everything later at home when you can look at everything, okay?"

"Sure. What about your bizarre day you mentioned. Tell me about that."

"Well, that was related, in a way, to the letter. So I'll tell you the whole story after you read that."

"Okay, you've got me eager to read this letter and hear about your day, but I'm resigned to waiting till after we get home. I surrender."

Amanda laughed. "Good, because you told me you had plans for me when I got home. You didn't forget about that already, did you?"

"No, I haven't forgotten." She squeezed Amanda's hand. After a few moments of silence, Mallory asked. "So your business in California is concluded then?"

"Yes, for the most part. I'm just waiting for a check."

"Check? What check? For your share of the house, you mean?" When Amanda didn't reply, Mallory glanced over at her lover who was staring back at her with her eyebrows arched.

"Okay, I know. After I read the letter, right?"

"Now you've got it." She reached over to slide her hand up Mallory's thigh, tucking into the valley where her thigh met her torso. "Just in case you forgot while I was away, I love you very much."

"I didn't forget. Ditto." She knew that always made Amanda roll her eyes and was not disappointed when she glanced over at her lover. They both laughed at their inside joke. It was not too long until Mallory turned into the driveway.

Mallory got Amanda's bag from the trunk, took her hand, and led her into the house. Once inside, Mallory dropped the bag and pulled Amanda to her. "I missed you so much," she said after she kissed her thoroughly.

Once they divested themselves of their clothes, they snuggled together in bed. "It feels very decadent for us to be going to bed when everyone else is just getting up."

Amanda was curled against Mallory with her head resting on Mallory's shoulder. Her hand was lazily stroking her lover's body paying particular attention to her breasts. She breathed in Mallory's fresh scent and brushed her cheek against the soft skin of Mallory's nipple."

"If you don't stop that real soon, neither of us will be getting any sleep any time soon."

Amanda slid her hand down Mallory's stomach stopping with her fingers resting at the point just above the top of Mallory's most sensitive part. "Is that what you really want, sleep?" Amanda asked inching her hand slowly lower through the tight thatch of curls. Sliding her fingers lightly over the now erect and sensitive tissue, Mallory rewarded Amanda with a sudden intake of breath. Another stroke elicited a moan from Mallory and encouraged Amanda's further exploration. She slipped inside her lover who was already wet and ready for her. She slid in and out, slow and deep, curling her fingers as she stroked out, a touch that seemed to have a particularly positive effect on Mallory. Her hips began to rock in time with Amanda's thrusts. Amanda felt Mallory tighten around her and knew she was close, so she increased her tempo slightly. Mallory tipped over the top and reached down to still Amanda's hand.

Amanda pushed higher in the bed and pulled her lover to her cradling her in her arms. "Okay?"

"Mmm. More than okay." Once Mallory recovered her breath, she continued. "That was very different...intense, but gentle. I love how an essentially repetitious act can yield such different sensations...different results."

Amanda leaned back to look at Mallory, a puzzled look on her face. "Do you really want to have this conversation right now?"

Mallory chuckled. "Why, do you have a better idea?"

"I'm convinced that I could come up with one given the proper motivation."

"Hmm, let me see what I can come up with." Mallory began to kiss her way down Amanda's body, eventually settling between her legs. She used her tongue to stimulate Amanda to arousal before she slid her fingers inside.

"That's good. Don't make me wait. I need you."

Mallory increased her pace, stroking in and out with her fingers as she tongued Amanda's clitoris. When Amanda tensed and held her breath, Mallory added just a little pressure, which caused Amanda to scream Mallory's name as she came.

Finally satisfied, they rested quietly with arms and legs tangled together. Amanda drew a finger down the bridge of Mallory's nose, down over the tip, and traced the outline of her mouth. "You're very quiet. What are you thinking about?"

Mallory rolled to her side and propped up her head on her hand. "Now Amanda, what kind of romance writer are you? This is the afterglow. Of course, I was thinking about how much I like spending time with you. You have such good ideas for how to spend idle time."

"Okay, how's this for an idea?" Amanda tickled Mallory until she begged for mercy.

"I surrender. I surrender," Mallory squeaked, finally calming as Amanda stopped, reaching out to pull Amanda into her embrace. "Got any other ideas I might like better?"

"In fact, I do. You said, before I left, that when I got back you wanted to talk about where we were headed...about our future together."

"Yes, I did. When do you want to do that?"

"Now?"

Recognizing that Amanda was serious, Mallory sat up and leaned against the headboard. "All right, what do you want to discuss?"

"Where do you see us five, ten, twenty years from now?"

"I don't know where we'll be living. I would like to think, that wherever it is, we'd be together...and happy. Yes, we'll definitely be happy. What about you?"

"I see the same thing. I love you, Mallory and I'd like to make you happy."

"Just being here with me and loving me like you do, makes me happy."

"What about work? Do you see yourself staying in nursing?"

Mallory pursed her lips, an indication that she was giving the question serious consideration before she responded. "I'm not sure about that. It's what I've been trained to do. I could be a nurse practitioner, or I could teach. But I don't think I'd like to make either of those changes at this point in my life. I think if I could ever afford it financially, I would love to give up administration and go back to patient care. That's a hard job, but in a different way, because it's much more physically demanding...administration is more stressful. I can't see myself as an old woman being a floor nurse, providing direct care. As much as I'd rather do that, it becomes extremely difficult as one gets older. So, despite the stress, administration will probably be what I do for as long as I work."

"If you didn't stay in nursing, what would you do?"

"Gee, I never gave it much thought. Other than nursing, I don't think of myself as having any marketable skills, although there are probably a million options open that I never considered."

"Don't be so literal. Dream bigger. If you didn't have to work, would you?"

Mallory thought seriously about the question before she responded. "Although the thought of not working is attractive, I think I might grow a bit bored after a while. So I think I'd want to do something, maybe part-time. Whatever it might be,

I'd want to be my own boss...no more begging the powers that be for permission for anything."

"Okay, so you'd want to be your own boss. Self-employed, part-time."

"Yes, but that's not realistic...there wouldn't be enough income and more than likely no benefits. Why all the questions?"

"I think it's healthy to have dreams and goals. Come on. Imagine that anything is possible. If that were so, what business would you own?"

Finally getting into the fun of the exercise, Mallory turned towards her lover, propping her head on her hand. She allowed herself to dream and imagine a future where she could have anything she wanted. "Hmm. Okay, I think I'd definitely want to do something service oriented...something where people would be happy with a project because it's something they couldn't do for themselves. A built in satisfaction factor." She grinned. "I'm sick of people complaining."

"I hear you."

"What about you?"

"I'd take care of you and write full time...things I want to write, not necessarily things I have to write to support myself. A subtle, but very critical difference," Amanda noted with a smile.

"So what does this exercise accomplish again, except to depress me?"

Amanda laughed. "Don't be depressed. I can see into your future, you know."

"Well, Carnac, we have something in common then, because I know what you'll be doing later on today while I'm toiling away in the salt mine."

Amanda smiled at Mallory's joke about Johnny Carson's prescient character, Carnac the Magnificent, shifting to allow herself a better position so she could look into Mallory's eyes. "Tell me then, other than keeping the home fires burning, what would it be that I would be doing?"

Mallory took Amanda's hand into her own smiling as she made eye contact, "Planning our wedding. I love you and want to spend the rest of our lives together. I want us to get married. Now that it's legal here in New York, I want us to have that. Will you marry me, Amanda?"

Amanda turned to face Mallory, draping herself over Mallory's naked chest before sliding her arms around her lover. "It would be my extreme pleasure to marry you. Yes! Definitely yes!"

## Chapter 23

Mallory and Amanda fell asleep wrapped together. When they woke up, Mallory asked, "So, let's talk some more about our wedding. Do you want an engagement ring or just matching bands?"

"I don't know. Never gave it any thought before. What about you?"

"Jewelry has never been my thing. For sure no diamond engagement ring for me. I want a white gold band, but with some sort of character, not just plain. I'd like either a design or some sort of ornamentation, but it has to be flat. I don't like something sticking up so it catches on things."

"Yes, I agree. So matching bands it is." Amanda hugged her lover.

"On my next day off we can go shopping for them if you want, but in the meantime, keep an eye out in your shopping excursions for something we might like. You'll know them when you see them and I'll be happy with whatever you pick."

"I'll look, but you get final approval. We can shop together, too."

"That sounds like fun. Still, if you see something, don't let my not being there stop you." Mallory craned her neck to look at the time on the bedside table. "I'm getting hungry. Let's get something to eat and we can think about our wedding. Big or small?"

They continued their conversation on the way to the kitchen. "Small, definitely small. My brother won't come, so the only person I really need there is you. Well, maybe Dana and Nic, and a few of our other friends. I'm sure you'd like Ren and Lindy there. Maybe we could ask Jo and the others who helped us when I had my accident. What about your family?"

They chatted as they moved effortlessly around the kitchen, preparing lunch. Taking the items needed to make lunch from the cupboards and fridge, Amanda said, "Here, you make the salad and I'll fix us a sandwich."

"Okay. Yeah, I'm not sure my dad would come, but I'd love my mom to be there. I know my dad loves me...but he chose for most of the time Piper and I were together, to pretend that my relationship with her was just a friendship. It was easier for him to deal with it that way. Mom is okay with me being a lesbian. Dad loves me—he just doesn't really approve. He did come to love Piper and seemed to understand that I loved her like he loves my mother when he saw how heartbroken I was when Piper died. I don't know, maybe Mom and I together could convince him to come."

Amanda took a bite of her sandwich and poured some oil and vinegar on her salad giving Mallory time to think about Amanda's brother being unwilling to come. Mallory volunteered, "Maybe I can ask your brother to come instead of you asking?"

"I'm not sure about that. Spencer might be rude to you."

Mallory shrugged. "He certainly wouldn't be the first and most likely not the last. Since he won't talk to you, having me call is the only option open to us if you want him to come for a visit. I'm willing to take the chance if you want me to," Mallory offered.

"Let me think about it, okay?"

Recalling her family's rejection of her after she confessed to them that she was a lesbian, Amanda could feel the knot growing in her stomach. She exhaled a long slow breath in an effort to control the gut-wrenching physical response the remembrance of that event always caused. Amanda changed the subject. They finished eating and cleaned up the kitchen.

Amanda got them each a glass of wine. "Come join me in the dining room. I have something for you to read."

She went to her carry-on bag, got the letters from Bernie, and handed them to Mallory to read. Mallory read the letter to the part that Bernie said she began a relationship with Amanda despite her involvement with Aline.

"That bitch!" Mallory glanced up with tears glistening in her eyes, knowing how painful it must have been for Amanda to read the revelation. "Oh, honey, I'm so sorry." She used her hand to wipe the tears from her face. "I know it's said that it's not right to speak ill of the dead, but this woman certainly had a warped sense of the meaning of fidelity, didn't she? What pictures did she leave for you?"

Amanda slid the picture of Bernie's family and the individual picture of their daughter across the table toward Mallory. All Mallory could manage was to shake her head.

"How could she do this?"

"I was so concerned when I thought she was cheating on me." Amanda sighed. "Who knew that all that time I was actually the other woman? You know, Aline knew about me."

"How?"

"She snooped into Bernie's emails. She seemed to know there were other women as well. She was no fool. She seemed to feel that she had no options but to remain in the relationship, not only for her own sake, but especially for the well being of her daughter."

"So you talked to her...to Aline?"

"Yes, on that day, was it just yesterday? Remember, I told you it was probably the most bizarre day of my life. She was really quite lovely and seemed to hold no ill will towards me. As unbelievable as it seems, she expressed genuine appreciation that I was good to Bernie. When I gave her the keys to the house, she hugged me good-bye and told me she thought we could have been friends under different circumstances."

Mallory uttered, "Humph! You certainly are right about it being bizarre. Too much like being a 'sister wife' for my taste."

"Well, there's one more little bit of the not normal left to show you." Amanda slid the insurance policy Bernie left her across the table to Mallory, then awaited her reaction.

"What's this?"

"Open it."

Mallory flipped open the document and scanned down the page. Suddenly, her eyebrows shot up. "My God! Amanda, this is unbelievable. You're a very wealthy woman." Then, as the realization struck her Amanda's financial status could have an impact on their lives together, she chuckled. With a broad grin on her face she said, "Just remember that I asked you to marry me before I knew you were rich as Croesus."

"So, now you know why I was asking you what you'd like to do for a living if you could do anything you wanted to do. You actually can."

"It's your money, not mine." Mallory shrugged.

"Oh, please. You're not going to take that attitude, are you?" Amanda came around to sit on Mallory's lap. She placed a light kiss on Mallory's lips then looked her in the eyes. "Truth is, money or no money, I'll end up doing the same thing I'm doing now. To me, having money will mean I can write what I want, not what others want or others pay me to produce. For me, the true value of having money is what I can do with it to benefit those I love."

Amanda gave Mallory a few moments to absorb the meaning of her words and to grasp the potential impact Amanda's inheritance could have on their lives.

"Obviously, I've had more time to think about this than you have...how would you like to go into business with me?" Amanda touched Mallory's face with her hand, a smile on her lips.

"Business? What business?"

"Well, I've been thinking and here's what I'm considering." Amanda shared her idea with her lover.

"That's sheer genius. Besides, I think it would be fun, too." Mallory reluctantly glanced down at her watch. "Damn! I've got to go to work. I'll stay later tonight so I can be home for a late dinner on Friday night. Let's have Nic and Dana over for dinner then and tell them all our news."

Amanda kissed Mallory goodbye and went to the phone to call their friends.

Nic answered the phone with a cheery, "Hello."

"Hey, Nic. Where's your other half?"

"She's not home from work yet, why?"

"I wondered if you'd join us for dinner Friday?"

Nic accepted the invitation on behalf of both of them. "It'll be good to see you and catch up. By the way, are you busy this afternoon?" Nic asked.

"No, what do you have in mind?"

"I've taken off early today, because I want to go shopping." Nic explained her plans.

An hour later, they were in the jewelry store searching through wedding jewelry. Based upon advice from Amanda, Nic picked out a beautiful deep blue sapphire ring with diamonds on either side of the main stone and bought matching white gold bands for each of them. The beautiful thin bands had a channel containing alternating diamonds and blue sapphires set flat into the ring.

"She'll love them, Nic. I promise. Sapphires are her favorite stone, but remember what they say about diamonds. So, you've definitely got a winner there." When the clerk wrapped Nic's purchase, Amanda hugged Nic and gave her a kiss on the cheek. "I'm so happy for you two."

While she was in the store, waiting for Nic to conclude her purchase, she found a wedding band she liked. She preferred plain bands, no diamonds, or other stones, but Mallory said she wanted some design in it. A unique band, three thin strands of white gold braided into a circle, caught her eye. She absolutely fell in love with it. Both she and Mallory had small hands, and this thin band would be perfect for both of them. Once she determined that she could get two of them, she placed a small deposit to hold them until she could return with Mallory to see if Mallory liked them as much as she did.

On the way home, she asked Nic, "How do you plan to propose? Do you have something special planned?"

"I don't know. I'm so excited, I don't know if I can wait to make special plans. I think I might just find an opportune time, drop to one knee, and beg her to take me on. Then, maybe we can all go celebrate over the weekend with a nice dinner somewhere fancy."

"I doubt there'll be much begging involved. But celebrating sounds like fun."

\*\*\*

Later that afternoon, Amanda began to research the information she needed to start up the new business. Confident that her friends would be interested in her idea, she called several real estate agents to get details on office space closer to, but not in, the city and made an appointment for an initial consultation with a lawyer for early the next day to learn what licenses and other legal papers she'd need to obtain.

The next morning, she checked out the two offices that were available within the area she wanted that fit her criteria for size, met with the lawyer, and was home in time to start dinner. While dinner was cooking, she typed up notes and printed out four copies of all the pertinent data she wanted to discuss after they had eaten. Then she waited for the meal to cook and her friends and Mallory to arrive home from work. She checked the time at least twenty times in the half hour before everyone arrived and read the notes over several times to be sure of her data. The meal was served and the four women chatted amiably through dinner.

"We'll clean up," Amanda said.

"Good," said Nic with a wink for Amanda.

Mallory looked at the two of them wondering what was going on, but said nothing.

When Dana and Nic headed for the living room, Amanda pulled Mallory to her and whispered in her ear, "I think Nic is going to ask Dana to marry her."

"Oh, I see...and how do you know this?"

"Because I helped her pick out their rings yesterday. Which reminds me, I found a set I liked for us. I put a deposit on them, but if you don't like them we can get the money back. I was afraid they wouldn't be there when we went back."

There was a shriek from the living room and Dana came charging into the kitchen. "Look! We're getting married." She proudly showed off her ring. "Nic couldn't have done better...it's like I picked it myself."

"We're very happy for you. Maybe we can have a double wedding," Amanda said hugging Dana.

Dana looked from Amanda to Mallory. "You too. That's wonderful news. We're all so lucky." She hugged them both.

Amanda pulled the cork on the chilled champagne she had put on ice earlier just in case Nic popped the question. They all agreed on the location of their celebration dinner and talked a bit about wanting to do a double wedding. After they toasted each other, they settled in the living room. When talk of weddings diminished and their chatter turned to casual topics, Amanda turned the conversation in a different direction.

"I'm happy to hear you two are planning to make your relationship permanent, because I asked you here tonight to discuss a business proposition I have for all of us. Let's go sit down at the table. I have things for you to read."

When they were all settled at the table, Amanda began. "As I mentioned, I have an offer to make that would be a dramatic change for all of us. I want us to start a business together."

Mallory already knew most of the details about Amanda's proposal. She focused her attention primarily on the reaction from Nic and Dana as Amanda began to reveal the details of her plan.

"I know the two of you don't want to travel any more. So, I am proposing that we enter into an equal partnership. Based on what I've read and the research I've done, with the world now one large global economy, projections are for an increase in the demand for people of different nationalities to be working together. They project a large increase in the demand for translation services. As translators, what do you believe our chances would be if we started our own company? If there is a need, how long would it be until we turn a profit sufficient to support all of us?"

Dana spoke first. "Well, as to if there is a need—there's always a need. I would imagine that with the contacts Nic and I have, we could have enough business to keep both of us busy within the first six months and enough to hire a couple of part-timers, within the first year. We only need a storefront for the office, as the work really could be done at home. If we're successful, we could add translators.. One offshoot might be to offer language classes and tutoring along with our translation services."

"Although not required to teach a foreign language in this situation, I have teaching credentials that might lend credence to our doing instruction." Nic suggested.

"I can do a website for us," Amanda offered.

Mallory shrugged. "I had four years of Spanish in college. Although I'm far from fluent, I can get by conversationally, certainly well enough that I could interact with clients seeking services. Plus, with my experience at the hospital, I'm sure if given some guidelines, I can do the office administration...make quotes, keep the books, do customer relations, and whatever other administrative duties there are to free the rest of you to do the translation and teaching."

Amanda handed a piece of paper to each of them along with a pen. "Write down the minimum amount of salary you each need so you can meet your financial obligations for the first year. Mix them up and pass them to me." She laughed when she saw the conservative numbers.

Dana asked, "What's so amusing?"

"Well, you're all within a couple of thousand dollars of each other and about fifteen thousand lower than I anticipated you'd be."

"Okay Amanda, this is a wonderful fantasy, but who is going to put up the money to help us go into business? I mean it would be great working together and even greater being our own bosses, but still..."

"I'm going to do it," Amanda said with a sweet smile.

"What did you do, rob a bank?" Dana asked. "This could be expensive for the first several months until we can generate some income."

"In a manner of speaking. Bernie ended up being very generous." She told them an abbreviated version of what had transpired in California. "So, you see, I need an investment and I want to invest in my friends. It's not totally an altruistic investment. In exchange for a twenty-five percent share of whatever profit we make after the first year, I'll guarantee everyone's salary for the first two years at the salary specified here." She handed each of them the business proposal she had typed up that afternoon. "If we're profitable sooner, we split everything evenly."

"This is very generous, Amanda. Why do that? You'll not be getting your initial investment back. We should be paying you back for that," Nic said.

"No. Over time, I'll get it back. I know it'll take up much of my time initially, to get things up and running. Then, as we become more established, I'd see my involvement substantially curtailed. After that, for as long as we own the business, I'm getting a full quarter share for a minimal initial investment of time and start up costs. I want to be free to write and this will enable me to do that." She gave them some time to look over the notes and figures she had compiled for their review and suggestions.

That was the first meeting of many the group had. They finally agreed to all the specifics, had their agreement formalized, and began to develop and implement their plan.

\*\*\*

They began preparing for Christmas. Nic's mom accepted their invitation to come for the holidays, as did Mallory's mom and dad. Her dad was a little reluctant, but they managed to convince him.

Amanda wrote her brother with an invitation to come visit for the holidays. She explained that she had entered into a very happy relationship with a woman named Dr. Mallory Barnes and that the two of them were hopeful he would come up and bring his wife and the kids. When she had no response from him, Mallory offered to call him. Mallory knew almost immediately that the conversation would not be pleasant when Spencer answered the phone.

"Hello. Is this Spencer James?" asked Mallory.

"Yes, who is this?"

"Hello, Spencer. This is Mallory Barnes, your sister's partner."

"Oh, yeah. The dyke my sister lives with."

She was pissed at him before she made the call for the way he had treated Amanda over the years, and his surly manner on the phone forced Mallory to lose her temper. "That would be Doctor Dyke to you," she replied sharply. She was surprised when he laughed.

"Well, not only are you a lesbian, but you're a lesbian with an attitude. So what do you want from me?"

She exhaled a long slow breath in an effort to calm her anger. "Well, although this seems rather pointless now, we were hoping you and your family would consider coming up for a visit this Christmas. I'd like very much to meet Amanda's family."

"Are you kidding me? Why? I love Amanda, but she knows I don't approve of her lifestyle. I didn't approve when she first told us she was gay, and I haven't changed my mind over the years that have passed. So, she might as well stop sending the notes to the kids and me. It makes me sick to think of what she does."

"What she does?" Knowing exactly what he meant, she came back innocently with, "You mean that she's a successful author?"

"Don't be a smart ass. You know what I mean. That she screws women."

"Well, technically that's not true. It's just me that she screws, as you so delicately put it, so the use of the plural tense of woman is really incorrect."

"Look, you're wasting my time, although I have to give you credit for perseverance. You don't give up."

"Well, I have a good reason. I love your sister and I know that Amanda misses having family although, now that we've talked, I can't imagine why she misses having you in her life."

Mallory was surprised by another hearty laugh from Amanda's brother. "You know, Doctor Dyke, if you weren't a lesbian, I might just like you. You've got guts."

"I'm sure you are aware, Spencer, that this country is populated by Republicans and Democrats who sit on opposite sides of the political fence. I hear tell that many of them are friends. They just agree to not talk about politics. Can't you do the same with your sister? Just not talk about her being a lesbian, I mean?"

"Nice try, but it's just not the exactly the same, now is it?"

"No, I guess not, not exactly. It's just that it does seem a little silly that you both profess to love each other, yet you can't seem to overlook this one little detail about her life." Mallory pushed on. "I know I'm probably wasting my time, but I'm going to ask you a favor." Before Spencer could protest or make another surly comment, Mallory cut him off. "I know you're going to say why, what for, or something like that. You see, Spencer, I'm not asking for me, I'm asking one last time for your sister's sake. Don't answer me right now...just think about this. Are you proud of yourself for having disowned your sister? You've had the blessing of hearing from her regularly, knowing that she's okay because she writes. What would you feel if she were to stop writing to you? Would you wonder if she were still alive? Wonder if she was okay?" She paused for a few minutes to let him consider the questions.

"Of course I'd wonder. I'm not a monster."

"Then stop acting like one and send her a note or pictures of the kids...something...anything. She loves your kids and God only knows why, but she still loves you even after all these years you've failed to respond to her."

There was silence on the other end of the phone.

"You still there, Spencer?"

"Yes, I'm here. Okay, I'll think about what you've said, but don't get your hopes up too high."

"Funny thing about hope, Spencer. It is innately, by definition, an elevated expectation for an otherwise less than desirable situation, isn't it? So, I speak for Amanda when I say, she hopes to hear from you for Christmas. Her email address is ajames@amandajames.com. Will you think about sending her a picture of the kids for Christmas at least?"

"I'll think about it, Doctor Dyke."

"Spencer, in a rather masochistic way, this has been an interesting conversation." She laughed. "Merry Christmas, Spencer."

There was a pause before he responded. Mallory thought he would just hang up, but Spencer chuckled. "Okay, Doc. Merry Christmas to you. I promise I'll think about all you said, but don't..."

Mallory interrupted, "I know...don't get my hopes up." She laughed. "Good-bye Spencer. I do genuinely hope you and your family have a wonderful holiday."

She hung up the phone. *That was probably a huge waste of my time. At least I tried and, to his credit, Spencer had heard me out to the end.*

They were all in the Christmas spirit. Mallory got a call from Ren and Lindy shortly before the holidays. She and Lindy were planning a visit into the city to do some Christmas shopping, see a couple of shows, and visit some museums. They declined Amanda's offer to stay with them for this visit, since their stay was short and they had already made too many commitments in the city for it to be convenient. However, they wanted to meet for dinner while they were in town. Amanda suggested that they come to Mallory's house for dinner instead. Amanda also asked Nic and Dana to join them for the meal. They also invited Amanda's rescuers, Pam, Jean, Meg, and Jo to join them. Pam and Meg weren't available, but both Jean and Jo accepted. Lindy and Ren were pleased they would get to meet some of Mallory and Amanda's friends.

The group of women spent an enjoyable time together. Gradually, over the course of the evening's conversation, Lindy got an opportunity to address Jo. "Mallory tells me that you're a policewoman. The new novel I'm working on has a policewoman as a main character. Later, I'd like to ask you some questions if it's okay."

"Sure. I'd be happy to help."

When dinner concluded, Lindy and Jo huddled in the corner of the living room for a few minutes while Lindy described the next book she was working on. The others continued the conversation about the new business the women were starting before the talk turned to a number of other topics.

As their conversation drew to a close, Lindy asked Jo, "Do you have a card with you?" When Jo shook her head, Lindy handed Jo two of her business cards and a pen. "Here's mine, and if you don't mind, could you put your phone number on the back of the extra one? I'd love to interview you about procedures and, maybe when I'm finished, you'd be willing to read my book and let me know if it sounds authentic? As a police officer you'd be the perfect person to help me develop my main character, and I could use some help with all of the technical details."

"I'd be pleased to help in any way I can." Jo replied.

Maybe when I'm farther along in my story, you'll consider coming to visit Ren and me at the Inn. We'd love to have you. Company is always welcome in the winter when we don't have guests."

As they prepared to leave, Ren repeated the invitation Lindy had made to Jo earlier, telling everyone to come up for a visit. "We've shortened our season, so it's just the two of us rattling around up there a good part of the year. We'd love to have the company. It's beautiful up in Maine, if you'll forgive our bragging."

Amanda responded for both herself and Mallory. "We both enjoyed our last visit with you while we were on the cruise and have talked about driving up that way for our next vacation."

Turning towards Nic, Dana, Jo, and Jean, Lindy added to Ren's invitation. "We are serious. We hope you'll all come along, too. We have ample room for everyone." She smiled warmly.

Ren and Lindy hugged everyone good-bye before they left. Jo and Jean departed next. On their ride home, before Jo dropped Jean off at her home, they discussed what a great time they'd had that evening. Jo talked about how excited she was that Lindy had asked for her number so she could ask her about her profession as a policewoman. Jean was almost as excited for her friend as Jo was for herself.

"Maybe she'll include your name in the credits. Wouldn't that be neat?"

"Yeah, I guess it would, but I really look forward to just getting to spend some more time talking to her. She's a lot of fun, and she and Ren make a great couple." They continued talking about the evening all the way home.

After the others left, Nic and Dana lingered to do their own recap of the evening with their friends. "Ren and Lindy are a lovely couple, Mallory. Thanks for including us tonight. Too bad they don't live closer," Nic said.

Everyone agreed.

Dana said, "Wouldn't it be fun to do a caravan up to their place in Maine later this year? It really isn't that far from here and it would be a fun trip for a long weekend."

"It does sound like fun. Let's revisit the idea once we have the business up and running." Mallory added, squelching a smile, "We'll talk to the bosses and see if we can all get a long weekend off together!"

***

Christmas was a happy time for Nic, Dana, Mallory, and Amanda. Nic's mother came for a few days over the holiday, as did Mallory's mom and dad. They had a wonderful time with their family members. Mallory's dad was reluctant to leave home for the holidays at first, but once he arrived, he seemed cheered by all the good Christmas spirit and feelings. Everyone pitched in to decorate both houses, and on Christmas Eve, they gathered around the tree and each told of their favorite Christmas memory.

As they retired for the evening, Mallory encouraged Amanda to check her email one last time. "Maybe Spencer wrote or sent something. We knew he wouldn't come, but maybe..." She shrugged leaving the hope unstated.

Amanda opened her email and exclaimed, "Oh, Mallory, look." Her brother had sent a picture of him, his wife, and the kids. The message read..."Merry Christmas Sis, to you and the Doc. Tell her to keep a rein on those hopes, and tell her that I'm working hard to try not to think about politics. She'll know what I mean."

Mallory, laughed when she read the message.

"Mallory, what's he talking about?" Mallory briefly explained the conversation she had with Spencer the previous week.

"Thank you, sweetheart. That's the best present you could ever have given me." Amanda kissed her lover and drew her close. "Now, this elf has one more present for you." She led her to the bed to deliver her gift.

*\*\**

"We've done pretty well for ourselves in such a short time, haven't we?" Amanda said as she snuggled against Mallory's neck. "In the short time we've been together, we've developed a wonderful group of friends, have plans for some dramatic changes to our careers, and because of your efforts my brother is back in touch with me. I'm so excited about our life together that I can't wait for tomorrow. There's so much to look forward to and so much to do."

Mallory nodded her agreement. With a twinkle in her eye, Mallory suggested, "But before we tackle tomorrow, there are some things left for you to do tonight."

Not catching Mallory's meaning right away, Amanda frowned. "Really?"

"Absolutely." Mallory pointed to her lips. "You need to place a kiss here." Amanda complied and Mallory pointed to her left breast. "And here."

She did as requested, but raised her eyes to Mallory's, one eyebrow elevated, waiting. When no further instructions came right away, Amanda smiled. "I love you. She kissed her lover softly. "And?"

Mallory pulled Amanda closer. "And, what?"

"Nothing, just waiting."

"Waiting, what for?"

Amanda leaned closer. "I'm awaiting my assignment." She didn't have to wait long as Mallory pulled Amanda on top of her to whisper into her ear her next request.

## The End

## *About AJ Adaire*

If you had told me, when I was struggling to write a one page story for my high school writing composition class, that I would one day write seven novels, I would have bet everything that would never happen. No one, especially me, ever considered it a remote possibility. Thirty years later, during a blizzard, having read all the lesbian fiction books I had in the house, I declared to my surprised partner, "I think I could write one of these." So you see, I wrote my first book just to see if I could do it. The completed novel occupied space on my bookshelf, untouched for many years. One day while in a cleaning frenzy, I considered disposing of the neatly stacked but now age-yellowed pages. As I began to read the long forgotten work, I was surprised to discover that the story was enjoyable. Editing and retyping the first book provided a new sense of accomplishment and additional tales followed.

Now retired, I live on the east coast with my partner of twenty-nine years. Because we love a challenge we provide a loving home for two spoiled cats instead of a dog. In addition to writing, any spare time is devoted to editing, reading, mastering new computer programs, and socializing with friends.

My published romance novels include books one and two of the Friends Series: Sunset Island (September 2013) and Awaiting My Assignment (November 2013). The Interim, a novelette that provides additional details about the life of Sunset Island's Ren Madison, was released in November 2013. Anything Your Heart Desires, the third book in the Friends Series, will be available early in 2014. I have four other novels in process.

### Contact Information

E-mail: aj@ajadaire.com
Website: http://www.ajadaire.com
Facebook: https://www.facebook.com/pages/AJ
Desert Palm Press: www.desertpalmpress.com

# SNEAK PEAK

# *ANYTHING YOUR HEART DESIRES*

## *Chapter 1*

Meg slid an arm across Jo Martin's stomach and snuggled closer. Jo could tell by the woman's regular breathing that she was, thankfully, still asleep. *Oh God, what have I done now? Shit, shit, shit! I should have stopped this...before we had sex. Why didn't I?* Jo groaned inwardly and exhaled a long sigh. *I could have just pushed her away, or simply said 'no.' What the hell have I done? How could I be so stupid?* The events of the afternoon raced through her mind. She wanted to put her fingers to her forehead and massage away the headache that was forming between her eyebrows but refrained, fearful of waking the sleeping woman next to her.

Earlier in the day, Jo had just returned from Christmas vacation with her family at their cabin in the mountains near Edinborough, New York. She had not even unpacked her suitcase when Meg stopped by unannounced. Jo opened the door for her friend expecting their usual brief greeting. A split second later, their normally casual hug and kiss hello took on a totally new dimension. Meg, definitely the aggressor, wouldn't release Jo after their brief hug. Instead, she pulled Jo firmly against her, pinned her against the wall, and kissed her thoroughly.

"I missed you more than you'll ever know," Meg uttered before pulling Jo against her to kiss her again.

Jo's mind wandered through the earlier events acknowledging that she'd responded more out of loneliness and surprise than out of desire for her friend. With the deed done, it was too late now to undo her error. Guilt and regret gnawed at her for what she'd allowed to happen. In her heart, she knew she didn't want a relationship with Meg. Until the kiss in the hall earlier, she hadn't even really thought of Meg as a potential sexual partner. They were friends, never more than that.

Jo was normally attracted to women who were smaller in stature and shorter than her own height of five-eight. Meg was an imposing figure of a woman, standing just a bit less than six feet tall with ice blue eyes, and nearly white short cropped hair. Her muscular, almost masculine, build attested to her avid interest in weight lifting. Meg had told Jo how much she'd missed her before kissing her. Unfortunately, Jo hadn't thought of Meg once during the time she vacationed with her family. She groaned mentally.

Why did I kiss her back...hell, more to the point, why did I have sex with her? Well, the answer is obvious, really. When was the last time I had a date or sex with anyone other than my vibrator? Jo calculated the answer to the question. Can it be true that I really haven't dated anyone in over two years? The last person I've even been attracted to was the Director of Nursing at the hospital, Mallory Barnes.

Jo and Mallory both worked shift work. Between their two crazy work schedules, they had rarely been able to get together with each other outside the hospital. Jo often brought prisoners in for medical treatment and they had become friendly during a two-week period when Jo was guarding one of the prisoners. As time passed, their initial attraction eventually turned into friendship and Mallory and her new partner Amanda had both become Jo's friends.

Mallory Barnes was much more her type than Meg. Short and petite, easy-going, dazzling smile, great giggle...yes, definitely her type. Jo quickly shook away her regret. Someone paired was definitely off limits. Besides, Jo liked Mallory's partner Amanda too. Once they'd established their relationship, Jo had quickly contented herself with a friendship with the couple. Jo had her two rules she never broke...never get involved with anyone already in a relationship, and never, never, never, date a straight woman.

Come on, stop digressing and get back to the issue at hand. Meg...how do I handle this? It's not that Meg is unattractive...she's certainly comely enough, even if she's not my type. She's intelligent, kind, interesting, and unattached. Unfortunately there's just something missing in my feelings for this woman sleeping next to me, ,me and I don't see the potential for my feelings to change.

Their lovemaking had been sweet, although Meg was definitely more into it than she was. Why on earth didn't I stop Meg after the first kiss? Because I didn't want to hurt her feelings--plain and simple, I'm an idiot. Now it'll be worse. She's going to wake up all huggy and kissy and I'm going to want to do a disappearing act. Only I blew it this time...this is my house. She's here. That means I have to ask her to leave. No...too cold. I can spend the rest of the day with her and beg off early saying I'm too tired. She'll want to go back to bed with me and spend the night. Well, I can't treat her like she's some meaningless one-night stand.  Surely I remember those days...let me see...when was the last time...oh yeah what...three, no more like four years ago? Oh no, she's waking up.

The tall woman stirred and turned toward Jo. "Hi," Meg said with a sleepy grin. "Are you okay?"

Jo smiled. "Yes, fine...you?"

"I'm good." she smiled weakly. Before Jo could extricate herself from the uncomfortable situation, Meg solved her dilemma. "Look, Jo, I think I'm more into you than you are into me."

Honesty is the best policy...but be kind. Jo nodded. "I'm sorry."

Meg shook her head. "No. I'm sorry if I made it hard for you to say no. It's okay, really. It's just that I've had the hots for you since we met, and I knew if I didn't make a move, you never would. I thought if we well, you know, did this, maybe you'd start to feel something for me."

"I do feel something for you, Meg. You are a lovely, kind, and loyal friend. I care for you very much, and treasure your friendship. But, I think this may have been a mistake. I'm sorry."

Meg exhaled a long sigh. "Please don't think it was a mistake. I enjoyed myself, and I hope you did too. I know you feel differently about it than I do, still I'm glad we made love. Maybe it'll help me get you out of my system."

Concerned about the ramifications of what they'd done, Jo put her hand on Meg's arm, "I hope this won't ruin our friendship?"

"Why should it?"

"Well, I don't know...will you feel awkward?"

Meg shook her head. "Look, we're both single adults. We like each other. I'd hoped for more unfortunately it's not going to happen. I'm still not sorry we did it and I hope you won't be either. Now, before you give me the 'it's not you it's me' speech, let's get up and go get something to eat."

Wow! She's a mind reader...I'm famished. Phew! Maybe this'll be okay after all. "Sounds good to me--I'm hungry. Are you on call tonight?"

Meg was a volunteer on the EMS squad. She rode in the ambulance with another paramedic and was on call three nights a week and every other weekend. She truly was a good soul to volunteer so much of her time.

"No, not on call, but I left my glasses in the ambulance and I'd like to stop by and pick them up if I can. Want to go with me? We can stop and get some pizza. I can drop you back here on my way to my house. I have an early shift tomorrow at the office." She held a responsible position as a Physician's Assistant.

"Yes, sounds good."

They rolled out of bed, turning their backs to each other as they quickly dressed.

Meg checked with Jo. "You want to eat first, or find out where the ambulance is?"

"Let's get your glasses first, before we eat. Even though I'm hungry, it's still a little early for dinner."

"I'll call and find out if they're at the EMS squad room or out on a call." She flipped open her phone and punched in the number of the regular driver. "They're at the hospital. They just picked up a gunshot victim and are taking him to the ER. We can catch up with them there."

Jo tucked in her T-shirt as she walked to the breadbox where she kept her off duty pistol and holster. She picked up her off duty weapon, reached behind her back, and clipped the holster and Glock into the waistband of her jeans. Then she put on a shirt, which she left unbuttoned. It was her standard off duty attire.

Meg and she made small talk on the way to the hospital. Maybe making love with Meg hadn't been such a terrible mistake after all. Meg actually did seem okay that sex would not be a regular component of their friendship, and with the fact that this experience definitely would not result in any kind of ongoing or committed relationship between them.

The two women entered the emergency room and spotted the EMS team across the room. The team members who had just delivered the patient were talking to one of the doctors on duty, explaining the emergency treatment they had provided to the patient on route. Meg gestured with her head to Jo that she would be heading in that direction to talk with her friends when they were free. Jo looked around and saw Mallory standing behind the main desk.

"Hey, Mallory. Busy tonight?"

"No, it's been strangely quiet. That's our first serious case, a shooting--some kind of domestic dispute between two friends over some woman. Apparently she slept with both of them, and one took particular offense."

"I hate those domestic dispute calls. You never know what you'll run into. One time..."

Before Jo could finish her story, there was a crash at the door and in an instant, a flash of motion. The crazed man rushed in past the shocked EMTs. He grabbed Meg and held a gun to her head.

"Where is he? I want to know where that bastard Smitty is."

Jo could hear Meg's reply. "I'm a visitor here, I swear I don't know."

While his attention was focused elsewhere, sticking to the perimeter of the room, Jo started to slowly make her way across the ER, moving nearer to the upset man. As she edged closer, his attention started to shift in her direction, but stopped to focus on Mallory when she dropped the chart she was holding in an effort to distract his attention from Jo.

Worried for Mallory's safety, Jo quickly moved closer to the gunman. Jo's hand flashed behind her back and emerged from under the shirt with her pistol in hand. She shouted, "Police! I'm a police officer. Drop your weapon, or I'll shoot."

The scene unfolded in what seemed like frame-by-frame action. The gunman pushed Meg viciously aside. As she fell, she smacked her head on the edge of the stretcher and dropped, unconscious before she hit the floor.

As Meg lay unmoving, the gunman's focus shifted to Mallory. The man raised his weapon to fire, apparently not sure who had called out or where she was standing. Jo tried to distract the gunman and yelled at the top of her lungs. "Hey you! Over here!" As if in slow motion, he fired once wildly before he zeroed in on Jo, turned toward her and pulled the trigger at the exact same time she did. They both fell to the floor. He was dead. She was seriously injured and bleeding heavily.

The EMS team as well as the hospital staff sprang into action. The wild shot he'd squeezed off had hit Mallory but, fortunately, only skimmed her arm causing a slight flesh wound. The hospital staff and EMS team lifted both Meg and Jo onto stretchers and began a quick assessment of their conditions.

The action was over in an instant. *Thank God Jo was here*, Mallory thought as she watched them wheel everyone away. Meg, who was still unconscious, was admitted for observation. Jo was rushed into surgery to repair the serious wound to her thigh.

Mallory normally would not be working this shift, but she was trying to catch up knowing she would be leaving her position as Director of Nursing soon. She and her partner, Amanda, and their two closest friends Nic and Dana would soon be starting their own business. Thanks to a large inheritance Amanda recently received when a former lover passed away unexpectedly, she was investing in a business for the four of them so they could be in charge of their own professional lives.

Mallory reached for the phone. Amanda...I'd better give her a call before she hears this on the radio and worries.

Eager for Mallory to return home, Amanda answered her phone on the first ring. "Hi honey, coming home soon?"

"Hey babe. No, but I didn't want you to be concerned. There's been a shooting at the hospital. But I'm okay, I only got a flesh wound."

"Flesh wound! What do you mean? You've been shot!"

"Yes, but I'm okay," Mallory emphasized. "Honest. I'm not sure about Meg and Jo, though. They were both injured. Jo killed the gunman. She was very brave and really impressive. If not for her I might have been more seriously injured, and certainly more lives would have been lost. If she hadn't called out to him to get his attention, I might not be making this call to you."

"My God! Are you coming home now? Should I come get you?"

"No, the police are on their way here, and I'll need to answer some questions, I'm sure. Also, I want to check on Meg and Jo's condition."

"I'll come there to you, then. I'm leaving right now."

"There's no need for you to come...really, I'm okay."

Amanda strongly protested. Mallory recognized a losing battle, and quickly gave in. "All right. I'll be in the surgery waiting room, waiting to see how Jo's surgery went."

## Chapter 2

Amanda rushed in and checked Mallory out thoroughly before wrapping her in her arms. "Are you really okay?" She whispered into her lover's neck as she held her tightly.

"Yes," Mallory assured her, "I'm really fine. I will say that, if Jo hadn't distracted him by yelling at him, I'm sure it could have definitely been much worse. It could have been me on that operating table. This was close, honey, I'm still shaking."

Amanda grabbed Mallory's hands. "I'll be forever grateful to Jo for saving your life. We owe her. How are Meg and Jo doing?"

"Meg took a terrible hit to her head. She's still unconscious, last I heard."

"And Jo? Have you heard anything about her condition?"

"Yes, she's still in surgery. She was shot in the thigh. If you have to be shot, the hospital is the best place for it to happen. If she'd been shot anywhere else, she might not have lived. I know she lost a lot of blood. Fortunately she was in the operating room in a matter of minutes."

A tall, well-built man with neatly trimmed grey hair and a well-trained mustache rushed in.

"Hi John," Mallory said. "Amanda, this is Captain John Strayer. He's Jo's boss."

Amanda and the police captain shook hands and exchanged greetings.

As they were chatting, the surgeon exited from the operating room. He recognized Mallory and the police chief and approached. "Has anyone contacted Jo's family yet?"

"No, not yet." The chief replied. "I thought I'd wait until I had something definite to tell them."

"Well, you know, as her physician, I can't legally give you any information. I think you can safely tell them that she made it through surgery and I'm guardedly optimistic. Have them give me a call for the details. I'm transferring her to the ICU. Mallory, I assume I'll see you up there?"

"I'll take care of that right away, thanks doc," the Chief promised.

"Take care, Mallory. Amanda," he said nodding in her direction.

"Come on, Amanda, we're going to the ICU. In so many words, he just gave me permission to read her chart. I'll find out what's going on."

The Chief pulled out his phone. "I'll catch up with you as soon as I can, Mallory. We'll need to ask you some questions about what happened."

Amanda sat in the ICU waiting room while Mallory entered the restricted area. Ten minutes later Mallory came out and sat down next to her lover. "She came through the surgery okay, but it may be a career ending injury. She lost a lot of blood and they suspect she'll have some numbness, at least initially. She had a lot of muscle and nerve damage. Some of the feeling will return but probably not all. They worry now about infection, and she'll need rehab to get functional use of her leg back."

"Mal, does she have any family here?"

Mallory shook her head. "I know she's close to her parents. But they live in Pennsylvania, I think. Why?"

"She saved your life. Maybe we should offer to take care of her while she recovers. I feel like we owe her something for that, don't you?"

"Well, we already have a chair." Mallory laughed about the reference to the motorized reclining chair with the seat that helped raise a person sitting in it to a standing position. They'd bought for Amanda after she'd injured her leg in her biking accident.

"Was she awake yet?"

"In and out. I expect that she'll have a lot of pain. They'll keep her pretty doped up for a couple of days."

"Can you sit with her or do you have to go back to your office?"

"I need to check in. I still haven't talked to the police, and I'm sure they're waiting to see me."

"Can you get me in there?" Amanda asked referring to the ICU.

Mallory smiled then pulled Amanda to her for a quick hug. "Time will be limited, but I can get you in there. You're a fortunate woman you know, to have a friend in high places."

Amanda raised her eyebrow. "And don't I know it."

* * *

A couple of hours later, Jo woke up. Amanda smiled at her. "How are you feeling?"

Jo gave a wan smile. "Kinda like I've been assaulted by a bullet."

"Well, we're all glad that guy wasn't a better shot."

"How are Mallory and Meg?"

"Mal only got nicked on the arm, thanks to you. Last I heard Meg hadn't awakened yet. But that was a couple of hours ago. I can check on her for you, if you'd like."

"Yes, in a little while. Can you stay with me for a bit?"

"Sure. Can I get you anything?"

"How about some water?"

"I'll ask the nurse."

When the nurse finished checking on Jo, she allowed Amanda back in to visit with her.

"Has anyone called my parents?"

"I think your Captain planned to call. Would you like me to follow up and call them?"

"Could you? I'd appreciate it. My mom will want to come, as will my dad. They just returned home from a trip to the cabin, so I know they'll be exhausted. I'm concerned about them turning around and making the trip here. Taking care of my dad is a full time job for mom. I know she'll want to take care of me. I really don't want her to...I think it's too much for her." Jo clicked the trigger to release a dose of pain meds.

"Well," Amanda said. "I have a solution. I'd like to invite your parents, and you when you're well enough, to stay with Mallory and me. Mallory and I can take care of you, and your mom and dad can visit until they feel comfortable that you're on the mend."

"Amanda. I couldn't possibly take advantage of you that way."

"When it's offered freely, how is it taking advantage? Please trust me when I say it's something we can do. Besides, Dana and Nic will help too, I'm sure."

"Well, I really appreciate it. Would you call my mom and tell her I'm going to be okay and tell her not to worry."

"I'll take care of everything. Now, you rest. I'll call Dana and Nic first to update them before I call your mom. I'll be back later after I've talked to everyone. Try to get some rest."

"Thanks. My mom's number is on my phone." Jo relaxed, thankful and reassured by Amanda's promise that she would have the support of her friends for what she knew might be a difficult recovery.

## Chapter 3

"Mrs. Martin? This is Amanda James. I am a friend of your daughter's. I just came from seeing her. I know her Captain called you, and you're probably concerned. Jo wanted you to know that she's awake and worried about you and her father making the trip to see her."

"Hello Amanda, and please call me Josette. Thank you for calling, dear. We've been so worried. I just talked to her supervisor a couple of hours ago, but he hadn't seen her. How is Joanna?"

Amanda smiled at the formal name hardly anyone used to refer to their friend and was surprised to hear Mrs. Martin had a strong French accent. Jo had never mentioned that her mother was French.

"Your daughter is doing okay. I have good news. They just informed us that, now that they have her stable, they plan to move her to the step-down unit soon. They'll keep a careful watch on her there, and assuming she continues to improve, they'll probably move her to a private room tomorrow or the day after. Jo wanted me to assure you that although she still has discomfort from the surgery, she's getting the best of care and she doesn't want you to worry."

"Thank you for calling. I feel reassured. No doubt I'll feel better when I can see her. My husband, Ben, and I plan to drive there to be with her tomorrow. I have trouble seeing at night, so we have to wait until morning to leave."

"I would like to invite you and your husband to stay with my partner, Mallory, and myself. We've already offered to take care of Jo, so if you will stay with us, we can all pitch in and help."

"I appreciate your offer, and I'm grateful. I feel better knowing that Jo has such good friends there to help watch over her. Thank you. Please tell her that we're coming as soon as we can and that her father and I love her. And thank you so much for your call."

Amanda returned to find Mallory next to Jo's bedside, talking softly with her. The nurse on duty said, "You can go in, but keep it quiet in there, please."

"Not a problem." Amanda slid her arm around Mallory's shoulder and Mallory circled Amanda's waist with her arm. Amanda related the details of her conversation with Jo's mother.

"Now, don't you worry about your parents. We'll take care of everything. You just worry about getting better."

Mallory squeezed Jo's hand. "Thank you for saving me."

Jo smiled. "Thank you both for being here for me." Relieved, Jo closed her eyes and drifted.

"We can't stay too long. Technically, we shouldn't be here. I'll check in with you again before we leave."

"Thanks."

***

Mr. and Mrs. Martin arrived at the hospital the next afternoon. Mallory met them when she went to visit Jo and check on her condition. Their day had been long and tiring. They'd left home early that morning, driven to the hospital to see their daughter, and spent several hours there in the uncomfortable chairs in the waiting room and visiting their daughter. With Jo's encouragement, her parents reluctantly agreed to leave before the end of visiting hours.

"Really, Mom and Dad, I'm fine. Please go get something to eat and get some rest."

Mallory drove them home at the end of her shift. Amanda had dinner ready shortly after they arrived. Nic and Dana, their neighbors and close friends joined them for dinner.

"Ben, Josette, we'd like to offer you to stay next door with us in our second floor guest quarters. We've all talked, and agree that it will be best to put Jo in the first floor guest bedroom here. The second floor in Nic's and my place will provide you with a private area of your own, and we think you'll be more comfortable there. We know you don't know any of us, but we are friends of Jo's and hope you'll feel comfortable staying with Nic and me."

Josette smiled at Dana and nodded. "Well, we know we've never met you all before, but we feel we know you. Jo talks about you all enough."

"Thank you for your kindness," Ben said. "I think, if you don't mind, we'd like to get settled now and make it an early night. We've had a long day."

"Of course," Dana said. "I'll show you to our house."

Nic extended her hand palm up. "If you'll give me your car keys, I'll get your bags,"

\* \* \*

A week later, Mallory picked Jo up from the hospital for her trip home. She was still on antibiotics and being monitored carefully for infection, but she had progressed sufficiently that the doctor felt she was well enough to be released to the care of her family and friends. He was reassured knowing that Mallory would be directly involved in Jo's care. The physical therapy Jo received during her hospitalization helped her become comfortable with the crutches she required to support and stabilize her when she walked. Getting in and out of the wheelchair was still something she required assistance to do. The trip home was uncomfortable despite Mallory's attempt to avoid any bumps.

Jo sighed as she sat in the living room chair surrounded by family and friends. "I'm glad that's over."

Mallory brought Jo a drink of water, a few crackers, and her pain pill, a kindness for which she received a huge smile in thanks. "I've made arrangements with the PT department to send someone out. Your insurance will cover the visits until you're comfortable enough to make the trip in to rehab for your therapy."

"That's a relief. I know you tried to be careful, but the ride home was no walk in the park."

"I know, sweetie, but it should be less problematic now that we have you settled."

The day after her return to Amanda and Mallory's place, Jo and her mother had an opportunity to speak privately. They lapsed into French, Jo's mother's native language. "I'm glad that you have such good friends, honey. I feel happier with you living here alone knowing that you have all of your friends to help you and support you."

"So, you like my friends?"

"Your Dad and I like your friends very much. You are lucky to have so many competent people around you."

"How is Dad holding up being around so many lesbians?" Jo winked at her mother.

"You know, I think it's been good for him. He was very quiet at first, but he's really hit it off with Nic and Dana, and told me that he's impressed with Mallory and Amanda taking such good care of you. He's been telling jokes, so I know he's feeling comfortable.

After staying in Nic and Dana's house for nearly a week, with some encouragement, Jo's mother and father felt comfortable leaving their daughter. They agreed to return home once Jo promised to call them with a daily progress report.

"We don't know how we can ever thank you," Ben said to the group of women.

"It's truly been our pleasure." Nic helped Jo's father with the bags. Nic, Dana, Amanda and Mallory left Jo and her parents alone for their goodbyes. They all waved goodbye as Jo's parents left for home.

They all adjusted quickly to a new routine with two fewer guests and one semi-invalid to care for. Jo did everything she could to be useful. She peeled vegetables and helped to the best of her ability in preparing meals. Her physical therapist came every other day until Jo could comfortably make the trip to the rehab center. Mallory had never seen anyone work as hard or as diligently to improve and to regain her strength as Jo did. Mallory did all she could by giving Jo daily massages to help stimulate the nerves and to relieve some of the stiffness and pain Jo felt in her injured leg.

As Jo recovered, Amanda, Mallory, Dana, and Nic were deeply involved in plans for their new translation business. Even though she wasn't actually involved in any of the planning for the business, because she was present, she listened to their discussions as they reported their progress. "I've rented us a small space for our offices and classroom about a half hour from their homes, closer to the city," Amanda reported. "Mallory and I are splitting the responsibility of overseeing the painting and furnishing of the new office space. I've already put up a website and made all the necessary arrangements for advertising which is scheduled to begin in eight weeks."

Nic reached for Dana's hand. "We're lining up other translators who can moonlight for us once we get established."

With everyone involved in jobs, and Jo involved in her rehab, time passed rapidly. Before they knew it, Jo had been on leave from work nearly two months. Mallory went with her for her check up with the surgeon. He didn't sugar coat his prognosis for her recovery. "Jo, I know you've worked extremely hard to make the amazing progress you've achieved in such a short time. I'm sorry to have to tell you that no matter how hard you work you'll never regain sufficient strength in her leg to return to your job on the police force. Don't get me wrong, you'll continue to improve, although I believe you may always have a slight limp and your leg will definitely help you predict the weather." He smiled kindly as he delivered the bad news. "I'll sign the necessary paperwork to allow you to retire on disability from the force."

"Thanks, doctor. It's not the outcome I'd hoped for, although it's kind of what I expected you'd say..I appreciate that you saved my life and my leg."

Jo and Mallory left the doctor's office with Mallory pushing Jo's wheelchair. Normally, she usually used crutches. However, they'd found that it was much less tiring if they used the chair when she had to cover larger distances or when the terrain made using her crutches too difficult. A short way down the hallway, Mallory quickly pushed Jo into a vacant office and closed the door, pulling up a chair next to Jo. "Are you okay?"

Jo sniffed once and wiped her eyes with her sleeves. "Yes. I've been expecting this news. I've worked as hard as I could to regain full use of my leg. Unfortunately I just can't seem to beat the odds on this one. The physical therapist told me basically the same thing. My limp should diminish over time as I strengthened the leg. She'd cautioned me though, to not hold out hope that I'd ever regain totally normal function. She said I'd always favor my bad leg. So I've been anticipating the bad news."

Returning home, they discovered that Meg was there for a visit. She had recovered her health, although she'd lost her memory of events for most of the week before the accident. Jo thought it was a blessing in a way. Their friendship seemed to be back to where they were before the fateful night of the shooting. They passed the time chatting together until dinnertime when the four of them talked about lighter subjects.

Two weeks later, Jo's captain came to visit her bringing the necessary paperwork for her to apply for a disability retirement. She was due to turn forty-three on her next birthday.

"If you were closer to full retirement, I could keep you on, but I don't think I can manage it for another two and a half years. I'm really sorry."

"I know, Chief. I appreciate your keeping me on this long."

After the captain left, Amanda came to the living room to sit with Jo. "Have you given any thought about what you want to do with the rest of your life?"

Jo shook her head. "I have no clue. I could probably be a part time dispatcher, I guess. I can't do that full time because they have the same pension plan I have. But I might be able to do up to twenty hours a week at that job without having to join the pension fund. Between that and my pension, I think I can earn enough money to keep me afloat at virtually no risk to my life and limb like I used to have. And my experience on the force should provide good background for dispatch work."

"Is that something you'd enjoy?"

"I guess it would be okay. At least I'd still be involved in helping people in a bad situation. I'd feel useful, I think." Jo ran her fingers through her hair. "Well, I've taken up space here long enough. I need to start thinking about moving back home. First thing I need to do is sell my car. With my left leg injured, I can't use a clutch any more...I'll need an automatic."

"I think Mallory would be better suited to help with that. Let's see if she'd like to go new car shopping."

Jo, Mallory, and Amanda took Jo's car and went shopping for a new vehicle that afternoon. Jo had obviously given some thought to her needs regarding a new car. "I think I want a small pickup truck. I'd like to be able to throw my bike in the back and not have to bother with a bike rack. My intention is to ride as much as I can as soon as the weather breaks. I think it'll help me strengthen my leg."

"Okay, let's look around. They went to several dealerships looking for the perfect vehicle. "I don't want a huge truck. They're too high for me to get into," Jo declared. "I need something small.

They drove through the local car dealership but didn't see any pickups out front. "Hey, look at that," Amanda said pointing to a small pickup at the back of the lot. There was no sign on it listing its price.

Mallory looked in the direction Amanda was pointing. "I wonder what the story is on that one."

Jo looked interested. "Let's go check it out."

Mallory navigated the lot and parked next to the little silver truck. The three women got out of Jo's car and with cupped hands peered inside the vehicle.

"This is neat," Jo said. "It's just the right size, seats four people, has a small bed, but it looks like this little rack flips back to extend the bed. I think my bike will fit in there. Let's talk to a salesman and see what the story is."

As if on cue, the tall, lanky salesman approached the group of women and after a warm greeting he asked, "How can I help you?"

Jo drew the salesman's attention. "We saw the truck parked here and are curious about this vehicle. Can you give us any information about it?"

"Sure. That's a 2006. I sold it as a new vehicle to an older man four years ago. He recently died, and his family just sold it back to us. We're getting ready to clean it up and put it out front for sale. It has really low mileage, only has eighteen thousand some odd miles on it."

"Next best thing to it was driven by a little old school teacher," Mallory joked causing everyone to chuckle.

"Exactly." replied the salesman adding a genuine smile. "I'm Dan." He shook hands with each woman in turn. "Which of you is interested?"

Jo raised her hand. "That would be me."

"Okay, let me show you some of the other features of the vehicle." He opened the door and allowed Jo to get in. "This is the turbo model. It has an electric driver's seat." He pointed to another car on the lot, "It's built on the same frame as that model over there, so it rides like a car but has four wheel drive and the added functionality of a truck."

"That's good, Jo," Mallory commented. "It'll be good in bad weather."

"Yeah, and the power seat will be perfect for me. I can push it back to get out and in and adjust it easily to drive." Turning to the salesman, she asked the price. It was within the ballpark of what she thought she could afford with her trade. "Can we take it for a ride?"

"Sure, let me get a tag. If you give me the keys to your car, I can have it appraised for you while you take this one for a spin."

While he was gone, the trio looked over the neat little truck. Mallory lowered the tailgate and flipped the bed extender back. "Look, she added, the back seat folds forward and that little door folds down making the back open to the bed so you can put longer items inside. That's pretty neat."

The salesman returned with a tag. Mallory and Amanda got in the back seat and Jo drove. She was barely out on the road when she decided she wanted the neat little truck. It answered all her needs. When they returned to the lot, they negotiated price, and Jo made the deal.

"I don't think you stole it, but you probably got a fair price. Perhaps had you not been drooling on the hood when we started dickering about price, we could have done a little better," Mallory teased.

Jo glanced at Mallory. "I would probably have paid full price if not for your intervention. It's exactly what I need. I'm really happy. It has low mileage, the extended warranty at a reasonable cost, and that nice bed cover that'll be good in the bad weather. It'll be nice to be able to lock things in the bed. I'm a happy camper." A huge grin spread across her face.

On the way home, the women stopped so Jo could treat them to dinner. As they were eating, Jo announced, "I think it's time for me to go home, ladies. I can get around on my own now and should be able to care for myself. I might need help with shopping for a few more weeks, but other than that I think I can manage." Jo had graduated to using a cane for stability and for the past couple of weeks had been navigating fairly well.

"We'll help you as long as you need us." Amanda promised. When she got home, Amanda offered and Jo accepted that she call their cleaning service and arrange for Jo's house to have a thorough cleaning. She could see if she could maintain it on her own and make her own decision about whether to keep them on or not.

"I hope I'll be able to do it myself. Surely, I'll have the time." A wisp of sadness insinuated itself into her voice, but she quickly forced herself to brighten her tone. "Just think, no more alarm clocks for me."

Mallory and Amanda had talked with Dana and Nic about the job offer they were about to make Jo. In the time Jo had spent at Amanda and Mallory's house, Jo had become a member of their extended family.

"Jo, we have an offer to make you. Initially, we won't need you much, but we're planning on opening the business in the next couple of weeks. Mallory is going to be the office manager, but she'll still working part time at the hospital for a while, and won't be available to be at the desk for all the hours we'll be open. Even after she leaves the hospital, there will be too many hours for us to cover. Especially after business increases and Nic gets busier, we'll need someone to help us out. We were wondering if you would be interested in working for us part time to start, with increasing hours as the business grows. We'll need someone who knows the business anyway because, as it becomes successful, Mallory and I will want to be able to take time off to get away together, as will Nic and Dana. We'll need someone we can trust to take care of the business when we're unavailable."

Jo had heard the women talking about the business. She was appreciative of all they had done for her, and she jumped at the opportunity to be able to help them in return. "Sure, I'll even do it for free. I owe you guys so much, how will I ever repay you?"

"We won't hear of it. We feel we owe you more for saving Mallory's life. We're extremely glad you'll be with us in our new venture."

## Chapter 4

Stacy Alexander sat at her desk located in front of a large window in her office. The window overlooked the main street of her little town, located just outside the New York City. Shops and restaurants lined both sides of the street. Her apartment was in a freestanding house above a little store that sold shoes and leather purses. She loved opening the door and stepping into the landing leading to the stairwell to her second floor space. When entering, she always inhaled deeply absorbing the aroma of the leather that seeped into the hallway there. She had chosen the little town she lived in for its small-town feel but also appreciated its proximity to the city. As an author, she enjoyed that she was able to be near her publisher for meetings when necessary, but coming from a small town in Virginia, she appreciated living outside of the frenzy and hectic pace common to big cities.

Stacy enjoyed the process of writing. She loved solving the challenges each story presented and especially loved the research involved. Actually, she had started as a researcher for an international company that did surveys and market research, a job she continued to do on a freelance basis between novels. She was currently working on doing the data analysis for some French surveys. Having taken the language in high school and college, her French was passable, but not what she considered fluent for professional purposes. She felt more comfortable writing than speaking the language. Still, she lacked confidence in her skills.

As she worked, Stacy glanced out the window every so often to watch the progress on the new shop across the street. Workmen had been in and out over the previous weeks, painting and bringing in furniture. Today, the cable people had been there all morning and seemed to have finished up making their connections.

Stacy was working on the plot outline for her fourth mystery novel and was stuck for a motive. As a result, for most of the morning, she'd sat staring out the window just thinking. In her first book the motive had been adultery and, in the second, a crime of passion and opportunity. The third had been robbery. *What other reasons were there, that would cause one person to take another's life?* She ruminated on the subject, seeking another motive for the crime. *Blackmail...yes, that's it. Blackmail. So, what could her victim, a twenty-five year old young woman living in a townhouse in a small town possibly have done that someone could be blackmailing her about at such a young age? She searched her brain for something different, something that would spice up her storyline.* Nothing came to mind immediately. *Tea. I need tea. That always helps.* Seeking inspiration, Stacy headed for the kitchen.

Thoughts drifted through her head as she waited for the water to boil and tea preparation. Cup in hand, she meandered her way back to the office and settled herself again. Leaning her chin on her palm, she glanced out the window. The same short, auburn-haired woman, who had been in and out of the shop across the street for the past few weeks, was waiting at the door. A tall, dark-haired, slender man dressed in trousers and a long Chesterfield styled coat strode up the walkway. They hugged each other in greeting. When they both turned towards the street, Stacy was surprised to notice that the taller person was a woman, not a man as she had first thought. Her hair was short but stylishly cut. It was a few minutes until the two women waiting at the door welcomed two other women, one short and blondish and, the other, a strawberry haired woman of medium height. After hugs, they paired off, the two shorter women together and the taller woman with the mid sized woman. They all joined hands and went through the door together. Stacy watched them, through the large front window of the shop. Once inside, the two couples paired off and kissed each other on the lips.

They're all lesbians! She watched in fascination as the women kissed each other, then separated to hug each other. She was surprised by the tingle she felt between her legs when the women kissed. She found it an erotic sight. *Wonder what business they're going to open*, she thought idly. Then it hit her. *Blackmail...her murder victim could be blackmailed for being a lesbian. Hmm. That might be a good reason for blackmail. But, what do I know about being a lesbian? Nothing. She smiled to herself. Research. I'll need to do research.* She watched for a while, hoping the women would kiss again, but they seemed to be over the greeting stage and were starting to organize the office.

Soon a sign painter showed up and began painting the name of the business on the shop window. *Oui Madame* slowly began to appear letter by letter. *Hmm, wonder what type of business that is?* Her question was soon answered as the sign painter added *Translation Services and Language School* below the name of the business. She muttered aloud, "Now isn't that convenient?"

Stacy put the novel aside for the time being, finally motivated to finish up the report she was writing. She would finish it, translate the report as best she could and ask the women at the new business to proof it for her.

**Read more of Jo's story in AJ Adaire's soon to be released novel, *Anything Your Heart Desires* coming in 2014.**

# Other books from Desert Palm Press

## The Guardian Series by Stein Willard
A Guardian's Touch – Book 1
A Guardian's Love – Book 2
A Guardian's Passion – Book 3

## Scarred for Life by SL Kassidy

## Friends Series by AJ Adaire
Sunset Island — Book 1
The Interim — a novelette

**Available now from Smashwords and Amazon**

**Coming soon**
Anything Your Heart Desires – Friends Book 3 by AJ Adaire
A Guardian's Salvation – Book 4 by Stein Willard
The Unbroken Warrior by Stein Willard
Phantom of the Heart by Stein Willard
Afterglow by Stein Willard

www.desertpalmpress.com

Made in the USA
Charleston, SC
23 September 2016